THE Mahjong Mavens OF Boca Raton

a novel

Ruth E. Weiner

The Mahjong Mavens of Boca Raton
Copyright © 2023 Ruth E. Weiner.

Produced and printed by Stillwater River Publications. All rights reserved. Written and produced in the United States of America. This book may not be reproduced or sold in any form without the expressed, written permission of the author(s) and publisher.

Visit our website at www.StillwaterPress.com for more information.

First Stillwater River Publications Edition.

ISBN: 978-1-958217-95-5

1 2 3 4 5 6 7 8 9 10
Written by Ruth E. Weiner.
Cover design & interior typesetting by Matthew St. Jean.
Published by Stillwater River Publications, Pawtucket, RI, USA.

The views and opinions expressed in this book are solely those of the author(s) and do not necessarily reflect the views and opinions of the publisher.

The Mahjong Mavens
of Boca Raton

Chapter One

SCHMENDRIKS: FOOLISH OR INCOMPETENT PEOPLE

The policemen charged into the South Tower Senior Center in Boca Raton and confiscated the incriminating purses lying open on the tables. They swept quarters, dimes and nickels into plastic bags and told the women to go home.

"Section 849.085 of the Florida Statutes prohibits gambling in a public arena. Pack it in, ladies," said the officer in charge.

Mavis Gruber stood, all fiery five feet-two inches, every hair on her chin alert. "We're playing penny-ante mahjong. You can't tell me that's a crime." Under her breath, she hissed, "You goddamned *schmendriks.*"

The officer hefted the bags of coins. "There's more than pennies here, Ma'am."

"Don't Ma'am us," said Gertrude Friedman, her lips turned so low, her bottom teeth did the talking. She leered, cross-armed with her chest heaving.

"This is bull crap," squawked Mavis.

"I'm sorry, ladies, but there's been a complaint and until it's settled, you can't play here."

Grumbles bounced throughout the common room. "Big shots. *Knuckers.* Picking on little old ladies. *Meshugennehs!* Idiots. You'll be hearing from my son the lawyer. He'll put YOU in jail." The women gathered up their racks and tiles, and put away their mahjong sets. "We'll play at my house. The cops can't bother us there." The women broke into groups of four, some shuffling with walkers and canes, others spry in defiance of their ages, their voices heightened to maximum pitch, their eyes on fire.

None of the departing women had asked either Mavis or Gertrude to join them.

Oysvorfs: The Outcasts

The clubhouse grew quiet—no click-clacking of mahjong tiles, no laughter, griping, or table-slapping as Mavis and Gertrude sized each other up from across the room.

At seventy-eight, Mavis Gruber dominated a room. Yellow-haired, tattooed, loud-mouthed and crude, she slammed down the mahjong tiles like they were bullets. She gloated when she pocketed a loser's money. "Take that, *schmegegi.*"

Gertrude Friedman, sixty-eight, complained about everyone and everything, whining, "Hurry up. You're taking all day to play one tile! Talk louder! Pay attention, *dumkop.* Your mahjong hand is dead. D - E - A - D." Gertrude had no tolerance for slow players, mumbling players, dumb players, or anyone disrespectful of the game.

At a game table near the door, Blooma Gottlieb, a tiny eighty-three year old granny, huddled low in her chair, looking lost. She held a tray of cookies, none of them eaten and wondered what ingredient she had forgotten this time.

Near the wall of windows, Winnie Reichman, a slender straight-backed woman of seventy-two, tried to get reception on her cell. Her face was stone-cold, her lips thin and tight. She gave up on the signal and drummed a text, like she was on a sinking ship and this message was the last she'd ever make.

The four females who had remained in the room squared off in the four corners. None invited the other to her house to play.

A few Wednesdays later, a note hung from the door at the South Tower Senior Center:

Mahjong games may resume as long as the total winnings of any player do not exceed $10. Statute 949.085, penny-ante game restrictions will be strictly enforced.
—Boca Raton Police

Word spread quickly throughout the complex, but the South Tower room felt violated, so the women resumed play at the North Tower, a more spacious area with a kitchenette and eight playing tables, well-spaced and covered with sound-muting cloths.

Not every mahjong woman got the message.

Mavis—The *Gantseh Macher*: The Big Shot

Mavis revved up to the familiar South Tower clubhouse in her pink Harley-Davidson Sportster eager to get back to the game. The day was bright and she was early. She sat on the large soft saddle of her beloved motorcycle and lit her stogie. Maybe a little *schnapps* before she took their money. She'd been known to walk away with thirty bucks, wiping out everyone at her table. Now there was a limit of $10. *Feh!* It wasn't about the money, she thought. But how she loved taking those *alter kakers* for a ride.

She swigged spicy whiskey from a silver flask and stared into the midday sun. She'd just hang there a few more minutes. Let the prune-faced blue hairs get their shit together.

Blooma—The *Ziseh Neshomeh*: The Sweet Soul

Afraid of being late, Blooma was seated inside the clubhouse, having arrived at noon, even though the game began at one. She dug into her pocketbook for her mahjong card, but it wasn't there. Neither was her purse of nickels and dimes and quarters. *Oy gevult*, she sighed. She must have left them in her condo. She hobbled out the rear entrance and rushed home, her short bowlegs doing the best they could. She gulped deep breaths when she got to her door, but she couldn't open it.

Where were those *farshtunkene* keys? She dumped everything from her oversized purse onto the walkway. Her wallet. Her pills. Her eyedrops. Her Vaseline. Tissues. More tissues. Sweet N' Low packets. Her cell phone, off of course. She shouldn't waste the batteries. Shreds of paper with scribbled lists. A crusty dinner roll in a crumpled napkin. Her Saint Anthony prayer card, a gift from the mailman when she got lost on the wrong block of the complex. "The houses all look alike," she told him as he drove her home. Was that only last week? Ah, finally, her mahjong card. And her keys. And her purse of coins.

Now what else had she forgotten? The *babke* on the counter. She hoped she hadn't substituted salt for sugar this time.

Winnie—*Ongeshtopt Mit Gelt*: The Rich One

In the Palace Suite section of Sunrise Village, Winnie paced her penthouse apartment listening for her driver Sal to buzz the intercom. Her long legs made short work of the space even if her home had three thousand square feet. The mahjong game would start without her if she didn't get there soon. Then she'd have to sit out a full round before she could rotate in. Where the blazes was that man? It was already one o'clock. She took the elevator downstairs, her shellacked red fingernails tapping the wall like a drumbeat. The Lincoln Town

Car was at the corner. Sal leaned against it smoking a Marlboro, jabbering into his cell.

He held the phone away from his ear when he saw her. "Where to now?" he snarled.

"The Clubhouse!" She wanted to add 'you surly moron,' but she didn't drive and Sal was part of her inheritance from her late husband, may he rest in peace.

"I thought you ladies were expelled from playing there." A smirk slid over his lips. Winnie wanted to slap it away.

She felt personally responsible for reopening the senior center. "I'll have you know, I wrote a scathing editorial to the *Sunrise Gazette* telling how we don't wager our jewelry or our Cadillacs. We play for nickels and dimes." Winnie straightened her shoulders; her chin shot up high. "Then I called the Boca Raton Chief of Police and gave him an earful. He had no right closing us down. I told him we'd file a class action suit against him if he didn't reopen the building for our mahjong game."

"Well, good for you." Sal swept open the rear door of the Lincoln Town Car with a flourish of his arm and an exaggerated bow from the waist. "It is my unrequited privilege to take you wherever you'd like to go."

Winnie heard his snicker, but ignored it.

Gertrude—The *Kvetch*: The Complainer

Pedaling her three wheeler to the South Tower clubhouse, Gertrude sweated with the effort. Her thighs rubbed. Her back hurt. She hated the flab around her midsection. She'd always been so proud of her trim figure, but since turning sixty, everything she ate padded her belly, hips and thighs. She looked like a pregnant woman when she turned sideways. She never regretted not having a child, never mind never having a husband, never mind rarely having sex.

Out of breath and perspiring, Gertrude arrived at the clubhouse.

Without pausing to look around, she ran into the bathroom and stripped off her Spanx underwear, stuffing it in her purse. Ah, she could breathe. She knew what would really cure her, a good *shtupping*, something that hadn't happened since she was fifty, almost twenty years ago. No man was good enough. But geez, she was horny. Playing mahjong always calmed her down. She'd had a scare last month when the police raided them, fearing she wouldn't have her regular Wednesday game. And what was that raid all about? Calling them gamblers? For quarters! Such *mishegas*! Foolishness. She wrote a good long letter to the Condominium Board detailing how every woman in the complex had a pension or social security or enough money from their dead husband's insurance. None of them played to gamble. It was a social game. Period.

When a reporter caught wind of the hubbub, he took Gertrude's photograph and put the entire story in the *Sunrise Gazette*. "Jewish Bubbes Busted for Gambling." She was quoted right there on the first page: "Ridiculous," said Gertrude Friedman, "we've been treated like criminals, not upstanding, respected tax-payers. Besides, playing mahjong is good for our brains." Gertrude felt like a celebrity with her picture front and center in the newspaper. It was about time she received positive attention.

With her body swinging loose, Gertrude swaggered into the common room. The seats were neat around their tables, but much to her surprise, no one was there.

"Where is everybody?" asked an out-of-breath voice from the doorway. "*Oy gevult*! I thought I was late!" Blooma set the cinnamon bread on the counter.

Gertrude recognized the old lady who brought pastry each week and who smiled even if she lost every game. "It's Wednesday. Where the hell are they all?"

Blooma shrugged. "I've got my card! Do you have a mahjong set? I never bring one."

"I got a set," said a smoker's voice, deep and throaty. Mavis strutted in like a cowgirl, smelling like poker games and saloons.

Gertrude pursed her lips and her face grew dark, her eyes beady and dagger-like. She didn't like that hussy. She'd be damned if she was going to play with her. "We can't play three. Might as well go home."

Blooma's eyes welled. "I remember playing three. We can figure it out."

Gertrude's lips flattened, widening her jowls. That old woman can't figure out how to button her shirt so it's even. Gertrude wasn't going to waste another minute in this room.

The door opened and in strode Winnie, her gold bracelets jangling, her eyes growing larger with each step, surprised that there were only three other women in the room, and weird ones at that. The mean-faced grouch who always complained. The wild one, all duded up like a man, smelling like smoke and whiskey. And the one with the *loch in kop*, a hole in her head, who put up wrong hands or gave everyone mahjong in the last wall and cost each player double.

"Might as well make the most of it," said Mavis, reaching into her pocket for her flask.

"Do you want a *bissel* cake?" asked Blooma. "A little slice?" She regarded Gertrude. "Or a big one?"

Gertrude made the face her mother warned would freeze like that. She took out a tissue, wiped her forehead then stuffed the wrinkled ball up her sleeve. She decided she would win every game and feel damned good about herself.

Winnie's fingernails stabbed into each other like they were at war. She didn't want to play with these low-class outcasts. She turned toward the door but saw her driver speed away. Perhaps one round, she thought. She folded her skirt under her skinny rear and sat down, her back straight, her narrow chest heaving.

Mavis straddled a chair. "Let's get to it, ladies." She snapped open the mahjong case and dumped out its contents.

With the eagerness of a puppy, Blooma brought out her mahjong card and her purse of coins. She hurried to sit, as if her chair would disappear if she didn't claim it.

The women sat square at the table, their mahjong cards in front of them. They mixed the tiles and set up their racks. Mavis declared herself dealer and meted out thirteen tiles to each of them with fourteen for herself because she was East. The Charleston began: three tiles to the right, three over, first left, second left, three over, last right.

"Let the games begin," squawked Mavis.

"*Farmach dos moyl!* Shut up while we play," warned Gertrude.

Mavis flipped her the bird.

Round and round they went, creating melds and kongs of similar suits—cracs, bams, dots, winds, dragons and flowers—picking, discarding, calling a needed tile, hoping for a joker, and then piping up "mahjong!" when a hand exactly matched a formula on the score card.

Hours passed like minutes. Mavis won six games, Gertrude four, Winnie two, and Blooma none. Mavis might have amassed the most quarters, but each left the game richer for having played.

Chapter Two

NUDNICKS: ANNOYING PEOPLE

The following Wednesday, Mavis, Blooma, and Gertrude waited at the South Tower for Winnie for close to an hour.

Blooma didn't mind; she sat on the couch, closed her eyes and dreamt about her grandsons—two sweet *boychics* whom she'd only seen in photos.

Mavis paced in circles, squawking out swears on each rotation like a person with Turrets syndrome. Gertrude compared her to a yellow jacket buzzing around the room with a grating Fran Drescher voice.

When the Lincoln Town Car screeched to a halt, a man with steel-grey hair and a square jaw opened the door for Winnie. She tapped her watch repeatedly with those red fingernails and strode off with her gold-threaded scarf flapping in the wind. She swept into the clubhouse without an apology.

Gertrude bit her tongue, but her jaw kept up a silent chatter.

Mavis sucked in her hollow cheeks.

Blooma's cheeks dimpled as her smile widened.

Winnie took out her mahjong card from a rhinestone-studded purse, set her bag of coins on the table, and pronounced herself ready to begin.

"*Schmeckle* head," murmured Mavis, but lost no time getting down to business. She broke the wall, dealt the tiles, and concentrated on making a hand. Mavis easily won the first four games, then relaxed and played differently, reminding Blooma to pick a tile when it was her turn or helping her deal, even as Gertrude grumbled under her breath. Gertrude went on to win three hands and Winnie won two.

Blooma hadn't won any, but she didn't care. She was there to escape her mind, not clutter it. Her joy was serving her home-baked chocolate chip mandel bread sprinkled with cinnamon and sugar.

"Next week, be on time," Mavis told Winnie as they packed up.

"Tell my driver. It's his fault, always making me late."

"Let me at that *schlub*. He won't be late again," squawked Mavis.

"I'll take care of it," said Winnie and meant it. She would stand up to that man for once and for all.

Indeed, she was early the next Wednesday, but said she had to leave at 3:00. Their usual game went till 4:00.

"Then sit your bony ass down and play," said Gertrude under her breath, but loud enough for Winnie to hear.

Winnie tensed but did as she was told. She wasn't going to give that snarling woman the satisfaction of a reply.

Mavis set up Blooma's rack as she stared into space. Mavis snapped her fingers and Blooma startled awake. "Sorry. I was just thinking."

"You could have fooled me," said Mavis, who stuffed a piece of Blooma's mandel bread into her mouth, followed by a swig from her flask.

Since Winnie left early and Gertrude refused to play three, Mavis cruised the community on her motorcycle before heading home. *Judge Judy* wasn't on until 4:30, so she had time to wander. The complex was flat with ponds and fountains flanking a golf course. The condos were grouped according to size and height, with the original boxy two stories on the south side, the high rises on the north side, and townhouses on the cross streets. Each section boasted its own clubhouse and pool.

Mavis rode the circumference of the village and ended up at the opposite end near the North Tower. Leaving the building, a gaggle of women *kvetched* about the mahjong sets stored in the closet. "The numbers are fading," complained one. "The jokers have stickers on them like the old days," said another. Mavis slowed her motorcycle as she passed them and they looked away like they hadn't see her. As if. Those *mamzers*! she thought. It was Wednesday and they had been playing mahjong without telling her group, leaving them out intentionally like they were *schleppers*.

Mavis stewed until the following Wednesday rolled around and she told the others what she had seen.

"Who the hell needs those *kakers* anyway?" said Gertrude.

"They can kiss my *tuches*," said Mavis.

"Wouldn't it be fun to create a little trouble?" asked Blooma.

They all stared at her.

Blooma? Winnie couldn't believe it. The sweet one? The only one she could almost like, even though Blooma couldn't play mahjong worth a damn.

Mavis dreamed up a plan; the women listened as she explained. Each felt a thrill burst through her.

Gertrude never tired of revenge.

Blooma giggled.

Winnie almost smiled.

Mavis knew the complex and its habits. Friday night was *Shabbos* dinner—chopped liver and crackers, soup and *knadlach*, challah, a chicken dinner with carrots and celery, and chocolate babke. The place was packed, and they stayed for the movie. Mavis had the run of the streets with no one the wiser.

So at sunset on Friday, Mavis parked her pink Harley at the handicap spot in the north wing of the Boca Raton Senior Living Center. She took a final pull from her flask before dismounting and greeting the others.

First came Gertrude, pedaling her three-wheeler with Blooma secure on a foam pillow in the back basket.

Then Winnie's driver dropped her off with strict instructions to pick her up in exactly forty-five minutes, which would give them enough time to complete their mission and get away without detection.

Together, the women entered the common room where the villagers had been meeting regularly to play mahjong. Tables were set up with remnants of recents games: a mahjong card, a forgotten scarf, a silver cane with a black rubber base.

"*Feh*, it's just another boxy room," said Mavis.

"And it smells like old lady perfume," said Gertrude.

Winnie raised an eyebrow. "And look at the walls. Cheap paintings of butterflies and droopy sunflowers. The still lifes are stiff and dull! Where's the color? The vibrancy? The inspiration?"

Blooma thought about the paintings in the South Tower room. Butterflies and flowers hung there too. Maybe Winnie thought those paintings lacked artistry as well but she never mentioned it. Blooma's inspiration was food, so her attention was drawn to the kitchen. She withdrew the plate of double-prune cupcakes with cream cheese frosting from her pocketbook and left them in the refrigerator with a "Help Yourself" note on top of them.

Mavis strutted to the rear of the room and opened the cabinet where the mahjong cases were stored. Each contained perfect sets of one hundred and fifty-two tiles.

"The first thing we have to do is find sets that have the same color of tiles," said Gertrude, always the organizer.

"Now you're the boss of me?" squawked Mavis, but she set to work unsnapping the cases.

Winnie examined what they found. Three sets had ivory tiles, two had lavender, and four had yellow. Mavis and Blooma chose the yellows; Gertrude grabbed the ivory; and Winnie took the lavender.

"Let's get to work," said Winnie.

The women redistributed the tiles in their cases, making sure there were still one hundred and fifty-two tiles. They jumbled them up just enough so that no one would notice at first. They added extra jokers to some sets and replaced them with flowers from other sets. They exchanged red dragons for greens, cracs for bams, dots for cracs, and norths for easts.

When the job was complete and the cases were returned to the cabinet, the women high-fived each other, something Gertrude had always wanted to do but never had the opportunity.

Mavis raised her flask, "*L'Chaim*. To life! May the games begin."

The following week, rumors circulated that the North Tower mahjong group was in turmoil. Nessa had won a hand that included six flowers, but Rita had four flowers in her hand at the same time! Ten flowers? Impossible! There were only eight to a set! Wendy called mahjong and exposed two green dragons with two jokers. Two players redeemed the jokers on their turns, but Bertha sat there stunned. She had another green dragon in her hand and desperately needed that joker. Five green dragons? Impossible! There were only four to a set. What was happening? Who had sabotaged the game? Everyone eyed each other with suspicion. *Gonifs*. Scoundrels! Thieves! Before long everyone was accusing each other of cheating.

Pay back was sweet.

Chapter Three

TSURRIS: PSYCHOLOGICAL SUFFERING

When the High Holy Day service for Rosh Hashanah was held in the North Tower, the four rebels refused to sit in the same room with the other mahjong ladies as they scanned the area for the culprit, zeroing in on a suspect, giving her the evil eye. They knew they'd giggle and give themselves away, especially since the prayers were solemn on this most sacred of days.

They decided to hold their own private High Holy Day service.

The day before Rosh Hashanah, Winnie gave each of her partners in crime her own monogrammed cloth purse. "I used to make these. I still have boxes of them in my closet, so I pasted your initial on it."

Gertrude grimaced. With all her money, she gave them a worthless *schmattie*? What about one of those silk purses with those pink beads? Weren't they good enough?

Mavis squirmed. She hated gifts. Now she'd have to give Winnie something in return.

Blooma studied the purse and had an aha moment. "On Rosh Hashanah, there's a special service called Tashlicht. You go to a body of water and throw away your sins."

"Sounds like a pagan ritual," said Gertrude.

"*Feh!* A *farkakte* idea! I got no sins," squawked Mavis.

"Bull shit," said Gertrude. "You have tattoos."

"So?"

"If you're Jewish, that's a sin," sniggered Gertrude.

"So I should put my tattoos in a goddamn purse and throw them in the ocean?"

"Ladies, we have an opportunity here," Winnie said, her voice like pearls. "The purse is a symbol, like Tashlicht. We can put our regrets and sins and sadness in the purse and set it afloat."

"That's a goddamned ridiculous idea," said Gertrude.

Blooma had tears in her eyes. "*Oy gevult.* Don't you understand that God desires kindness?"

Winnie took Blooma's hands in hers. Winnie was five-eight and with her Italian leather pumps, she towered over the little woman. "I'd need a sack for all my *tsurris*, but I'll winnow down my sorrows into one purse just for you."

"That's the spirit," said Blooma.

On the morning of Rosh Hashanah, the women wore their High Holiday clothing, except for Mavis. Her shorts exposed her wrinkled legs and the outline of her thong. Blooma's black shirtwaist was starched stiff and smelled like mothballs. The last time she wore it was at her husband Isaac's funeral. Gertrude poured herself into a business suit, leaving the waist band unbuttoned and her shirt flowing free. Winnie dressed in a silk chemise. The four women looked Temple ready, except for their sneakers, although Winnie's were designer chic.

Winnie's driver was summoned to take them to Red Reef Beach. As they neared the ocean, they decided they'd each find a meditative spot to talk out their sins and regrets. Then symbolically, they'd put them in the purse and toss them out to sea.

After getting out of the car, the women walked down a short slope.

"Smells like rotten fish," said Gertrude.

"Like dead armpits," said Mavis.

They removed their socks and sneakers and left them in a pile.

Winnie strode to a nearby sandbar. Mavis kicked, stomped and splashed at the ocean's edge. Blooma tiptoed in, lifting the hem of her skirt, and Gertrude headed for an outcrop of rocks.

Once Gertrude knew no one was within hearing distance, she turned her back and reached into her pocket for the purse. Then she let out a deep belly laugh that made her body shake. She would put nothing in it. Nothing good. Nothing bad. *Bupkis.* Nothing. She amounted to nothing.

She had been a woman of numbers, a retired bookkeeper by profession, and she added up to zero. When it came to her retirement, the bosses gave her a gold-plated pen, some generic good luck cards, and a wooden plaque with her name on it, which they spelled wrong. Friedman instead of Freidman. Her email account was cancelled the minute she walked out the door. She left no impression and no one would miss her. Without realizing it, she was crying, big bloated tears that dropped into the purse. She tossed it away, angry at it for capturing something so personal. She stood a long time staring at the horizon.

Further down the beach, Blooma's dress swished in the surf as she searched inside her cavernous pocketbook for the purse. She removed it like it contained rocks, so heavy, like the burden in her heart. She dipped two fingers and a thumb inside and pulled out a gold ring. All morning she had debated about removing it, but with a *bissel* of Vaseline, it twisted right off. With her chin down, her voice soft, and the ring held up to *Ha Shem*, she spoke the truth. "I resented my husband Isaac for making me feel small like a grain of sand. Today, I release the guilt I've carried for not standing up to him and for not protecting my daughter."

She could hear Isaac's accusations, the pounding insistence that he was right and Blooma was wrong." That girl was a handful from the moment she was born. Crying like we were killing her. Always the loudest kid in any room. And when she was older, she smoked on the corner and kissed boys in front of the house. A *shunda* for all the neighbors to see. And then she married that dark-skinned *schvatze*? How could she disgrace us? Nothing but trouble. And you, *dumkop*, you stupid woman, you catered to her every whim. The blame's on you, Blooma, that our daughter turned on us. You spoiled her rotten." He'd go on and on until he stormed out of the house and slammed the door and left Blooma crying. He forbade her to contact Sarah after he tore his clothing, declared his daughter dead to him, and sat *shiva* for a week. He demanded Blooma wear black for a year, which Blooma obeyed. But she wore white panties and a white bra and felt her skin blossom pink whenever she thought of Sarah.

Blooma wiped the tears from her eyes and cleared her voice. "I am no longer attached to you, Isaac. I break our circle today and forever." She returned the ring to the purse. Then she recited *Kaddish*, the prayer for the dead. "Amen," she said aloud and tossed the purse into the ocean. "*Gey avek*," she shouted into space, "Go away, go far, far away." She unbuttoned her dress and took it off, stuffing it into a plastic bag in her pocketbook; she didn't want to litter. She had worn a bright yellow housedress beneath the mourning clothes. She stood in the water like it was a new dawn.

On the other side of the sandbar, Winnie reached into her pocket for the purse and found the four coins she had placed there. She chose the shiniest one first. "You were my golden boy, my dearest love Samuel." She kissed it softly. "Imagine the life we could have had if only you had lived." Gently, she placed the coin back and withdrew another, tarnished and dull like it had been wallowing in mud. "Brian, you *schtunk*. The only good that came from you was our son BJ. How did you talk me into naming him Brian Junior and not circumcising him?" She flung the coin into the ocean then scrubbed her fingers clean. The third coin looked tear-stained, like it had already been dipped in the ocean. "BJ, my beautiful son, I am so sorry I was too weak to raise you properly. I cared more about me than you. Now I am old and I need you in my life. Please find it in your heart to forgive me." She held the fourth coin to the sun. "Jev. My husband Jevela. So kind and thoughtful. Surrounding me with magnificent artwork. At least you didn't suffer when you died. I will find you in heaven." Winnie settled the three coins in the purse and shook it gently, mixing loss and longing and love. She waited for the pull of the tide and set it afloat; it dipped and surfaced and dipped again before it disappeared.

Mavis continued to kick the water. She didn't believe in Tashlicht or Rosh Hashanah or the purse. A *schtickle drek*, a piece of shit. She had a whopper of a regret, burning down her parents' home. But it was an accident, not a sin. Jail time? Well, she got caught with a few ounces of pot. Dumb fuck luck. So now, she should thank the purse-gods? She should praise the new year and usher it in by saying she had sinned. Fucking bullshit. She put the purse to her mouth and shouted into it: "I am Mavis Gruber. One of a kind. No one screws with me. Not ever. Not even purses." She stuffed it in her shorts, turned her back on the ocean and walked along the sand.

She leered at the other women as they tossed their sins into the ocean. Damn them, Mavis thought, and yanked the nip of whiskey from her bra and drank it deep. She thought back to her college psych class when she learned an acronym for the seven deadly sins: PEWSAGL. Pride, envy, wrath, sloth, avarice, gluttony, and lust. She was never greedy for money or food, and was always willing to share her booze and drugs. Sure she lusted, often, but it was not sinful to have lovers. She never gave a good goddamn what anyone else thought and enjoyed shocking others. She danced on tabletops, mooned old fogies, and lied for the fun of it. But in her heart of hearts she had one overriding sin and it wasn't on anyone's list. Mavis put the purse to her lips again and whispered her deepest truth: "Mavis Gruber is a coward." Then she launched it into the ocean like a rocket and watched it sink.

The women gathered together on the shore drawing close to Blooma.

"Why Blooma, you're a ray of sunshine," said Winnie. "What did you do?"

"I took off my mourning clothes. Eighty-two is not too late to start again." A dimpled grin spread across her face. "In the spirit of Tashlicht, I have something special for each of you."

"More *chazarai*," said Mavis. "Another piece of trash to dump in the ocean?" For Christ sakes, she should shut the hell up. "I'm sorry, Blooma. Go ahead. Whaddaya got?"

Blooma brought out a loaf of bread. "I baked this challah this morning." She tore off a piece for each woman. "*Essen*, eat, and while you do, think about what we did to those mahjong ladies who wouldn't let us play with them."

"They deserved whatever they got," said Gertrude. "We didn't hurt them, we just played a little prank."

"And enjoyed every minute," said Winnie.

"Isn't that the point of sinning?" said Blooma. "You do something wicked, get pleasure from it, and congratulate yourself at how clever you are?"

The women nodded.

"But look at the bigger picture. We took away the pleasure of winning from those ladies. We created a false set of playing tiles and giggled that they would be confused and angry and they'd go home suspecting each other of cheating. Isn't that a sin?" asked Blooma.

"Sin, shmin," said Mavis. "We goofed them and had fun doing it."

"But what if you were on the receiving end. Would it still be funny?" asked Blooma.

"So we should run to the Rosh Hashanah service and go up on the Bimah and beg forgiveness from those *farbissineh* biddies?" snorted Gertrude.

Blooma tore off another piece of bread for each woman. "Did you know that fish have no eyelids and that their eyes are always open?"

Mavis whispered to Gertrude, "Is the woman off her rocker?"

Gertrude shrugged.

Blooma forged on. "We're here to rid ourselves of sin, to ensure that our names are written in the Book of Life and that we have another full year to make amends."

"Amen," said Winnie, thinking that Blooma had made sense for a change.

"I'm not finished," said Blooma. "Let's throw our challah into the water and think about what we can do to be nicer to others. The ocean will sweep away our sins and at the same time feed the fish."

"It's a win-win," said Winnie.

"Win-win-Winnie!" said Mavis.

They all laughed, but inside they understood the custom of going to the ocean on Rosh Hashanah. The sins of today did not have to be there tomorrow. Sins, like the current, will move on.

Blooma raised her piece of challah. "I cast away the sin of deception." She had lived for decades in Isaac's shadow, pretending to love and obey him. No longer did she have to lie.

Gertrude turned down her lips. "I cast away the sin of pride." What difference did it make if she wasn't honored by her colleagues? She knew her value.

Winnie lowered her chin. "I cast away the sin of selfishness." What she wouldn't give to have her son back in her life again.

Mavis wanted to bolt, but she knew she had to say something. "I cast away the sin of anger." Was it wrath that boiled inside her? Or was she missing the point altogether?

They tossed the bread into the ocean, then formed a circle—tiny Blooma, bow-legged Mavis, wide-hipped Gertrude, and statuesque Winnie. They held hands, each absorbing the other's energy. From a distance they looked like rag dolls, ready to be swept away by a rogue wave. But up close there was a fierceness to each of them, a determination to hold onto the moment.

They hummed Hebrew songs from their childhood: *Adon Olam*, the *Shma*, *Ayn Caloheinu*. Some got some of the words, none got all, but it didn't matter. Their voices rolled out to sea with their sorrows.

Chapter Four

PLOTZ: OVERCOME WITH STRONG EMOTION

On a sunny Wednesday in late October, while the four outcasts were playing mahjong, the door to the South Tower clubhouse opened, and a woman entered, her platinum hair done up like Venus. She had high cheekbones, lush glossy lips, and a bosom that didn't sag.

Mavis' eyes popped. Gertrude's jaw dropped. They gaped at her supple skin, her unwrinkled neck, and her strong jaw. Blooma ran for the tray of rugelach. Even Winnie tipped her chin in a nod.

"I heard this is the game room. I just moved to the complex and I like games. Can I join you?"

"Sure thing," said Gertrude, in a higher pitch than normal. "Do you play mahjong?"

"I don't, Sugar, but I'm a fast learner." She winked at Gertrude, who blushed like a schoolgirl. "I'm Jayne," the woman said in a Southern drawl, her voice like a song.

"I'm Mavis. She's Gertrude. She's Blooma, and that's Winnie. Why don't you sit beside me and watch for a while. I'll show you how to play." Mavis scooted to put a chair between her and Gertrude, whose jaw still had not closed.

"Pleased to meet y'all. Now don't let me interfere. I'll be as quiet as a church mouse."

We're claiming her, thought Gertrude, imagining the envious reactions of the North Tower sourpusses when they saw her group's new player. She's all ours.

Mavis rolled the dice and dealt the tiles. As she set up her hand, she whispered details about the game into Jayne's ear, imbibing the smell of vanilla on the woman's hair and skin. Creamy soft, sweet enough to taste, thought Mavis. She'd never much cared for women, but this Jayne Mansfield look-alike was different. Helpless in a strong way. Even how she sat said power, with a hint of take-care-of-me. Mavis liked to be in control, but she admired spunk. None of the mahjong women had spunk. Winnie was cold and smelled like money. Gertrude was stiff and smelled like vinegar, and Blooma was a cupcake.

Jayne studied the mahjong card. "So I pick a hand and then collect tiles that match it. Something like gin rummy, except there are three suits—bams, dots and cracs. Right?"

"You catch on fast," said Mavis.

"And each suit has a matching dragon," said Gertrude, who had moved her chair closer to Jayne's. "And there are winds and flowers." Gertrude pointed out the symbols, wishing she had filed her nails that morning; they were jagged and mottled with color, not manicured like Jayne's. And those perky boobs. Gertrude hadn't had breasts like that since grade school. She liked the way this Jayne studied the mahjong card, like she was absorbing it, her sculptured brows rising and lowering with meaning, her eyes focused and concentrating. Gertrude admired smart people, even if they did have Southern accents. She resisted the urge to take the woman's hand and hold it and not let it go.

Winnie inspected Jayne from a distance. She liked how classy she was. Not like these women who wore *schmatties*, raggy old clothes.

And Blooma was so happy to see a new face, someone else who might enjoy her babke. She would bake her special almond strudel with cinnamon and raspberries, she thought. It would round out Jayne's skinny hips.

"Maybe you need a private lesson, Jayne?" Mavis winked and grinned, confusing all her wrinkles.

"If you want to teach me the finer points, I'd be obliged." Jayne batted her thick eyelashes at Mavis, but addressed the table. "When's the next game?"

"Wednesday at 1:00," said Winnie.

"And you should know," squawked Mavis, unable to contain her inner parrot. "The woman is never on time."

"Maybe you'd like to sit in while we wait for her?" asked Gertrude.

"Stop pestering me about being late. It's Sal's fault, not mine." Winnie glared at Mavis and Gertrude with her eyes, but smiled at Jayne with her lips. "You can sit beside me next week and I'll show you how to organize your rack."

"I showed her just fine," said Mavis, drumming on her chest like an alpha-male.

"You're too fast. She needs a patient teacher," said Winnie.

"And you're too damned slow," snarled Mavis.

Jayne stood up. "Oy! I could *plotz* from you ladies."

The women's mouths dropped. A blond, with no *tuches*, and no chin hairs knew Yiddish? Who would have believed it?

"See you next week," cooed Jayne and swept out of the room like a feather on the wind.

Chapter Five

OY GEVULT: UH-OH! ENOUGH ALREADY!

Whenever Jayne showed up, she flirted with each woman as they sat around the table. She complimented Mavis on the matching rose tattoos on her forearms.

"Oh, those are in honor of my fiftieth birthday when they were all I wore to bed with Charlie Sheen."

In her dreams, thought Gertrude. The woman was a pompous *nudnik*. Charlie Sheen was half her age. Now Cary Grant or Spencer Tracy, that she might have believed.

"That was before he became a star," crooned Mavis. Mavis took off her shirt. Her halter top revealed the tattoo of a parrot on her left shoulder. "Meet Sammy." Mavis gave a sharp squawk. "He's my alter ego."

More like an excuse to be an asshole, thought Gertrude.

To Winnie, Jayne said, "Your hat is as lovely as a daffodil in spring."

More like a peacock in heat, thought Gertrude. No one wore hats anymore, especially ones that shadowed her face like the Wicked Witch of the West. Gertrude's face took on an evil glow, like she was going to eat anyone within biting distance.

For Blooma, Jayne complimented her baking. "Yummy strudel, Doll-Face."

More like prune face, tittered Gertrude, when she's not wearing her dentures. Jayne caught Gertrude's eye and Gertrude felt a pang of guilt for being so catty. Good thing Jayne couldn't read her thoughts.

Jayne patted Gertrude's hand and played with a strand of her hair. "You remind me of Alice on the *Brady Bunch*. What a honey she was."

Gertrude gulped. She had met Ann Davis and had her picture and autograph. In person, she wasn't plain at all. Her eyes sparkled and her laugh was infectious. Gertrude took out her pocket mirror and noticed the resemblance. That night she'd find that photo and frame it.

Jayne knew what her girls liked, and they had become her girls. They each took special pains to please her. Blooma gave her the best slice of cake. Winnie made sure she didn't need a key to get into the exclusive lounge on the fifteenth floor of the high-rise. Gertrude offered tips on the stock market while Mavis took her for joy rides on her motorcycle.

One day, Jayne decided they should all go to the Watering Hole, a hot spot on Jog Drive. Jayne said there was Karaoke and it would be fun for them to sing together. That's all it took for the shouting to begin, except for Blooma, who would never raise her voice.

"A Beatles song," said Gertrude. "*Let It Be*."

"Rolling Stones!" said Mavis. "Way cool."

"A classic by Sinatra," said Winnie. "How about *High Hopes*."

"Only if I'm smoking a doobie," said Mavis.

"A what?" asked Blooma. "A Boobie? How does that work?"

Jayne threw back her head and laughed. The women stared at her smooth neck and touched their own, ironing them out. "We're going to sing *Man Eater* by Hall and Oates." Jayne stood, her strong frame swaying, her white t-shirt dazzling. She belted out the words:

> *Watch out boy she'll chew you up*
> *Oh, here she comes*
> *She's a man eater.*

"Man Eater? I've done that," said Mavis. The tattooed parrot on her shoulder shimmied.

"I can add a little spice," said Gertrude, shaking her *tuches*.

"*Oy gevult!* My husband should turn over in his grave," said Blooma, blushing.

"That song's about women in total control," said Winnie, her glasses slipping over her nose, her eyes peering over the lenses. "My style completely."

"Time to practice," said Jayne.

On the night of the big event, Jayne met the women at the South Tower for a final rehearsal. Winnie strode in wearing a wide-brimmed lavender hat that dipped and flowed like a wave. Blooma draped her lucky shawl around her shoulders, the one she wore to *shul* and all the women had oohed and aahed. Mavis had on a halter top exposing Sammy the Parrot. Gertrude wore a button-down white cotton shirt and a navy blue skirt.

Jayne was dressed in a tight sequined top, gold pants and open-toed stilettos. She spread her make-up kit out on the table. Mavis had never seen so many sexy shades of red: electric crimson, wild orchid, vivid cerise, ruby woo.

One by one, Jayne transformed each of them.

"You have champagne eyes," she told Winnie. "Pale gold with a tinge of orange." Jayne feathered purple shadow mixed with yellow on Winnie's lids and applied a silky peach to her lips. "Your hat needs to accent your assets, like a frame adds to the beauty of art."

Winnie thought about the artwork in her apartment, how each was framed differently, how the most elaborate frames called too much attention to themselves. Winnie reached into her purse for the alternate hat she had packed, the yellow beret. She felt like a model when she wore it and it magnified her champagne eyes.

"Now you're a masterpiece." Jayne told Winnie.

For Blooma, Jayne brushed cornflower shadow onto her lids. "You have forget-me-not blue eyes," said Jayne.

Blooma wished she had a forget-me-not brain instead. What good was all this color on the outside, if her insides were fading? She pulled her shawl tight.

Jayne took a fluffy brush and dipped it in soft plum powder, then caressed Blooma's face and neck. "Relax, Sweetie, you're going to look ten years younger when I'm done. You'll be opening your top button and throwing off the shawl."

Oy gevult! At eighty-two she'd look seventy-two? She enjoyed feeling Jayne's light touch dressing up her skin. The last time she'd had this much attention was when she fainted at the pool and the EMTs hovered over her.

"Blooma's in bloom," said Jayne. "A hot-house hottie!"

Jayne massaged foundation onto Gertrude's face. No one had touched her in decades, not a doctor, not a dentist, barely a fleeting wisp from the wind. Gertrude tingled down to her toes.

"Gun-metal gray for you, Gertie," said Jayne staring into Gertrude's eyes. "I think you and I should shop for new eyeglass frames, something to show how powerful you are. Periwinkle is your new color." Jayne lined Gertrude's eyes with blue and added mascara. "You're a beauty under all that bluster," Jayne whispered.

Gertrude couldn't believe what Jayne said. She knew she had clear skin, never a blemish, but her jowls sagged and her frown lines ran deep. But for Jayne to say she was a beauty! Never had anyone mistaken her for a beauty. Sure, she was a beaut. She'd been called that a million times. Gertrude blinked her steely eyes and wondered if she had imagined Jayne's words, because the woman was working on Mavis' face and complimenting her rebellious style and Mavis wasn't rebelling, not one bit.

"Red is your color, Mavis, like the redwing thrush," said Jayne. She hummed a tune, then sang a melody seemingly just for Mavis: "'That's the wise thrush; he sings each song twice over.' I bet once is never enough for a woman like you," winked Jayne.

You're damn right, thought Mavis, once is never enough for me. Two-timing was her style. How was she to know if she liked something if she only tried it once? Once was a tease; twice was a commitment. Three times was never an option.

The women's faces beamed honey-golds and pinks; their eyes sparkled and glittered. No brown spots or deep wrinkles—hot spice and salty seasoning instead.

Mavis was reminded of a story she had read in high school, *Dr. Heideggar's Experiment,* how old farts were duped into thinking they were young again. Hell, she could go along with this makeover for a little while. It tickled her fancy.

At 8:00 PM, Sal dropped the women at the karaoke bar with strict instructions from Winnie to be back in two hours. The women emerged from the car like they were on display for a red carpet event. They paraded into the nightclub, each face radiant with anticipation.

Chapter Six

VEY IZ MIR: WOE IS ME!

Inside the Watering Hole, the air thrummed with static. A bearded man wearing Oshkosh by Gosh overalls held the mic so close to his lips that the sound system shuttered as he sang *I Can't Get No Satisfaction.*

"No surprise there that he can't get no girlie action," Gertrude shouted to Mavis.

"A *nebbish* like him never got no girlie action," Mavis shouted back.

"Shush!" scolded Winnie. "It's not easy to get up on stage like that."

"Sure it is, Sweetie. All you need is confidence," said Jayne.

The OshKosh man bowed and a smattering of people in the audience and at the bar pounded their fists on their tables. Mavis hog-whistled and stomped her feet.

"Shush," said Winnie again. "Stop creating a ruckus."

Mavis waggled her shoulders at Winnie and squawked a few times until Winnie cracked a tiny smile.

"Those champagne eyes need some life behind them," said Mavis to Winnie.

Mavis waltzed toward the bar and stopped short. Four women were strutting to the stage: one was barrel-round with stick legs; one had a mop of grey frizz; another was rail thin; and the fourth was tiny and ratchet-faced. They wore frilly white shirts and red skirts, polka dot bows in their hair, and painted on Cupie-Pie lips. Giggling like teenagers, they blew kisses at the *alta kaker* men at the bar.

Mavis poked Gertrude. "Lookie, lookie. The mahjong *farbissinehs*, the four meanies. Let's spit on them."

"*Oy vey iz mir*," said Blooma, putting her hands to her cheeks and shaking her head back and forth. "Shush! We'll get in trouble."

"What's going on?" asked Jayne.

Winnie pulled herself to her full height and turned her nose down at the same time. "They're the North Tower mahjong women who won't play with us."

Mavis and Gertrude hissed.

"*Oy!* Stop it," Blooma said. "Don't make a scene."

Jayne corralled the ladies into a booth. "We'll get them soon enough, you'll see."

On the stage, the music started. The Cupie Pie North Tower mean mahjong women wiggled their *tucheses* and made pouty faces. They kicked their legs Rockette style and belted out

Ain't She Sweet. See her coming down the street.
Now I ask you very confidentially, ain't she sweet.

Mavis stood, ready to throw peanuts at them, but Jayne strong-armed her. "Honey, I'm telling you. We'll knock 'em dead." She signaled the waiter. "A bottle of your best house red wine."

"I haven't had *schnapps* since Passover ten years ago!" said Blooma, sipping it slowly, but steadily.

"This is grape juice," said Mavis, who chugged it, then ordered bourbon.

"Ladies," said Winnie, "it's liquid courage. Drink up."

"I don't need alcohol for courage," said Gertrude, "I have natural energy." Liquor made her groggy. She hated being less than herself.

THE MAHJONG MAVENS OF BOCA RATON

Then it was showtime. On the stage, the women flanked Jayne like ambient light. She was the sun. The women snapped their fingers and the words came tumbling out.

> *She'll only come out at night*
> *The lean and hungry type*
> *Watch out boys she'll chew you up*
> *She's a man eater.*

Through dentured teeth, hoots and whistles filled the room.

"That woke them up," shouted Jayne.

"More! More! Bravo!" came the catcalls.

"We'll be back," said Jayne. The women took a bow. Mavis shimmied, Blooma's eyes twinkled, Winnie saluted, and Gertrude jiggled her ample hips.

The Cupie Pies hadn't moved, not a muscle until one of them broke the spell and spit into the air three times. "Poo, Poo, Poo. *Vilder chaiah!* Wild animals!"

Gertrude and Mavis wanted to moon them, but Blooma slapped their hands. "We are *mensches*. Remember that."

"Man-eating *mensches!*" Jayne roared and the men at the bar shrank. "A round of cognac for my girls."

"My treat!" called Winnie.

Mavis poured hers into her flask for later and ordered another round. "Let's do shots."

"Who's a *putz?*" asked Blooma.

"Shots, Blooma, shots. You know chug the drink like men," Gertrude said. She sent caution to the wind and tossed one back.

Blooma stroked her shawl like she was removing crumbs from it. "I never did that before." She picked up the glass, took a lip-smacking sip, then gulped it down. Her eyes bugged and her bottom lip dropped. "Darn tootin,' that's good."

"Dial Sal and tell him to give us another hour," said Mavis.

But before Winnie could make the call, Blooma toppled off her bar stool.

Jayne swept in and lifted Blooma like a feather. "Doll Face, are you all right?"

Blooma's head swayed. "Am I dead?"

Jayne laughed, but it wasn't a throaty laugh, more like a nervous titter. "Too much excitement for one night. We'd better get you home."

Jayne carried Blooma outside, and for once Sal was actually there, talking with some young men and smoking a Marlboro. Winnie opened the doors and the women piled in. Jayne set Blooma in the front, reclined the seat and opened the window.

Sal stomped out his cigarette and got in the car. "What happened to the old broad?"

"Too much *schnapps!*" said Mavis.

Chapter Seven

EMMIS: THE TRUTH

When the Lincoln Town Car pulled up to Blooma's condo, she insisted she'd be all right. "I just need a little air."

The women knew better. They wanted to get her into bed and make sure she was okay. The apartment was one of the smaller ones and four people fluttering around Blooma would be too much, so Mavis volunteered to stay.

"My place is in the next row of houses. I can walk home after she's settled," said Mavis.

"And I'm only two streets away. I'll stay too," said Gertrude.

Winnie let out a sigh and looked at Jayne. "No need wasting good clothing and a face full of make up putting an old woman to bed," she whispered. "Let's get a nightcap at the exec club."

After retrieving the keys from Blooma's pocketbook—tossing out old tissues, cough drop wrappers, a half-eaten bulke roll, and three plastic forks with suspicious crumbs on them—Mavis unlocked the door and turned on the lights. Gertrude guided Blooma into the apartment.

A heavy sweetness filtered through the air. Honey and blueberries. Candy and cookies and love. Mavis expected lollipops to dangle from the ceiling and flowers made of chocolate and cherries to sprout from the floor. Nothing like the kitchens where Mavis had ever lived, heavy with beer and whiskey and smoke.

Gertrude found the sweetness cloying. It smelled sticky like syrup, unlike Gertrude's apartment which was antiseptic clean, scrubbed weekly on her hands and knees. Gertrude had grown up with three older sisters and three younger brothers. Their house stank of dirty socks and hair spray and piglets. That's what her parents did. They ran a pig farm. Hers was the only Jewish family within fifty miles and her mother and father wanted to assimilate. What better way than with *tref*, forbidden food, strictly non-kosher. The big pigs stayed outside in pens, but the babies were so cute that her father brought them into the house to play. But pigs rolled in mud and attracted flies. Everywhere in Gertrude's childhood home there were fly strips that smelled like castor oil. Flies were squashed and legs were severed and wings dangled. Blooma's little apartment was too sugary for Gertrude. She closed her nose and breathed through her mouth.

Mavis and Gertrude helped Blooma into bed. They meant to tiptoe out the front door and head to their own places, but Blooma started coughing, her tiny body shaking under the covers. They just couldn't leave her there by herself. They took turns keeping watch.

Neither Mavis nor Gertrude had ever been in one another's homes, so this was a major opportunity to poke around. Mavis checked out the living room first. The couch was large with plastic over its cushions, as if no one had sat there for decades. On the coffee table were several stacks of envelopes wrapped in rubber bands and a few magazines: *Hadassah*, *The Moment*, and a beaten up copy of *Yankee* with a cheerful woman on the cover who looked remarkably like Blooma. Could it be?

Mavis scanned the pages until she came to a story about a regional contest requiring Brewer's yeast for baking. A middle-aged woman with brown hair and sparkling blue eyes showed off a key-shaped challah the color of honey and wheat. "The winning recipe by Blooma Gottlieb is called 'Schlissel Bread,' symbolic of unlocking the gates of heaven and filling your home with blessings." It was Blooma, all right.

Mavis shared the article with Gertrude. "Our personal Betty Crocker!" she said, studying the picture. "Blooma had crooked teeth. Amazing what dentures will do."

Mavis shrugged. She had never bothered with false teeth. Six uppers and six lowers were plenty good for her.

Blooma was resting more easily, so the women took a break and sat together at the kitchen table devouring a blueberry crumb cake. Both women dropped their jaws when they noticed the picture on the refrigerator. Two bright smiles beamed from two dark-skinned boys. Behind them stood a biracial couple: a tall, thin black man and a tiny porcelain white woman.

"The girl looks a lot like Blooma," said Mavis.

"*Emmis*," said Gertrude, "that's the truth."

"I didn't know she had a daughter," said Mavis.

There's a lot we don't know about each other, thought Gertrude, and a lot you'll never know. "Blooma's private life is none of our business," said Gertrude.

"You don't say? I saw you snooping," said Mavis.

"But I didn't open any cabinets like you did."

"You're just waiting for me to fall asleep," said Mavis. "I got big ears."

"*Emmis*," said Gertrude again. And a big mouth, she thought, but didn't say it. She stomped to Blooma's room to check on her. She was snoring lightly, in soft rhythmic puffs.

Gertrude found a blanket in the closet and lay down on the unmade twin bed. "How do you like that? Blooma and her husband had slept separately."

When Blooma woke the next morning, she saw a body spread out on Isaac's bed. "Have I gone to Hell? *Ahfteloches*, just my luck to end up beside that man for eternity." Then she saw Gertrude raise her head and heard the tinkling of glasses in the kitchen. "Why are you here? What's going on?"

Gertrude sat up and yawned like she had nowhere else to go. "What's going on is you collapsed last night after drinking too much and we brought you home and put you to bed. We didn't want to leave you alone, so Mavis and I took turns making sure you were all right."

"You didn't have to do that."

"But we did," said Mavis, who strutted into the bedroom. "What if you didn't wake up and we weren't here? We'd blame ourselves for killing you."

"You wouldn't have killed me. Besides, I'm ready to die."

Mavis and Gertrude went into action, flurrying around the bed, fluffing the pillow, feeling her forehead. Mavis brought a straw to Blooma's mouth. "Drink some water. You'll feel better."

"We should get in touch with that beautiful girl on the refrigerator. Is she your daughter?" asked Gertrude. "We didn't know you had a daughter."

"It's none of your beeswax," said Blooma.

"We're just trying to help," said Gertrude.

"We helped ourselves to the blueberry cake on the counter," said Mavis. "You can't die yet. I haven't tasted your Schlissel Bread."

That brought a smile to Blooma's face. Maybe she'd live to bake another day. "Thanks, girls. You've done enough." Blooma swung her legs off the bed and onto the floor. She stood up straight, ignoring the sway in her head and the need to collapse. "I'll be fine. Go home now."

"Are you sure?" asked Mavis.

"Call 911 if you feel faint. They built a station house in the complex, they get so many calls," said Gertrude.

"I'll see you at mahjong. Thank you. Really. I just need a little time to myself."

Mavis knew the feeling. So did Gertrude. They each gave Blooma a light hug.

Blooma waited until the front door closed before falling back onto the bed. She was surprised to see that she was in her nightgown. Who had done that for her? Mavis and Gertrude together? Laughing at her bony body. The blood rushed to her face. She was relieved that she still had on her bra and panties. They had the decency not to have stripped her down. But they had been in her house. All night! Digging into her drawers and closets. The *yentas*. Gossiping together. Then tattling to Winnie and Jayne about her secrets: the picture on the refrigerator, her daughter Sarah, Sarah's black husband, their dark-skinned boys.

Blooma got out of bed, her head pounding like a hammer had banged it. She put on her slippers and shuffled to the bathroom and then into the kitchen. She boiled a pot of water, made a cup of tea, and put what was left of the blueberry cake in front of her with a fork. She was so hungry.

When she was ready, she sat across from the refrigerator and stared at the photo. After her husband died, Blooma allowed a seed of hope to grow. It began when the photo arrived in an envelope addressed to Blooma Gold, her maiden name, not Gottlieb—Sarah's way of saying that Blooma was free of Isaac. Blooma felt color come alive in her for the first time in the ten years that Sarah had been banished. But that was four years ago already. And still Sarah hadn't come to Florida. And Blooma couldn't go to New York alone. How could she manage through an airport? Taking off her shoes. Getting patted down. Flying in a tube of toothpaste! Blooma needed to put her arms around those *boychics*, her grandsons, Andrew and Mark. She needed to bake them monkey bread drizzled with sugar. "When?" Blooma cried. "When! Is Sarah so busy with her doctor-life that she can't visit her mother? Isaac doesn't breathe here any longer. It's just me."

Blooma did not show up for mahjong on Wednesday. Her heart was in the wrong place, and she had misplaced her dentures. She wouldn't leave home without them. When did I have them last, she thought? Did Mavis or Gertrude take them when they were in my house?

Instead of searching, Blooma took the picture of Sarah and her family, put it under her pillow, lay in bed with the covers pulled over her sunken face, and slept.

Chapter Eight

MENSCH: A PERSON OF HONOR AND INTEGRITY

"Should we go to Blooma's house?" asked Mavis.

"She could be dead!" said Gertrude.

"We're going to need a fourth for mahjong," said Winnie. Mavis and Gertrude glared at her. "Well, it's true. No one else will play with us."

And then they all thought about Jayne, the lovely, youthful, slinky Jayne. But she wasn't at the clubhouse on Wednesday afternoon either and the women refused to play three.

"Only *schmendriks* play three," said Mavis, whose bowlegs made their way out of the clubhouse and onto her pink Harley. She skirted past Blooma's to check on her. The blinds were open, so she was still alive. No need to bother her, Mavis thought. She was all right. She just had to catch up with herself.

Mavis parked her motorcycle in her driveway, got out her sponges and Armor All and polished her wheels. She loved that motorcycle. It reminded her of her free-flowing days when all she cared about was her next high or her next lay or her next full-out brawl, duking it out with some *fashtukenah* bitch over who got a better parking space. Those were the days. Until she got stuck here, in this dingy condo with old coots living all around her. No *baytzim* on any of these ancient people. No balls. What she wouldn't give for a day of speed.

Winnie called her driver to take her home from the clubhouse. She barely nodded good-bye to Gertrude, who stared stone-faced at the mahjong tiles, the racks set up for a game.

Gertrude sat there for a long time before deciding to play all four hands, by herself, hopping from one chair to the other, vying for the best play, pretending she didn't know what the other hands contained. It dawned on her that each hand was deliberately different and each was close to mahjong because it needed different tiles to complete it. She picked and threw until the seat where Blooma usually sat got the winning tile. She would have been paid double-double because she got it herself and her hand contained no jokers. Blooma would have floated to the ceiling. Maybe she should visit the old woman to see how she was doing, but she didn't have her phone number, and she didn't want to knock on her door like a *buttinski*. Instead, she played more games until her own seat had won four in a row.

The next Wednesday, Blooma still hadn't shown up, but Jayne had. She came in holding a bag of ice to the side of her cheek. "Damn pain in my right molars. Maybe I don't need them at this age anyway."

"Who are you kidding?" asked Gertrude. "We got men to eat!"

Jayne eked out a laugh then looked around. "Where's Blooma?"

The women shrugged.

"Haven't seen her since we stayed overnight at her house. She shooed us out the next morning like we were pests invading her privacy," said Gertrude.

"We need a fourth. Do you want to play mahjong?" asked Winnie.

Jayne had caught on to the game well enough. Certainly she was a better player than Blooma. There were no snacks or babke or rugelech to nosh, but Jayne said her jaw was tender anyway.

Gertrude wanted to stroke her cheek and spoon-feed her apple-sauce and make the pain go away. She sat to the left of Jayne and imbibed the lavender of her skin. She touched a knee to Jayne's thigh and laughed it off, but Jayne followed up by not moving and allowing Gertrude's leg to remain close.

"Do any of you know a good dentist who doesn't charge much?" asked Jayne.

"Such a question. Does a bear shit in the woods?" asked Mavis.

"Insurance pays for it anyway," said Winnie, "so what does it matter?"

"Never got dental," said Jayne.

Winnie stared at her like she had two heads. Jayne might be in good condition for a woman in her early sixties, but she was looking for trouble if she didn't have insurance. Then again, her husband Jev had made sure Winnie had the best of the best. "Humana for healthy living," he told her. A lot of good it did him. Dying so suddenly. Winnie's eyes welled thinking of that last day. How Jev had come to breakfast smooth-cheeked, his mustache turned up like a smile. "How's the love of my life?" he'd ask each morning and kiss her cheek. He smelled like cardamom and white flowers, patchouli and cocoa. Winnie marveled at how well groomed he kept himself, right down to his mani-pedi every other week. He even had his brows waxed. A true gentleman. A *gantseh mensch* in every way.

"My late husband Jev swore by his dentist, even if the man was a *faygele*," Winnie said.

"I don't care if he's gay," said Jayne, "as long as he doesn't charge me an arm and a leg."

She has such nice legs, thought Gertrude, smooth and shapely, with muscular calves. She loved that in a woman. "Teeth are always in style," said Gertrude. "I can lend you a few bucks."

Jayne arched her brows. "You'd do that for me? Such a *mensch* you are."

Funny how Winnie was just thinking that word. Jev would have given Jayne the money outright. He was generous like that. "How much do you need?" asked Winnie. "I'll just write you a check. Consider it a gift."

Gertrude felt like she'd been slapped. Winnie, *ongeshtopt mit gelt*, loaded with money. It was just like that woman to upstage her, stealing Jayne away from her. She'd show Winnie who had the dough. Gertrude had saved every penny since she was a kid. She had more than that woman any day. "You just let me know what you need and I'll be there for you," said Gertrude to Jayne. "We don't want our new mahjong player out of commission because of a toothache."

"You're both too generous! I'll pay you back. I promise," said Jayne, and blew air kisses at Winnie and Gertrude.

Just then, Blooma hobbled in. "Is it Wednesday?" She was carrying a tray of pastry. When she saw the four women sitting around the mahjong table, their racks filled with tiles, their cards open for play, her face crumpled. "I see you started without me."

Jayne leaped to her feet. "Sit down," she insisted, pulling out her chair for Blooma.

"Have a piece of mandel bread," Blooma crooned, offering the hard wafer that was baked with chocolate and raisins.

Mavis spoke up. "Jayne's got a hurting tooth. She's eating oatmeal and mush."

"Then I'll make a *glezel tai* and she can dip the mandel bread in it, just like I like it," said Blooma.

Each heart softened. They imagined Blooma sipping hot tea and savoring the treat like Oreos dipped in milk.

The mahjong game began with each woman rotating in. Whenever they sat out, they'd help Blooma with her tiles. To her delight, Blooma even claimed a few wins. "I'm hot today," she boasted and smiled, her dimples on display.

Chapter Nine

FARMISHTED: MIXED UP, CONFUSED

Jayne took Blooma's arm as she walked her home. "Just keeping you safe to bake another day."

"My sister and I used to walk home from school together when we were little. We shared our secrets." Blooma's face took on a glow. "Like the time Herbie Sathan kissed me at recess. Or when my sister picked her nose and put the booger in Russell Karl's sandwich. We giggled about that for years."

"Where's your sister now?"

"Long gone," Blooma patted Jayne's hand. "But I can pretend that you're her. What can we giggle about?"

"How about those Cupie Pies trying to sing karaoke?"

"Karaoke?" asked Blooma.

"At the Watering Hole? When we sang *Man Eater*?"

Blooma stopped short. "When we did what?"

Jayne hummed the tune and sang some of the words: *"She'll only come out at night, the lean and hungry type."*

Blooma's eyes grew wide. *"Watch out boys she'll chew you up!* I remember!" Blooma stared at Jayne as if seeing her for the first time. "You have a lovely voice. So rich. And you look a bit like ah, that blond woman from the 50s? Rose. Rosemary. Rosemary Clooney."

Blooma tripped through her memory, recalling songs Rosemary Clooney had sung: *You Make Me Feel So Young, Sisters,* and *I'll Be Seeing You.* Blooma's husband Isaac said Rosemary Clooney had a horsey face and thyroid eyes. But Blooma loved her high cheekbones and upswept hair and large bosom and thin waist. Isaac was at work when the Bing Crosby-Rosemary Clooney Show came on, so she was free to dance around the house and even whistle, which Isaac said was bad luck. *Narishkeit.* Foolishness. It was behavior like that that made her lose her babies before they were born, he said.

Blooma looked at Jayne, this Rosemary Clooney twin and was reminded of life without Isaac, and singing, and the young Blooma who had hope and a bounce to her step—not the old mindless biddy that she'd become.

"I'll tell you a secret," said Jayne. "I sang back up for some pretty famous stars, like Tina Turner and Cyndi Lauper when I was in my twenties and thirties. Mostly in New York, sometimes in Vegas and twice in L.A."

"That doesn't sound like a secret," said Blooma.

"It's what I did next that I'm afraid to share."

"I won't tell anyone. I barely remember your name. It's Jayne, right?"

Jayne laughed and held Blooma's hand. "Well, here goes. I sang back up at a Blondie gig. Debbie Harry was struggling on stage, all glassy-eyed and sneezing, so I told her to take a break and I'd perform instead. I had on my best blonde wig and a dress that looked just like hers, so I figured I could be her. Well, I went all in. Strutting and belting out '*The tide is high but I'm holding on. I'm gonna be your number one. I'm not the kind of girl who gives up just like that, oh no.*'" Jayne stopped talking and covered her eyes. "I was a skinny, flat-chested kid back then. I didn't have the curves I have now. And my voice just wasn't ready."

"I bet you killed it anyway," Blooma said.

"I got booed off the stage and blackballed by the booking agents. Good-bye big time. I've been a two-bit saloon singer ever since."

"It's not too late to try again. You know, there are cruise ships out of Fort Lauderdale looking for singers. I see the ads for open auditions in the *Sunrise Gazette* all the time. You should check it out. With a voice like yours, you'd knock them dead."

Jayne laughed, a hearty, throaty, deep-chested release. "Not the best choice of words, Lovey Pie." Jayne leaned in and gave Blooma a soft kiss on the cheek. "You're a dear for believing in me. Actually, I'm familiar with the *Sunrise Gazette*. I'll check it out. Now it's your turn to share a secret."

"Let me think." They were a block away from Blooma's house where there was a bench at the corner. The women sat side by side. "I do have one secret, one that I would only tell my sister, never the mahjong ladies. They'd think I was *farmishted*."

"Famished, is that like hungry?" asked Jayne.

"*Farmishted.*" Blooma repeated the word, accenting the second syllable. "It's Yiddish meaning mixed up in the brain. I'm going to tell you something crazy. A secret is sacred, you know, so you can't tell anyone."

"I won't tell anyone. Cross my heart and hope to die," said Jayne.

Blooma swallowed hard. "I killed my husband."

Jayne's face went white.

"He was having a heart attack. I knew it. Dripping sweat. Holding his chest. And I sat there staring at him like I was paralyzed."

"You were in shock."

"No, I was waiting to see what would happen."

"And what happened?"

"He keeled over and gasped, then he was quiet."

"But what could you have done?"

"Called 911 sooner."

"You were definitely in shock."

"For twenty minutes?"

"But then you called, right?"

"Of course, but by that time it was too late."

"How old was he when he died?"

"Eighty-one."

"So he had a long life and you had a lot of time together."

"Too long and too much. I'm glad to be alone."

"And this is your secret? That you killed your husband and now you're glad to be alone?"

"Yup. It feels good to say it out loud. I never was able to love him again after he let our daughter die."

Jayne gaped at Blooma. "He killed your daughter?"

"No. He ripped her out of our lives and declared her dead."

"That's terrible. Why?"

"Because she married out of our faith."

"But it's the twenty-first century!"

"He was stuck in the dark ages and never accepted her choice."

"But you do?"

"Only if she'll let me."

"Where's your daughter?"

"In New York."

"Has she come back alive to you?"

"She's given me a bit of peace these last few years since Isaac died, but she still won't visit. She won't set foot in any house that had him in it. I'm thinking of moving. But where would I go? That's so unfair. I'll never meet my grandsons."

"Why don't you go to New York?"

"Do you see me? *Farmishted* in the head. I barely remember where South Tower is for our mahjong games. I'm going to find New York?"

"Does your daughter realize this?"

"She doesn't seem to care." Blooma raised her brown-spotted hands to her face, her gnarled fingers rubbing her tear-stained eyes.

Jayne put her arm around the old woman and held her gently. "What if I told you I have pills that will increase your brain power. You could take them for a few months and then get on that plane, no problem."

"Pills?"

"Yup, they have estrogen in them. Mind boosters, among other things."

Blooma's face flushed and she felt faint. A solution? A way to get to New York to see Sarah and the boys and meet Sarah's husband? "And you'd give me these pills?"

"They're pricey. Fifty dollars a bottle. You'd probably need three months' worth before you were ready, but I can only get you a month's supply at a time."

"Thirty pills. That's one hundred and fifty dollars," said Blooma.

"Times two. You'd need two a day."

"Three hundred dollars?"

"See you're sharper already."

"And you'd do this for me? To help me? And you'd stay by me as I changed? Like that boy in that book I read when I was a teenager, *Flowers for Algernon*. How come I remember that and not what I had for lunch today. Did I eat lunch today?"

"Sweet Cheeks. I'm here for you. But going to New York is something you'll have to be brave enough to do by yourself," said Jayne.

"The pills are our little secret. All right?" said Blooma.

"Absolutely."

"Then time's a wasting. I've got cash in the house. Do I pay you now?"

Blooma bustled up her walkway, eager to get started. "*Come-on a my house, my house,*" Blooma sang from a Rosemary Clooney hit song.

Jayne finished the line, "*I'm a gonna give you candy.*"

北

Chapter Ten

NU: WHAT'S UP?

Gertrude gave up driving when she moved to the complex. She hated the expense and filth of cars. Too much pollution. Better to use her legs. Besides, there were too many crazy *meshugennehs* wanting to pass her on the right, throwing things out their windows and swearing at her, giving her the bird. If a sign said 25 MPH, she didn't go any higher and if someone started beeping at her, she'd slow down. She ruled the road when she drove but it got so exhausting. Much easier to pedal her three-wheeler. She even had an extra large basket for groceries. It was a civilized way to travel.

She left the clubhouse after playing mahjong, still tingling from Jayne's closeness. There was something about that woman that sparked Gertrude, a feeling she hadn't had since that silky soft man who looked like Tony Curtis sat across from her in the accounting firm, always looking at her when she wasn't looking. Nothing came of it though. He was fired. The bosses called him a dreamer.

As she pedaled, she noticed Blooma and Jayne deep in conversation. She waved, but they didn't notice her and she would not stop or shout out a howdy. They were engrossed. Gertrude felt a pang stab her heart. She could not bear having Jayne prefer Blooma over her.

Or Winnie. Or Mavis. She wanted Jayne as hers. That was the story of her life, always wanting, never getting. She pedaled the two blocks to her house in a fog. Why was she never good enough? Why was she always the intruder? That's what they had called her growing up. "Intrude," not "Gertrude." She wanted to be liked. She tried. Until she put up a shield and stopped caring. And now it was happening again. Just when she was feeling a bond between her and Jayne, a real friendship developing. Didn't she give her a thousand dollar check today for the dentist? Then that Winnie outshone her. Just like that. Gertrude needed a plan. Something more than money.

The following Wednesday, Jayne wasn't at mahjong when Gertrude arrived. She had hoped to get her alone to invite her to dinner, a *hamisha* meal from the deli on the corner: matzoh ball soup, brisket, and *tsimmes*, a Jewish meal that she could heat up and call her own.

"Where's Jaynie?" asked Mavis.

She was Jaynie now, thought Gertrude? What was Mavis' connection? Why hadn't Gertrude been included? Did they go to another karaoke bar without her?

"She'll be along. I saw her last night at the executive club. She said she'd be late to mahjong. Something to do with a doctor's appointment," said Winnie.

So everyone had captured a piece of Jayne but her, thought Gertrude. Always the intruder, the one left out. Gertrude pouted; her bottom lip sagged lower than usual.

Another week passed before Gertrude finally had a private moment with Jayne. Gertrude had seen Jayne sauntering down the street on her way to mahjong, so Gertrude paced her speed so that she'd pedal up behind Jayne when they got to the senior center.

"I'm wondering if you'd like to come to dinner this Friday night?" gulped Gertrude.

"At your home?" asked Jayne.

"Yes, 535 Elm Street." Gertrude couldn't believe she was actually asking and that this beautiful Venus would accept. Gertrude would have a lot of prepping for the visit, not only cycling to the corner for food, but she'd have to close off her trophy room. She didn't want Jayne to know how she spent her free time. Not that she was ashamed of it, but it was her lifelong secret, her private space, her haven of fantasy and glory and fame. Even Jayne wasn't welcome there. Not yet, anyway. And certainly she didn't want her telling those busy body *yentas* what she had accumulated. None of their *farkakte* business.

"What can I bring, Honey Pie?" Jayne asked.

Gertrude almost swooned. "Just yourself. Six o'clock sharp."

The next two days were a blur for Gertrude. She never invited company to her condo. It was larger than Blooma's, with three bedrooms and two baths, but the layout was similar. She once believed that her nieces and nephews might visit. But she long ago gave up hope of that. She hadn't heard from her brothers or sisters or their offspring since her parents died, and that was so many years ago, she lost count. She wasn't surprised. She never was part of the family. Smack middle. Never accepted by the three older brothers and never accepted by the three younger sisters. It wasn't that they were mean to her, they just had no need for her. So she put her mind to being the best in her class and moving out and on, which she did.

She had a great career at the accounting firm, crunching numbers and making the bosses happy. She'd gotten raise after raise and when it came to her retirement, they gave her a silver pen and a gold plaque and sent her out with a 401K and some generic "Happy Retirement" cards. So they spelled her name wrong. Anyone can get Friedman confused with Freidman. And what did it matter that her email account was cancelled the minute she walked out the door? She'd been a real asset to the company and saved them lots of money by refusing claims and collecting funds. She had been good at her job.

Once she moved to Florida, she had more time for her beloved hobby: photography. Not just of anybody, but of celebrities. She'd go to concerts and the theater, waiting outside the stage door or sitting in the lobby until everyone had left and she had time to chat up the star and snap their picture, but that didn't happen often. Her best photo was of Sidney Poitier, so handsome. *To Gertrude with love, Sid Poitier.* Sid! Her buddy!

Gertrude purged the hallway, kitchen and dining area of her framed photos, stacking her collection in the trophy room, which was wall-to-wall faces of luminaries from New England to California. Never foreign. Except for Baryshnikov. He had actually signed the picture, *To Gertrude in Dance.* Amazing. The real deal. On display for all to see. Except she was the only one who viewed the two hundred and twelve pictures on her walls of fame until each detail was memorized and sainted, over and over again every night, unless *Dancing with the Stars* was on or a rerun of *Hollywood Squares.*

She'd duplicated photos and put them in albums. She miniaturized photos and kept them in her purse. One of her favorite pastimes was selecting which pictures to accompany her. Grocery shopping was best with Rachel Ray, Kirstie Alley, and Julia Child. Sitting by the pool was shared with Christie Brinkley, Raquel Welsh, and Cindy Crawford. A great movie wasn't perfect without Meryl Streep, Robert Redford, and Clint Eastwood.

Maybe one day Gertrude would share her gallery with Jayne. Jayne, with her tight skin. *Had she had Botox?* Jayne, with her muscled arms. *When did she work out?* The complex had a paltry gym. Jayne, with her small *tuches—her mother could not have been Jewish.* Jayne was everything Gertrude was not: beautiful, desirous, youthful, with the singing voice somewhere between Tina Turner, whose photo she had, and Madonna, whose photo she didn't want. Gertrude had her standards, after all.

The day of the big dinner, Gertrude roamed through her apartment with a nagging itch in her head. She had a photo of Jayne Mansfield in one of her looseleaf notebooks. Gertrude retrieved it in seconds and felt a glow pass through her as she looked at it. The blond hair, the full lips, the body of a goddess, prettier than Marilyn Monroe, sexier than Bridgette Bardot.

Gertrude chose a gold frame that she had been saving for Tony Bennett's photograph. He was performing in Florida in January and she was ready for him. She googled Jayne Mansfield and there was an image with her signature, straight and sure with bold letters, the J large and flowery. Gertrude got her best pen and copied the name and added a note of her own: *Here's to life. Jayne Mansfield.*

Her Jayne arrived at 6:00 PM sharp. Gertrude wore a loose fitting chemise, a paisley plum and white. She added periwinkle blue eyeliner, just like Jayne taught her, and a dab of cherry lipstick.

The house was immaculate, the meal ready, and her confidence high that she could carry on a conversation about current events and local gossip. But Jayne seemed distracted, like she was there on a mission, to get in and get out. That set Gertrude's radar buzzing. Instead of a relaxing meal, Jayne fidgeted and picked. She begged off saying she needed surgery but couldn't afford it.

"I thought you were finished with the dentist," said Gertrude.

"This is something else. Something personal." Jayne pressed her fork into the carrots in the tzimmes to mush them up.

"And insurance doesn't cover it?"

"I don't have a steady job, and I'm sixty-three, two years shy of Medicare. Besides this is elective surgery."

"What kind of money are you talking about?" asked Gertrude.

"Over thirty thousand dollars. I don't have that kind of money," she cried.

Gertrude made a mental spreadsheet of her finances. Was it foolish of her to even consider helping Jayne out? Was she that desperate for someone to need her? Oh, what the hell, she thought. Call her crazy in the head, *a ritch in kop*, but geez, there was something special about this woman, something that made Gertrude want to help her. "Let's say I lend you fifteen thousand dollars and we work out a plan for you to pay me back."

"Really? Are you sure?" Jayne rushed to Gertrude's side and kissed her on the lips, not just once, but four big, loud, smacking kisses.

Gertrude practically fell off her chair. She had no idea what to do. To kiss back? To laugh? To cry?

"Thank you," Jayne cried. "I'll figure out a way to repay you. You can count on me. I don't know how I deserve such a wonderful friend."

A friend, Gertrude thought. A real friend.

When their meal resumed, Jayne ate with relish and Gertrude was thrilled. When someone knew that help was on its way, pain was diminished. Gertrude knew that to be true.

"I have something special for you," Gertrude said over coffee.

"You've already been so kind," Jayne drawled.

Gertrude presented Jayne with the autographed photo.

"Wow. She's a looker."

"That's Jayne Mansfield. I think you resemble her," said Gertrude.

"That's mighty sweet of you. Is she playing in a show around here?"

"She died in 1967 when she was thirty-four. Decapitated in a car accident."

"How gruesome!" Jayne stroked her smooth neck. "What an ironic thing to write: *Here's to life.*"

Gertrude thought she had been clever with that and loved that Jayne appreciated it.

"How did you get her to autograph the picture?"

"She was a relative on my dad's side. In the family, you know. I'd like you to have it."

"I'm honored and flattered." Jayne reached in for a hug. "You take my breath away with your kindness, Gertie. Thank you."

Jayne had called her Gertie. No one ever gave her a nickname. Not ever. Jayne thanked Gertrude again for a wonderful evening. When Gertrude leaned in for a hug, Gertrude did a body triangle, avoiding all the hot spots. But Jayne pulled her close. Heating up Gertrude. Shooting electricity through her body. Fifteen thousand dollars was a pittance compared to having a friend, especially one who made her feel good about herself.

Mavis loved spit-shining her Harley, polishing it for a road romp. She was engrossed in buffing the fenders when she heard a familiar drawl.

"What are you up to, Lovey? Can I help?"

Mavis saw Jayne standing just outside the carport, a small space lined with junk: tires, hubcaps, and an ancient Volkswagen growing vines, stems, leaves and flowers from its hull. The Condo Committee threatened to cart it all away, but Mavis argued that it was realistic sculpture and she had a right to express herself through automotive art.

Jayne's checkered capri pants were skin-tight. Her low top revealed mounds of bosom. Mavis imagined herself as Jayne. Ready to roll. Today Mavis' bosom was mottled with brown spots and wearing only a halter, her chest looked like a rippling ocean on a windy day.

Jayne took a rag, and without a word, made soft swirling motions on the rear of the motorcycle. Mavis' lips curled up.

"She's a beauty, isn't she," Mavis cooed.

"Sure is, but I never figured you for pink."

"The color's grown on me," said Mavis, who cringed inside at how she ended up with a pink motorcycle in the first place, certainly not her choice, but it was available so she grabbed it. "Red would be my color," said Mavis. "You said so yourself."

"Blue is mine," said Jayne.

Blue, thought Mavis. Like my husband Wally's eyes. Sadness and longing. Searching for me.

Jayne walked around the bike staring at its dimensions. "My father had a hog. Very possessive of it too. He let me sit on it when I was a kid, but I got so excited, I peed on the seat. He called me a sissy from that day forward. I never did like that man."

"My father was a butcher. Sliced beef into roasts and chops. He never had time to ride a motorcycle, and he'd be damned ashamed of me for riding a pink charmer like this," said Mavis. "Come on, Jaynie, hop on. Let's give 'em something to talk about."

Jayne straddled the rear seat and whooped like a teenager.

"Hold on, we're off," said Mavis.

Mavis careened around corners and sped through puddles. She skirted the exterior of the complex, along the golf course and the exercise trail. She loved the thrill of having Jayne cling to her, but she sensed that Jayne was no stranger to speed.

"Teach me how to handle this filly, will you?" Jayne asked.

Mavis stopped in a vacant lot on the west side of the complex where new construction had begun but no one was working after hours. She instructed Jayne as if they were in a horse ring, telling her how to push right, turn right, push left, turn left. Jayne was a natural.

"Let's drive to the beach," Jayne said.

"No, Ma'am. Never out of the village. Too many *meshugennehs* out there for my sanity. I got enough roads right here. Besides, I love scaring the old geezers. Gives me a charge."

Slugging freely from her flask, Mavis let Jayne drive back to the condo as she enjoyed the scenery. She hooted at anyone within earshot, watching the *alter kakers* shake their heads. Mavis thought she saw Gertrude scowling behind a window as they passed her house. The *farbissineh*. She could suck the sour out of sauerkraut in no time flat.

That *gonif* Sal, steamed Winnie, was in her side of the condo at dawn, like he had every right. He snatched her favorite painting right off the living room wall, like she had no say in the matter. Apparently, she didn't.

Winnie stared at the empty space. Why'd he have to take the *Couple in Love*? Her late husband Jev had been like the man in the painting: a *lange loksch*, tall and reedy like a stick, with horned-rimmed glasses and a trimmed mustache. In the picture, the man was kissing the hand of an aristocratic lady dressed in blue silk. Winnie saw herself and Jev in the artwork. Their gentle love. Their considerate coupling. How could Sal just waltz in and take it, as if it belonged to him? The bastard. She covered her mouth after she thought the word. Once she married Jev, she swore off swearing, but Sal got her blood boiling.

When she asked Sal to take a different painting instead, he looked over his nose at her. "I have a buyer."

Winnie refused to cry in front of Sal. She knew it was a matter of time before Sal sold all her paintings out from under her.

"We need the money," Sal said.

We? thought Winnie. Like they were a couple. A picture of the two of them would be of a demon overpowering a shrunken angel whose wings had closed in on her for protection. She never realized Sal's ruthless ambition when Jev was alive, probably because Sal kept his distance from her, even when he drove her and Jev places or joined them on vacation. Jev had trusted Sal's opinion, but Winnie didn't. He was a big snot, looking past her and through her.

Winnie's heart hurt when she recalled an overheard conversation between him and Jev.

"Can't you be nice to Winnifred?" asked Jev.

Hearing her full name had perked Winnie's attention.

"Winnifred is merely a woman of convenience," Sal hissed.

Winnie never heard more because the phone rang but those words banged around in her head. Woman of convenience? Was that a whore? She was no whore! Did he mean that Jev married her for show? as a trophy? She could be flattered at that. Sal didn't say marriage of convenience; woman of convenience meant something different. Maybe he was saying she was privileged, that she liked good things.

She had wanted to ask Jev, but then she'd be admitting that she'd broken his one and only rule: no eavesdropping. It was heinous and unforgivable, he said. It led to misunderstandings, hurt and resentment.

Winnie's mind spun out the same words over and over again like an ear worm: Woman of convenience. Woman of convenience. Why had Jev named that man executor of his will? Why was he in control? She was Jev's wife. She was Jev's wife. She was Jev's wife, not Sal.

For the five years since Jev had passed, Winnie progressively felt more imprisoned. Sal tracked everything she did, even ordering her to keep the curtains drawn throughout the day. Light was not good for the paintings, he said.

"Jev let me keep the shades open," she insisted.

"He's not in charge, now, is he?" he warned her.

When she and Jev had moved to Florida, they bought two penthouse condos in a new development in the toniest section of Boca Raton, one for her and Jev, the other for Sal. Then Jev broke through the walls and created one glorious home for the three of them. Jev said that it made good business sense because that way they could entertain potential buyers in one section and Winnie could have her private quarters in another. Right from the start, she felt uncomfortable and isolated. She rarely ventured through the connecting door, even if Jev spent most of his time there.

She looked at the wall clock: 12:35. Where was Sal? Didn't he realize it was Wednesday, mahjong day. She'd be late to mahjong again. Sal never honored her need to be on time.

"For those worthless old hags?" he chuckled.

Winnie might think the mahjong ladies had crazy habits and were *meshugenneh*, but Sal had no right calling them names. And the way he looked at Jayne! Shooting daggers at her, like he thought she was a trashy Barbie. He should only know that she gave Jayne a check for three thousand dollars for the dentist. Good thing she had a private checking account, even if her monthly allowance was monitored. She had accumulated a decent sum over the years. It was her money and Sal had no right to it.

Winnie watched out the window searching for the Town Car. With each passing moment, she pursed her lips tighter and pressed her manicured nails deeper into her palms. Why did Jev leave her the

Lincoln Town Car in his will with Sal as her driver for perpetuity? He knew that her eyesight was bad and would prevent her from driving, so was he protecting her? But when Winnie wanted a ride, she had to clear it with Sal. She was at his mercy unless she called an Uber or god-forbid, took a bus, which was so beneath her. Of course, she had a gold MasterCard, but Sal paid the bills and he questioned every purchase. What right did he have to do that?

Winnie raced from the elevator to the street floor and back again, her heels clicking like a time bomb. "Where is that moron no good thief?" she shouted. She'd never arrive on time to mahjong if he didn't come home soon. Mavis would snicker and Gertrude would scowl, not that Winnie cared, but she had a reputation to maintain.

Winnie went through the alphabet and called out every swear word she could muster. When she ran out of English words, she swore in Yiddish. At 1:25, Sal sat on the horn of the Lincoln Town car. When Winnie emerged from the building, she wanted to spit on him, but what would that prove? That her roots were as common as his?

When Winnie finally arrived, three silent women sat around the table. Blooma was studying her mahjong card and nibbling strudel. Gertrude was flipping through a magazine, her plate piled with pastry. And Mavis lay on the floor with her legs up on the chair doing stomach crunches. When she reached one hundred, she rewarded herself with a Snickers candybar.

The women were waiting for Jayne. Mavis had spit-shined her motorcycle, hoping for a spin through the complex. Gertrude's heart fluttered, eager to see her new best friend, and Blooma wanted to prove to Jayne how she was thinking smarter.

Every time the door creaked, the women's hearts thudded louder, but phantom shadows passed through, not the live and vibrant woman with high cheekbones and perky breasts. Not the golden haired Venus with long legs and supple skin and just enough wrinkles to qualify her as wise.

So when Winnie blasted in, the women's chins sank into their necks. "It's that worthless termite Sal's fault," said Winnie.

"Call him shit-head or asshole. Did you know that swearing takes away pain?" said Mavis, jumping into her seat and dealing out the tiles.

Winnie had been practicing her swears, but she hated to reveal that part of her nature to these women.

"*Mamzer* is a good one," said Gertrude, "*Farkakte mamzer* works even better."

Blooma blushed, knowing that saying fucking bastard never changed anything. In fact, she recalled telling Isaac that he was a *farkakte mamzer* once, but the man was asleep with his back to her and it didn't make her feel any better. It's amazing how much she had been remembering lately. She had taken two pills a day for the last four days, one with breakfast, the other with dinner. The pills were supposed to be twelve hours apart, so Blooma set her alarm for five in the morning. Dinner was the early bird special at the senior center, not to be missed.

Drink lots of water, Jayne had told her, and walk twice around the block. Then do a crossword puzzle or word search or something to stimulate the brain. Blooma studied her mahjong card during those times with a deck of cards she had bought. She simulated each hand, searching for the right combinations. Once the mahjong game finally got going, Blooma was shocked that each time she set up her rack, she had a hand to play, not just picking and throwing.

Blooma was on the verge of calling mahjong when that speed-demon Mavis won her fourth straight hand. Gertrude evil-eyed her and Winnie snorted. Blooma was happy though. Progress in a pill. That was mind-boggling to Blooma. Maybe she would finally get to New York and see those boys before they had their Bar Mitzvah. She wondered if Sarah was bringing them up Jewish. She wondered how surprised they'd all be when she arrived at their doorstep. A little old lady with gray curls and a bubke announcing that Bubbe Blooma had arrived!

Blooma had lost steam and her tiles betrayed her. She wished Jayne had shown up to help or she could take another of those mind pills, but Jayne warned her that two a day were more than enough and their effects were cumulative. So Blooma was content to think that if she was so improved in just a few days, imagine how she'd be in a month.

Chapter Eleven

FARKLEMPT: EMOTIONAL

The following Wednesday, on her way to play mahjong, Blooma heard a muffled cry come from the canal. She peered down, but saw nothing. She focused her ears. Sure enough, a whiny voice filtered up from the shoreline. The hillside was too steep for Blooma to descend, so she hobbled to the center clutching her babke and praying she wouldn't be too late.

"Help!" Blooma cried, hoping someone would hear her.

Mavis, Gertrude, and Winnie were setting up the tiles when they heard the scream. Racing out the door, they saw Blooma's face, scrunched up and wailing.

"*Oy gevult!* There's a baby in the water and it's dying," Blooma said, pointing toward the canal.

"What in the world?" said Gertrude.

"A baby?" said Mavis.

"Where?" asked Winnie.

"Sh. Sh. Listen," said Blooma.

The four women peered over the edge of the walkway. Sure enough, cries came from the shore. Mavis sprang into action by barreling down the side of the grassy hill. Gertrude followed, her sturdy shoes deliberate with every step. Blooma and Winnie stayed near the top, shouting encouragement.

"What do you see?" asked Winnie, tapping her foot and craning her neck.

Blooma started down the embankment on her tush. She knew she'd never get there on her arthritic feet, so she half slid and half crawled until she could hear the wailing up close. A keening pitch.

"Hold that limb steady, Gertrude, I'm going out there," said Mavis.

"You'll fall in!" said Gertrude.

"And then what? An alligator will eat me? I'll get a *bissel* wet? But we'll save a life," said Mavis.

Blooma rounded the area where branches had fallen from a tree. All she could see was Gertrude's wide backside. She was on her knees, with her arm stretched toward Mavis, who was crawling along a thin plank of wood. Mavis reached out and scooped a kitten into her hand, a tiny mewling kitten whose voice had carried like an echo up the embankment, onto the shore, and into Blooma's ears.

Mavis hugged it to her chest as Gertrude helped them to safety.

By that time, Winnie had tiptoed down the hillside, one slow step at a time, careful not to spike into the grass with her heels. "What's all the fuss about? A drowning kitten, for God's sake. Someone probably left the thing out there to die."

But when Mavis thrust the fur ball into Winnie's arms, Winnie's heart thawed. "Oh, the poor little baby." She took off her beret and settled the tiny being into it, swaddling it like an infant.

"Well, look at that. The ice queen has maternal instincts," said Mavis.

Blooma blew warm air into the little bundle. Gertrude cooed. Tears welled in everyone's eyes.

"What a bunch of *schmegegis* to get so *faklempt* over a pussycat," said Mavis.

"You did well, Mavis," said Blooma, patting her gently on the back.

"Yeah, now what? I hate cats and they hate me," said Mavis, recovering. "I'll probably break out in hives."

"She has a tiny collar," said Winnie. "And there's a phone number on it." Winnie took out her cell and called it. "Yes. Yes, a little gray kitten. Near the South Tower Senior Center. I'll be in the common room waiting for you."

"So you're taking all the credit, Winnifred?" Gertrude hissed. "Mavis and I risked our lives for a kitten, and you reap the glory?"

"Ladies, what difference does it make?" said Blooma. "We performed a *mitzvah* today, all of us. How often do people get to save an innocent life?"

"You're right, Blooma. One for all and all for one." Gertrude loved the three musketeers, especially the version by the Three Stooges. She'd be d'Artagnan.

The women brought the kitten into the senior center and poured some cream into a *shissel*. The cat lapped it up, licking its pink little nose with its tongue.

"I never had a cat of my own," said Blooma, looking out the window, waiting for the kitten's owners. "When we came over on the boat from Russia, there was a stray cat on board who took a liking to me. I was just six years old and so afraid of being on that huge ocean liner bound for who knows where. And she came to me at night and laid her head beside me on my pillow, which I think was rolled up newspapers. I petted her and told her stories. I named her Sarah, which means Princess. When we separated at Ellis Island, I saw her gray eyes stare at me from afar and she nodded. I saw it. She said to me, '*Zei mir frailich*! Go and be happy.'"

The kitten reminded Blooma of her childhood when she just started out in this country and had so much in front of her. Why was it that today she was looking back and not finding much satisfaction? Oh God, she shouldn't say that. Blooma's eyes welled wondering whether the little pussycat in Winnie's hat might be better off sinking and not having to search and seek and want and yearn and rarely be fulfilled. Why was everything so complicated? This little creature, mewling and crying, so basic, so needy, so insistent. Did that change with age? Wasn't Blooma still crying, needing to be wanted. Was that so wrong?

Mavis stood beside Blooma at the window. "I never had a cat," she said, "but I once had to cat-sit and it was disastrous. My cousin was away for two weeks and told me, not asked me, to take care of his ancient tabby. It wasn't really his. It belonged to his girlfriend and it was like a hundred years old. Well, I came by before he left and introduced myself, and it had these fleas biting it. Nothing about this cat said longevity. But I was young, in my twenties and single and said I'd watch the poor thing." Mavis realized that Gertrude and Winnie were listening, so she talked louder, enjoying the center of attention. "It was winter and they wanted me to keep it upstairs in a cold bedroom because that's where it was comfortable. But I wanted to go in and out as fast as possible, so I moved its bed to the first floor to a cozy corner. At least I thought so. And when I came to feed the cat, I couldn't find it. I searched the house and there it was. On the second floor on a stack of books. The top one's name was *Might as Well be Dead*. That's the god's honest truth. *Emmis*. The cat was stretched out stiff on a book."

"*Oy gevult!*" said Blooma. "What did you do?"

"The vet said to put the damn thing in the freezer. When my cousin came home, he called me a *farshtunkene* cat-killer. But it wasn't my fault. Who the hell goes away knowing their cat is on the precipice of death and leaves it to an idiot who knows nothing about pets?"

"And how long ago was this? Over five decades?" asked Gertrude. "What the hell difference does it make now?"

"When we're old, we want what's familiar," said Mavis. "We don't want to be moved for someone else's convenience. That cat died about a week too soon. Sure, it would have died anyway but on its own terms. Damn it, I'll never die in a corner that I didn't create."

"*Gottenyu!*" said Gertrude. "You sure know how to cheer a girl up!"

A car stopped near the front door and a couple got out. The man was a giant, the woman a peanut. They rushed into the senior center, tears streaming down their cheeks. "We thought Whiskers was gone forever. She got out of the lanai through a rip in the screen. She's so tiny, she could squeeze through anything. And we never saw her leave and by the time we realized she was gone, we didn't know what to do. Oh thank you for saving her!"

The four women stood taller as Winnie gave them Whiskers, and took back her hat.

The couple was gone in a shot and the four women stood cat-less. "A good deed never goes unpunished," said Winnie.

"What's that mean?" said Gertrude.

"They barely thanked us. They just took that kitten like we were going to cook it for dinner. They should have offered us cake or something," said Winnie.

"I have bubke," said Blooma.

"And I have wet shoes," said Mavis. "Winnie's right. They could have been nicer."

Winnie couldn't believe that Mavis agreed with her.

Gertrude waved her arms. "No matter. We did something right. That's reward enough."

"You sound like Blooma," said Mavis.

"Is that such a bad thing?" asked Blooma, as she sliced the babke and put on in four plates. "*Essen.* Eat. That little pussycat is safe now and we were responsible. It'll have a full rich life with those bubble-brained *dumkops.*"

The women ate and played mahjong and no one cared that Winnie was too deliberate, Mavis impatient, Gertrude fast, and Blooma slow.

That night each woman thought about cats.

Gertrude imagined finding photos of famous cats like Garfield, Sylvester, and Puss in Boots, and posting them around her house.

Mavis imagined her cousin and the long-deceased tabby meeting at a motorcycle rally and talking about flea meds and veterinarians.

Winnie found a childlike painting in her apartment of an orange and yellow cat. Its face was rectangular, its green diamond eyes were intense and its pink nose was triangular. She named her Whiskers.

And Blooma tried lapping a saucer of milk, just to see how it felt on her tongue.

Chapter Twelve

MISHEGAS: SENSELESS BEHAVIOR OR ACTIVITY

A notice posted on the bulletin board in each tower caught the attention of every mahjong player:

Mahjong Madness Cruise
on Royal's Freedom on the Ocean.
Leaving from Fort Lauderdale.
Two days, one night. December 6 – 7
Individual scoring.
Prizes for win, place, and show.
An additional 3 awards for high sessions
Even the lowest score wins.

Blooma wondered how many games she'd have to lose to be the overall loser. Could she at least win one and still take home a prize? With her improving brain, she felt a little smarter each day like the scarecrow in the Wizard of Oz. Maybe she should aim higher?

Mavis rubbed her hands together. She wondered what the prizes would be: booze? money? *chazzerei?* more shit that she never needed? Could she find out before she put all her energy into winning? *Feh.*

What difference did it make? She decided she'd win every game if she wanted to; she had a few strategies up her sleeve.

Winnie thought about being away from Sal for two days, free on the ocean, although he'd probably strip her house of artwork during that time. Maybe she shouldn't go. She hated leaving the house knowing he was prowling every corner. At least her bedroom suite was her haven. Jev never allowed him in there and Sal honored that, at least when she was home. What if he didn't? She had to hide the key in a better place. She needed that man out of her life.

Gertrude's wheels turned, figuring out how she might win the whole tournament and a high-session prize. What if she roomed with Jayne? Sleeping in the same cabin, watching Jayne's nighttime routine like brushing her teeth, removing her makeup, putting on PJs. Snoring. What did Jayne do with her hair, Gertrude wondered? Wrap it in rollers? in a bandana? leave it free? Gertrude wanted to know.

"I choose Jayne for my roommate," said Mavis.

Gertrude's lips turned down and a growl escaped her throat. "What are we ten years old? It's not up to you to choose."

"Touchy touchy," smirked Mavis, knowing she hit a sore spot.

Winnie grimaced. She'd book her own room, thank you very much.

"What's going on?" drawled a lilting voice.

The women parted and Jayne read the notice. "Doesn't that look like fun, but I'm a novice at the game. Besides, it's probably too expensive for my budget."

Gertrude decided to pay Jayne's way, but she didn't want the others to know. She'd take Jayne aside and tell her privately. Every fiber in Gertrude's body shuddered at the possibility.

Mavis watched Jayne's eyes flutter at Gertrude and noticed Gertrude's response, like the moon ogling the sun, content to be in its shadow. "Want to be my roomie? We can split the cost," Mavis asked Jayne.

Gertrude scowled at Mavis, but kept quiet. She wanted Jayne's full attention, but didn't know how to get it.

Jayne ran her long fingernails through her blond hair. "Freedom on the Ocean? Out of Fort Lauderdale? Funny thing about that." She looked at Blooma and gave her a knowing smile. "I saw an ad in the *Sunrise Gazette* about an open audition, so I went. Guess what? I got a spot on the Thanksgiving Day Cruise. If I'm any good, maybe they'll hire me for the tournament and I'll get a room for free."

Blooma clapped her hands like a child. "I knew you could do it! You took my advice. I'm so proud of you."

Jayne bestowed a coveted kiss on Blooma's cheek. "Doll Face, you encouraged me and I went for it. First decent gig in years. And I have you to thank."

The other women wished they knew what was going on, but they congratulated Jayne on something that obviously made her happy and had something to do with Blooma helping her.

Gertrude turned away, not wanting anyone to see how she really felt. So Blooma and Jayne had a thing going too? Gertrude feared the envy that boiled up in her would turn her face green. She remembered the afternoon when Blooma and Jayne sat on the bench while Gertrude pedaled by like a ghost. Whatever they talked about had made a difference in Jayne. How she wished she could make an impact like that. Gertrude's gaze fell again on Jayne, who was swaying like music danced inside of her.

"Ladies, the best part is I get to wear fancy wigs and sing a few tunes." Jayne twirled and bumped Mavis with her hip.

Mavis spun around and twerked into Winnie, who jumped out of her way.

"You're a *gansa meshugenneh!*" shouted Gertrude. She wanted Jayne's attention. She wanted to be twerked. She wanted to twirl with excitement. Instead, she stomped into the senior center, plunked herself down in front of the community's computer, and logged onto the Royal website.

After a lot of discussion, Mavis and Blooma decided to room together while Gertrude and Winnie each booked a private cabin.

Winnie was thrilled to be alone and Gertrude was hoping that Jayne might yet join her.

"Jaynie, you'll be the headliner on the ship! You'll see!" Blooma's eyes sparkled and she felt seventy again.

Thanksgiving dinner was a big deal in the complex. Families crowded in from across the country and reservations needed to be made. Gertrude sort of spent Thanksgiving alone, watching the Macy's Thanksgiving Day Parade on television. Once in a while, one of her siblings remembered to call her, but she didn't go out of her way to call them either. A niece or nephew might email one of those mass greeting cards with a singing turkey, but Gertrude didn't bother with a reply.

Gertrude's family were her photos. This year, she went for blonds whose names began with J. She propped their pictures around the dining room table: Jayne Mansfield, of course, with a newly printed picture from the Internet; James Dean, whose signature she had forged to perfection; Jodie Foster, who actually signed her photo, and Jane Lynch, whose character on the TV show *Glee* tickled Gertrude every time she watched it. Gertrude started the conversation by asking each what they thought of her Jayne.

James Dean told Gertrude to go for her dream. Why not, thought Gertrude. She'd never been with a woman and had never considered it, but something about Jayne got her old juices flowing. She asked Jane Lynch her advice. Her blue eyes snapped, "Be your own woman, Gertie. Don't let others make decisions for you." Jodie Foster interrupted, "Being understood is not the most essential thing in life, you know." Was there an underlying meaning going on that Gertrude wasn't getting? She was about to hear Jayne Mansfield's take when there was a knock at the door. She would be horrified if anyone saw her chatting with photographs.

"Gert-rude? Are you home? I went by Blooma's but no one

answered her door. Her curtains are drawn and no baking smells are coming from the kitchen. Should we be worried?"

Mavis wavered on Gertrude's landing, her legs about to give way. One nip too many. Thanksgiving was not a happy holiday for Mavis now that her family was gone. It was her fault that her parents never enjoyed their last Thanksgiving; both had been in the hospital suffering from smoke inhalation. She had come home blasted one evening and forgot to use the ashtray. The bed was a better extinguisher, except the ashes smoldered and the house went up in flames. She got her parents out before the place became an inferno, which didn't mean that their lungs hadn't been affected by the fire.

Before Gertrude opened the door, she whipped the photos off the chairs and tucked them behind a cushion on the sofa. She needn't have hurried, though, because by the time she confronted Mavis, the old woman was slumped against the wall, with her eyes closed, snoring like a soldier. Gertrude considered leaving her there, but it was Thanksgiving.

"Mavis, wake up." Gertrude shook her gently and Mavis' cheeks twitched.

"Goddamn Florida mosquitos." Mavis swatted her cheek. "They never let a woman sleep in peace."

"Mavis, come inside. Let me get you some water."

"Bourbon. Better yet, an Adavan, then bourbon."

Gertrude put her hands under Mavis' armpits and stood her upright, surprised at how light the woman felt. She had figured Mavis was made with muscle and grit and a heavy helping of coarse salt. Gertrude led Mavis into the living room, onto the reclining chair, and realized too late that when seated, Mavis would be staring into the dreamy eyes of male movie stars on the opposite wall: Cary Grant, Johnny Depp, and George Clooney, each with his signature, and a heart-shaped symbol with Gertrude's name inside.

"What did you say about Blooma?" Gertrude asked. "I took a spin by her house too and no one answered the door. Should we worry?"

"Nah, she's getting deaf, like the rest of us," said Mavis, worried more about her blackouts that were becoming daily occurrences.

Chapter Thirteen

BUBBE MEISEH: A MADE UP STORY

Without telling the other women, Blooma boarded Royal's Freedom of the Ocean cruise ship on Thanksgiving morning. She wanted to surprise Jayne and be in the audience for her debut performance. The cruise was a one-night turn-around from Fort Lauderdale to the Bahamas and back. Blooma couldn't believe that she had arranged this herself, even calling for a cab to take her to the dock. Those pills were magic.

She worried about the money she was spending, especially since it was from Isaac's life insurance policy, her nest egg, she called it. She should be saving it for her grandsons. Putting them through college. But surely she could use a thousand dollars for herself? She was eighty-two, after all, and she didn't know how many spending years she'd have left. Besides, Isaac invested in long-term care and she was still paying premiums.

She decided to employ words she'd heard tossed around but never uttered. "I'm worth it. I deserve it. I'm a good person." She was a product of the Depression where rubber bands and cotton balls had as much value as beef and sugar. To spend a few extra dollars on pills and cruises enhanced her life. Blooma kept talking herself out of her guilt.

She boarded the cruise in time for the festive meal where she sat with four other older women who talked on and on about their grandchildren and great-grandchildren. She wondered how Gertrude, Mavis and Winnie were spending their day and what it would have been like to sit with them. They were probably alone in their apartments looking at their empty walls, like she would have been.

After turkey, stuffing, potatoes, cranberry sauce and endless chit-chat, Blooma was exhausted. She needed a nap. Walking toward her cabin, she peered down the endless corridor as a blur grew into a force of energy and a wrinkled lady on a scooter blasted toward her. Blooma pressed herself against the wall as the wild woman passed.

"Where can I get one of those?" Blooma called.

"The Courtesy Desk! Go for it!" whooped the woman.

Before Blooma knew what she was doing, she was standing at a counter ordering a scooter and within ten minutes, she was revving the hand gears. "Watch out world, Blooma Gottlieb is coming. You got nothing on me, Wild Women! I'm da BOMB!"

She sped down her hallway—reaching 5 mph!—parked the scooter and ran inside for a quick nap. Even the adrenaline rush from the ride couldn't cause her eyes to stay open. After a necessary snooze, Blooma scanned the activity board for Jayne's performance but it wasn't until 10:00 that evening. What to do in between? B-I-N-G-O caught her eye. She'd always wanted to play bingo. So she scootered to the lounge on the sixth floor. She looked around the room for where to park and saw another scooter-lady maneuvering into a corner table. If she joined her, would she look as old as that woman did? Instead, she parked her scooter at the back of the room and walked to a table where a young pretty girl was texting on her phone.

The teen looked up and waved. Blooma waved back, thinking how nice to be acknowledged until Blooma saw an older gentleman approaching.

"Grandpa Murray, I've been waiting for - e v e r," said the girl. "I saved your lucky table."

The man kissed the girl's cheek.

"Grandpa, don't stay up late. Mom says we have to be off early in the morning."

"Such a *shana punim*," he pinched his granddaughter's cheek and kissed his fingers.

"Oh Grandpa, I'm too old for that."

"You're never too old for a little loving, my little Missy," he said as his granddaughter jumped up, her legs lean and tan, and was off like a deer.

Blooma thought the girl cute, but in her grandfather's eyes, she had a goddess' face.

The man bowed slightly toward Blooma. "And who's this beautiful flower gracing my special table?" he said, his voice lower and stronger than appeared possible from this barrel-chested, bald headed, bushy-browed dumpling.

Blooma's cheeks reddened. "I'm Blooma."

"An apt name for a rose," he said and sat beside her.

A crew member came by with bingo cards and chips. Blooma charged them to her room and felt very grown up. Isaac usually did all the credit card business and she sat dumbly beside him. Even now, years after his passing, she felt strange writing out checks and rarely paid anything by credit. She was an old-fashioned gal.

Out of the side of her eye, Blooma snuck a look at Murray as he organized his four bingo cards like a checkerboard, with coins at the ready in short piles in between.

How can he keep them all straight? This Murray must be a genius or maybe he has a stash of magic pills too.

Blooma watched him as the numbers were read aloud, the long hairs on his white brows flicking when he could cover a square. She was so busy studying him that she missed two numbers in a row, but Murray noticed and placed two of his red coins on her card to help.

Again Blooma's cheeks turned scarlet. Was she that *farblondzhet* that she couldn't even follow bingo action?

Finally, a woman at another table yelled "Bingo!" and Blooma felt her breath settle. One of the crew came around with another set of bingo cards, but Blooma stretched back and chose to watch Murray instead.

This time he spread out five cards, elbowed her lightly and said, "My Dear, this one's for you."

When hers was the winner, Blooma jumped out of her seat and clapped like she'd won the lottery. Murray puffed out his broad barrel chest with rooster pride.

"Maybe you'd like a nightcap before going back to your cabin?" Murray asked.

Blooma looked down to her hands as if they might answer for her. Her fingers twiddled and twitched and tapped themselves into sound.

"I'd be delighted," she said and had no idea where those words came from. "Do you think we could find the place where a singer named Jayne is performing tonight?"

"Apple solute me!" he said with a chuckle.

They walked out of the room arm in arm after Murray had hiked up his Bermuda shorts over his round belly. Blooma kept glancing at the power scooter she had parked in the corner of the room only an hour earlier.

They entered the lounge arm-in-arm, more for balance than for intimacy. Blooma wondered if the scooter would remain where it was and if she'd be charged extra for losing it. But she stopped worrying when she saw a stage and a sign saying: *Jayne's World* and a photo of her Jayne in a glitzy costume, all dolled up. A clock's hands announced the time of her show: 10:00. It was 9:45.

Where had the time gone? She was never out this late. She felt like she was in another universe. Murray chose a table at the back of the lounge, close to the restroom. She hadn't had a private conversation with a man since Isaac passed and toward the end of his life, she barely spoke to him. She had been so angry with him for forcing her to declare their daughter Sarah dead. No mother should have to do that. Isaac refused to say Sarah's name ever again and her name was all that sat on Blooma's tongue. Sarah. Sarah. Sarah.

"Do you like mint julips?" asked Murray.

"Tulips are lovely," said Blooma, wondering why he was asking about flowers.

His round face blossomed. "Then a mint tulip it is," he said and signaled a waiter.

"Your granddaughter is very sweet," said Blooma.

"My Missy is like a sugar plum," said Murray.

"I have two grandsons, Andrew and Mark. And a lovely daughter named Sarah." The name felt like a kiss from Blooma's lips. "Sarah, her husband and their boys live in New York." Blooma was surprised to be saying this to a stranger.

"So you're a snowbird?"

"No, I live in Boca Raton full time. For the last ten years, maybe more?"

Murray's chunky hands rested on his round belly. "I live with my daughter and granddaughter in Fort Lauderdale. My daughter works on this ship. She books the entertainment. Missy and I get to cruise a lot."

Blooma realized that Murray's daughter must have been in charge of hiring Jayne whose show would begin any minute.

The waiter brought two handsome drinks in fluted glasses. Blooma's had a little umbrella with a cherry. She felt new today, like she'd been born on the ship. Alone. In charge of herself. She was eager to see Jayne perform and sitting beside this man felt comfortable, like he was an old friend. Murray was a like a bear, all hairy and wide. He sprawled in the chair. Isaac had been narrow like a stick, with angles and hard edges. Before he died, he was crooked bones and yellow teeth. Murray was jolly. Blooma guessed he was still in his seventies. A young one.

Isaac was never young. He'd sit in her father's parlor debating portions of the Bible with him. When she served them tea, Isaac would turn his chin to the left, their private signal that she was being admired. How she waited for the chin tilt. Beside her now, Murray's chin was indistinguishable from his neck. She wondered what signal he might use to woo her, an eyebrow flicker like Groucho Marx?

Blooma sipped her mint tulip as the room darkened. A spotlight radiated a flag of colors.

"My daughter says Jayne's World will be all the rage. Rainbow rights and all that," Murray said.

Blooma loved the idea of rainbows. What a perfect background for her Jayne. Blooma sipped her mint tulip and became a shadow. She didn't want Jayne to know she was there. What if Jayne got booed off the stage? What if she bombed? Jayne wouldn't want Blooma watching if that happened.

The lights dimmed and Jayne promenaded onto the stage in a sequin dress tight at the waist, her breasts bubbling out of the top. Her curly blond hair was surrounded by a peacock-feathered hat that would make Winnie envious. As she stripped off her long white gloves, she belted out her first song, making eye contact with the men in the audience.

Hello Harry......Well, hello, Louie
It's so nice to be back where I belong
You're lookin' swell, Manny........I can tell, Danny
You're still glowin'...you're still crowin'...you're still goin' strong.

Murray let out a wolf whistle that caused Blooma to jump.

"My daughter tells me to get the crowd involved right off the top," Murray whispered to Blooma. "Trick of the trade."

But Jayne captured the audience immediately. She threw back her head, elongated her youthful neck, zippered out of her gown and stood in a black teddy and black silk stockings like Madonna. "Come on, boys," she purred, "I'm waiting." She strutted across the stage, winking at the men. Her eyes were moon glows, large and luminous.

Get into the groove
Boy, you've got to prove
Your love to me, yeah
Get up on your feet, yeah
Step to the beat
Boy, what will it be?

Young men paraded around the room in a conga line as Jayne followed up the song with *It's Raining Men* and *Y.M.C.A.*

Blooma watched as legs flew right and left, and butts jiggled. Energy pulsed through her as Jayne strutted and jumped on the stage.

"My daughter's gonna be thrilled with this act," said Murray, who had to shout to be heard.

Maybe she could mention the mahjong tournament to Murray, and his daughter would book Jayne for the cruise. Oh how fun that would be for her and the girls.

The next song was a ballad. The audience settled into their seats as Jayne covered her curves with a black robe and exchanged her blond locks for a short shaggy brown wig. She sat on a stool, crossing her legs just right so they peeked out from the silky fabric. She had changed her shoes to red high heels and melted the audience with *Somewhere Over the Rainbow*.

The spotlight panned to the piano player, but Blooma kept her eyes on Jayne, who zippered into a white jumpsuit and brushed the wig into a pompadour like Elvis Presley.

Grinding like Elvis, Jayne sang *Viva Las Vegas*, and again the conga line snaked through the room. Putting on a star-studded hat, Jayne morphed into Michael Jackson, doing the moonwalk across the stage. Something shook around in Blooma's mind, like a secret about to be told, but she couldn't put her finger on it. She wondered how Jayne could impersonate these singers so well. She wondered who Jayne was beneath those wigs and masks and makeup. All Blooma knew was that Jayne caught on quickly at mahjong and was becoming a friend, but the woman on the stage was larger than Blooma's understanding. This woman belted out words with a deep power. She held on to an audience with a magnetism that didn't jive with the senior center and mahjong. Why would a woman so beautiful and talented hang around with four old ladies?

A waiter set down another mint tulip, and somehow Blooma had sipped it until it was gone. Her head was woozy and she knew her legs would never make it down that long corridor to her cabin. She hoped she wasn't going to have another spell like at the Watering Hole. Jayne would have to save her again. Oh that would be so embarrassing.

Murray saw Blooma's distress and slipped his arm around her waist and let her rest her head on his shoulder. It was a warm shoulder, padded, and scented like Old Spice. She closed her eyes and Jayne faded, the room faded, and Blooma fell into a deep sleep. She stayed that way until Murray stroked her hair and whispered to her. "Blooma, my dear, it's time we get you home." She woke and Jayne was no longer on the stage. A few young people hung around the bar, laughing and drinking.

"I missed the finale," Blooma said. "I wanted to give Jayne a standing ovation."

"My daughter will book Jayne's World again, to be sure. The crowd loved it."

"We have a mahjong tournament on board in a few weeks. Do you think you could convince your daughter to hire Jayne for that?"

"I can ask," Murray said, his eyebrows fluttering. "Will you be there too?"

Blooma nodded. "I wouldn't miss it."

"Well, in that case, I'll insist."

Chapter Fourteen

KINEHORA: KNOCK ON WOOD

Mavis prepared for the upcoming tournament by playing online, her computer whirring throughout the night. On the ship, she was determined to win high score for each game. She would pack her halter tops because they showed off her Lucky Sammy tattoo. Every time she rotated to a new table at the tournament, she'd squawk like a parrot and tell a bawdy joke. It would piss off those *farkakte* women and throw their game.

Once upon a time, she'd say, I had a parrot I took everywhere, even to the club on Friday nights where I'd drink a little *schnapps* and let Sammy sip some too. Whenever we went onto the dance floor, Sammy would yell, "The roof, the roof, the roof is on fire, we don't need no water, let the muthafukkah burn!" The crowd on the dance floor would cheer and hoot, which would make Sammy yell even louder. The crowd went wild. One *Shabbos* I took Sammy to temple. When the choir started to sing, Sammy yelled, "The roof, the roof, the roof is on fire, we don't need no water, let the muthafukkah burn!" I scolded Sammy with a whack to his head, "Bad Sammy, you can't say that here!!" He looked around, puffed out his feathers and asked, "Why not? These are the same muthafukkahs that were at the club last night!"

Mavis would get those women so riled, they'd drop their mah-jong tiles, and then she'd win. Mavis went to sleep dreaming up more parrot jokes, laughing herself off the bed.

Gertrude intended to win too. She set up a card table in her living room. On each chair, she put a picture of a renown gambler—Omar Sharif, Ben Affleck, Gladys Knight—then she'd play mahjong with them, outsmarting them on every move. She made light conversation with them, practicing being sociable and friendly, qualities she knew were not natural to her. Needless to say, she won every game and gloated at the celebrities.

After returning home from the Thanksgiving Day Cruise, Blooma found an inner confidence. With Murray sweet-talking her and look-ing forward to seeing her again, she felt desirable, something she hadn't experienced since her wedding night sixty-two years ago, which ended in disappointment. She conjured up Murray at the mahjong tournament cheering her on. She wanted to make him proud, so she practiced with her deck of mahjong cards, trying combination after combination until her head hurt. Then she got confused and took a nap. When she woke, she took one of her magic pills, even if it wasn't at a twelve hour interval. Then she went through the mahjong cards again, memorizing the hands. She was determined not to place last.

Winnie didn't care if she won or lost, she just wanted to get away, away from her condo that stank with Sal's cloying rum aftershave. Every day now it seemed Sal was taking another painting off the wall. Sure, there were hundreds in the collection, but why take the ones that Jev had hung especially for her eyes, ones he thought she'd enjoy the most. She couldn't bear seeing the blank wall where two lovers had danced, or a mother and her children had walked a winter road, or three sandpipers stood toothpick-leg deep in conversation.

Winnie avoided talking to Sal, except to inform him that she required transportation. "You'll be driving me and my friends to the dock on Saturday, 8 AM sharp," she told him.

"What for?" he asked.

"We're playing in a mahjong tournament."

"That blond floozie too?"

"Of course Mavis is going."

Sal scowled. "Not that floozie. The wannabe dame. What's her name? Jay? The one who should be ashamed."

Winnie wanted to slap the man, hard. What right did he have criticizing her friends, especially Jayne, the epitome of womanhood, something Sal could never appreciate. Of course Jayne was going with them, but not to play mahjong. She was performing on stage in one of the lounges and was scheduled to sing at the tournament's opening event.

"I'll have you know, Jayne was hired to sing on the ship, a real headliner," Winnie gloated. But she saw Sal twist his mouth, raise one eyebrow, and nod, like he disapproved. Kill-joy. A *mamzer* who had tried every which way to take her Jev away from her, to win his attention. Jev allowed the man to think he approved of him, for business's sake. A harmless show of affection. After all, when the three of them were together, Jev barely gave Sal a second glance. Of course, the men had spent a lot of time without her, but she refused to think about that. Where would it get her? Angry at a dead man? Where was the margin in that!

The day before the tournament, Sal removed two more paintings from the common living area. The Picasso-style nude, which she never loved—it was too explicit in its abstraction—and the gorgeous raven-haired woman with golden arms and lush lips—which she adored. Her most precious artwork was in her private suite, where Sal never ventured. Maybe she'd hide her favorite pieces in her closet or under her bed. She'd double lock the door so he could never get in.

"I can't drive you women to your tournament tomorrow. I'm leaving on a business trip for a few days," he said, his voice adopting a British snottiness. "You'll have to figure out another way to get there, or drive the Lincoln Town Car yourself." He made a deep guttural noise and his Adam's apple bobbed, like he was holding down a laugh.

Her mind traveled back years. She was reminded of her darkest morning.

Jev and Sal had a business meeting downtown, and they were out the door at dawn in the white Rolls Royce they routinely rented—Jev believed the car was a better credential for wooing wealthy art dealers. Winnie didn't like to drive. She was confused by double yellow lines and short white lines and speeding up at traffic signals and green cars. Something about tail lights bothered her too.

Winnie felt stranded. She had a ten o'clock appointment with an astrologer and had expected Sal to take her. If the drive had been more than two miles, she would have called a cab, but she remembered the lean years, the penny-saving hollow-cheeked years before Jev. She gulped in courage, found the key she stashed in her jewelry box for the Lincoln Town Car, and descended the private elevator to their coveted parking space. She set her wide-brimmed hat on the passenger seat; she loved hats. There was something mysterious about a woman in the back seat of a Lincoln Town Car wearing a red wide-brimmed hat. She would put it on when she parked at the astrologer's salon.

Winnie eased out of the garage. No green cars in sight. No screaming taillights. No highway merges. Just a calm right-lane crawl. She could do this. She was doing it.

Driving around a corner near the salon, she swore she saw the white Rolls Royce in a parking lot. She didn't have the confidence to double back to check. Then she spotted the familiar thin frame of her husband about to enter a building. She slowed the car and tried to keep her eyes on the road and on her husband, deciding whether or not to beep the horn wildly and show him that she—Winnifred Lee Cohen Robbins Reichman—was actually driving.

But Sal's shadow lurched in front of Jev, opening the door. The large man leaned in to Jev and kissed the tip of his nose. Winnie saw Jev lift his chin. She thought she saw their lips meet.

Even as she drove home that morning, eyes blurred, mascara streaking her cheeks, green cars darting in front of her, and horns blasting, she shoved the image to the back of her brain. She had refused to drive since that day and made sure Sal took her wherever she wanted to go and waited until her errands were completed. She made it a priority to exclude Sal from Jev's life, even if they were business partners and lived in the same apartment. Winnie wasn't second fiddle to anyone, or so she believed. And then Jev suddenly died. In his will, he left fifty-five percent of the business to Sal. Winnie and Sal were to share the penthouse. She would get the Lincoln Town Car, with the provision that Sal would drive Winnie wherever and whenever she wanted. What was Jev thinking making her dependent on Sal? Every time he dropped her off somewhere, she spit on the ground, expelling her hatred for him.

Frozen in her chair as Sal plucked more paintings from the wall, Winnie set her lips in cement and refused to cry. When he took the one where sunflowers and pears thrived in a lush garden, she imagined what a painting of her own garden would look like: balled-up tissues, ground-down teeth, discarded fingernails, and black scowls. What an ugly picture that would make. She refused to let Sal get the better of her. She had to figure out how to banish him from her life.

The ringing of the phone stunned Winnie out of her funk.

"Winnie, dearest, I'll be at the clubhouse at 8 AM sharp on Saturday morning. Do you have enough room for a trunkful of costumes?" Jayne asked, her voice filled with glitter.

"Oh Jayne. I don't know what to do. That good-for-nothing *mamzer* Sal is leaving today on a business trip. How on earth will I get to the cruise ship? A common taxi? One of those Ubers? I wouldn't even know how to call them. I am just too overwhelmed to think. I have to cancel. You'll all have to make your way to the docks by yourselves."

"Nonsense," said Jayne. "I'll drive!"

"My Lincoln Town Car?"

"But of course, silly pooh! No need to change our plans because that bastard Sal is MIA."

Winnie's heart filled with heat. "So we'll still meet the girls at the clubhouse?"

"Let's be daring and pick each up at her condo," Jayne said.

"I'm not sure where everybody lives. All those condos look alike," Winnie said.

"No worries. I know my way around," assured Jayne.

Chapter Fifteen

SCHLIMAZEL: A PERSON WHO SUFFERS MISFORTUNE

On the day of the tournament, Jayne dropped the women off at the cruise ship entrance. "Go on ahead while I park. I have to check in through a processing door reserved for the working stiffs. I'll see you at the kick-off luncheon."

Gertrude dragged an ancient suitcase strapped round with a man's belt. She refused to let anyone near it. "Don't touch my stuff," she growled. The porters sidestepped her to help Blooma and Mavis with their modest bags. Winnie needed a cart for her luggage.

As they walked up the ship's gangway, the women carried dreams of winning and fears of losing, except for Winnie. She was happy simply to be away from Sal. The next few days would give her time to decide what to do next. To sell the penthouse? To move to a smaller place? To find her son BJ and reconcile with him? To take the remaining paintings and flee? She needed to think.

Winnie was so grateful that Jayne drove. She wondered how she could show her appreciation. Maybe she could buy her something on board the ship. She remembered all the perfumes and trinkets that Jev bought for her when they cruised. "Anything for my darling Winnie." She recalled how Sal would grimace. He joined them on cruises because they displayed pieces from their collection at the art galleries onboard. But Winnie kept a vigilant eye on the two men, although she had woken many nights to find Jev's side of the bed empty. She decided he'd be in the casino gambling and put the thought that he was with Sal way in the back of her mind. And she locked it there. Sealed. Not spoken about. No accusations. No sass. Jev was her husband, even if they rarely made love and only on those occasions after they'd watched sexy movies.

Blooma was proud that she knew what to do on the ocean liner. Her dry run from a few weeks earlier boosted her confidence. After Blooma embarked, she looked around for Murray, who had called her twice to chat and said he looked forward to seeing her again at the tournament cruise. She dreamed he'd be in the lobby waiting for her, but he wasn't. Disappointed, she located her cabin, a long walk from the elevator, but she decided she did not want another scooter. There was no need to appear older than she was. If Murray still showed an interest in her, she wanted to be free to stroll the deck with him.

The mahjong tournament's luncheon kicked off the event. All players would meet in the banquet room at noon for a buffet lunch. Afterward, the Director would go through the tournament rules. Finally, Jayne would perform three songs to get the players pumped.

Jayne had practiced the tunes in the South Tower common room with the ladies as her audience. First she strutted in a Tina Turner wig, sequined red dress and bright red lipstick, singing the optimistic tune *Simply the Best*. "If you're the best at what you do," said Jayne in preparation for introducing the song at the tournament, "you can hold your head up and shout it to the world."

For her next tune, she whipped off the wig, put on a fedora and a man's jacket and sang Sinatra's *High Hopes*. "Cause she had high hopes, she had high hopes, she had high apple pie in the sky hopes."

Blooma believed that Sinatra was right in the room with her. And Gertrude was *kvelling*; she was so proud at how Jayne could transform into one of Gertrude's favorites stars.

For the last tune, Jayne chucked the Sinatra disguise for oversized sunglasses, a blond wig, and a black pantsuit. She sang Madonna's *Lucky Star*. "You must be my lucky star 'cause you shine on me wherever you are."

"How will you make those clothing changes without boring the audience?" asked Winnie.

"It's all about timing," said Jayne.

"I could help you," said Winnie. "I have a great sense of fashion."

More like fashion cents, thought Gertrude. The more money you have, the more you think you're in style.

The women were excited about being in on the details ahead of time. They were equally thrilled with the luncheon buffet options. Mavis and Gertrude stacked their plates with meatballs, roast beef, potatoes au gratin, French fried potatoes, potato salad and potato fritters.

"Spud-tacular," Mavis squawked.

Winnie's plate was neatly separated into small portions of turkey, green beans, and sliced melon. Blooma made a beeline to the brisket, carrots, and raison pudding, her comfort foods. She noticed that Mavis nipped from her flask but not as openly as usual. She hid it behind her napkin to guzzle.

After the meal, a robust woman with a gold badge welcomed the players and stated the hard-fast rules of the tournament. "Welcome to Mahjong Madness. Today, Round One is four games, then you'll tally your points, pass in your sheets, and have twenty minutes before the second round begins with a whole new set of opponents. After Round Two, there will be an hour's break so we can check scores and post results before Round Three begins at precisely 4:00 PM. This evening you are on your own to enjoy this beautiful ship. Tomorrow morning, you'll play two rounds before lunch, and two rounds after lunch, then we'll have our awards ceremony and a sumptuous banquet."

The Director took a deep breath. So did Blooma. She thought she was prepared, but looking around the room she saw a hundred eager faces, some flawless, some weathered, some with full makeup, some plain, but all with fire in their eyes and can-do attitudes. No number of pills would keep her alert throughout the afternoon no matter how much she had practiced. She had seven pills left, enough for the tournament. But whenever her brain stalled, she popped another one. *Oy gevult!* She needed to buy more from Jayne, pronto.

The Director hushed the crowd who was murmuring at high volume. "Ladies, remember, you must wear your name tags whenever you're in the tournament room. There's no chatter while games are in progress. Participants are advised to be prompt. Ten penalty points will be deducted from any player not seated when the game bell begins. For every minute late, ten additional points will be deducted. If a player fails to show up after five minutes has passed, she forfeits the match. Check your schedules for times. If there are any questions, do not make decisions on your own. Ask me, Madam Director." She bowed, her bosom heaved, and her voice rose to a crescendo. "I have final say."

She didn't stop there but blah-blahed on about penalties and dead hands and bonuses. Mavis was ready to squawk.

Blooma closed her eyes, fending off fear.

Gertrude made notes in her journal, paying close attention to every detail.

And Winnie stared into space.

When Madam Director finally finished, there was a ten-minute break before the entertainment officially jump-started the tournament. Winnie, Blooma, Gertrude, and Mavis brought their chairs to the edge of the stage so Jayne's aura could shine on them. The *farbissinehs* in the crowd scowled at them.

More than ten minutes passed and the room grew rowdy. "Time to play!"; "Who cares about entertainment!"; "Get the show on the road!"

Seeing Murray at the back of the room whispering to a brown-haired woman, Blooma rose to her feet and waved to get his attention. But she was so tiny, she could barely be seen. She watched as the woman gave Murray a hug before she marched to the podium to speak privately with Madam Director.

The Director hustled from the stage and talked with some audience members, then bustled to the microphone. "And now," she crooned, "we take great pride in kicking off our tournament with our very own Cupie Pies! Let's give this talented quartet of ladies a rousing round of applause."

The four *farshtunkene* women who sang Karaoke at the Watering Hole skipped onto the stage all decked out in matching t-shirts with bright red polka letters shouting CUPIE PIES. More like the Dopey Pies, Gertrude thought. She could imagine the four of them with matching t-shirts. Mavis would write MAN EATERS or PUTZ SUCKERS or SCHLONG MASHERS, something outrageous to get a rise out of the opponent. Blooma would want cupcakes or rugelach or streusel. Winnie would embroider CLASSY LADIES with gold thread. For herself, Gertrude wanted a collage of her favorite movie stars on her chest rooting her on. Maybe just their lips or their noses or their eyes. Yes, definitely their eyes, staring down at whoever sat across from her.

Blooma raced up to the woman with whom Murray had spoken. "Do you know what happened to Jayne? She was supposed to sing at our tournament."

The woman glanced at Blooma's name tag. "You're the lovely Blooma my dad has been talking non-stop about for weeks. You two met on the Thanksgiving Day Cruise, right?" Her voice was like cherries and cream.

Blooma's face glowed, hearing that Murray actually had mentioned her, but this was a moment that required seriousness. "I'm really worried about Jayne."

"Jayne had a problem. My dad is helping to solve it."

Blooma frowned.

"Oh, nothing major. A costume malfunction. My dad's a whiz at fixing things, even at his age. He continuously surprises me at how much he can do."

Blooma blushed wondering if Murray had any surprises in store for her, even at her age. Blooma returned to her seat and told the girls that Jayne had some sort of costume problem and won't be performing. The women felt like an angel had tumbled off their shoulders. They wanted to pick it up, hold it, make it feel better; instead they had to sit through the Cupie Pies' screechy rendition of *Aint She Sweet* and a medley from *The Lion King*.

When they finished, everyone clapped wildly except for Blooma, Gertrude, Winnie and Mavis, who felt heart-heavy that Jayne had not sung and worried for her well-being. Before they knew it, however, they were assigned a table and the first round of the tournament had begun. Their minds had no choice but to tune in to their mahjong hands.

Blooma had trouble concentrating. She lost the first four hands and threw the winning tile all four times, losing one hundred points. She didn't care. She just wanted the first round to be over so she could find out what happened to Jayne. At last, when the hour finally ended, she rushed into the hallway, hoping to see Murray as she had in her daydream. She also had to use the bathroom, and by the time she finished, the next round was about to begin. She had no choice but to find her seat and play. She popped a pill, sat down, and focused. The first match was endless and mahjong wasn't called until the last tile in the last rack. One woman was unstoppable and called mahjong early in the second and third matches. And somehow, remarkably, Blooma won the fourth hand. Thrilled with her win and with added energy, she flew out of the room, where she saw Murray in the hallway waiting for her. Blooma's heart jumped and fluttered.

"I need your help," he said.

"Is Jayne all right?"

"Come with me."

Murray took Blooma's arm as they walked to the elevator.

"Will I have enough time or should I forfeit the session now?" asked Blooma.

"A few minutes of TLC should do the trick," said Murray.

They descended to the second deck, in the bowels of the ship where the hired help had their rooms. Murray knocked on a cabin door, but no one answered.

"Jaynie, open up. It's Murray."

Blooma heard shuffling and sniffling as the door unbolted. Before her stood Jayne, her hair pulled into a ponytail, mascara streaking her cheeks. She was dressed in a man's silk Hawaiian shirt that smelled faintly of Old Spice.

"Oh *Bubbeleh*, what happened?" asked Blooma, pulling Jayne into a hug.

"They're all lost! Gone! Stolen! Missing!"

"Slow down. I'm here to help you," said Blooma.

"My costumes! My wigs! My suitcases! I gave them to the porter before I parked the car," she hiccuped. "They never showed up at my cabin. We've scoured the ship and no one can find them. How can I perform? I'm naked on stage without them."

Murray handed Jayne a tissue. "My daughter is on it. She'll track them down."

Blooma recalled the costumes Jayne wore when she practiced and the others she had witnessed on the Thanksgiving Day Cruise: the Elvis jumpsuit, the Madonna corset, Judy Garland's red shoes. Why couldn't she just be Jayne, the woman with a stirring voice who would inspire the mahjong ladies to victory?

"*Mein kinder*," said Blooma hugging Jayne like a daughter, "you don't need to cover up in costumes to please a bunch of old ladies. We're happy just knowing you're singing for us."

"You don't understand, Blooma. This is my chance to be someone new, to prove myself." Jayne blew her nose like a foghorn.

Blooma patted the edge of the bed, urging Jayne to sit beside her. "Let me tell you a story. When I was a little girl, I couldn't ride a bike. No matter how hard I tried, I kept falling over. My father had no patience and my Orthodox mother felt it was a *shunda* to run alongside me in her long flowing skirt and perfectly coiffed wig. And do you know what?"

Jayne raised her tear-stained eyes to Blooma. "You learned to ride anyway?"

"Nope. I gave up. I never learned. I never had the *chutzpah* to get on that bike again. So I never felt the air stream through my hair. I never got to whip through Central Park with my friends. I never raced down a hill with my feet off the pedals, not knowing if I'd be safe at the bottom."

"So you're saying I should have gone out there anyway?"

"Exactly."

"But now it's too late. Lunch is over and I've let you all down."

Murray sat on the other side of Jayne. "By the time you perform tonight, your luggage will either show up or not, and it'll be your choice what you want to do."

Blooma marveled at Murray's words, how he offered Jayne options. She had never experienced options in her life. She married when her father said so. She got pregnant according to Isaac's timetable. And she lost three babies to miscarriage before her darling Sarah was born. She believed it was all destiny, *beshert*. When Isaac banished their daughter from their lives for marrying a black man, she obeyed Isaac's decree. And now she was alone, with an addled brain and no hope for ever riding a bicycle. Somehow that wasn't a fair deal. Maybe destiny wasn't predestined, if that even made sense.

"Believe in yourself, Jayne. In the end, we only have to prove to ourselves that we are worthy of love and admiration." Blooma's head hurt thinking about what she had just said. She'd been baking sweets all her life to make others happy. But was that the real reason? Didn't it make her happy too?

A knock at the door caused them all to jump. Murray ran to get it, and into the room came an enormous man maneuvering two suitcases and five hatboxes. As Jayne bounced from the bed, Blooma slid off, landing on her rear with a jolt and pitching backward, hitting her head on the floor. She had a weird point of reference as Jayne straddled above her, those long legs stretched out Liza Minelli style. Although Blooma averted her eyes, she could look right up Jayne's bare legs. Blooma saw an unexpected bulge in Jayne's underwear. Did Jayne have a tumor? Was she sick? Was her appearance on stage so important because this would be her final chance to shine?

Blooma closed her eyes as the giant man who had brought in the suitcases stretched her out on the bed.

"Blooma, Darling, are you all right?" Murray stroked her cheek.

Jayne hovered over her, fanning her face with a sandalwood scented wooden fan.

Blooma's eyes focused on the fan, which looked like the Chinese letters on a mahjong tile. "The tournament! I'm going to be late! Help me up. Get me to the playing room, Murray. Right away. I can't forfeit. I just can't."

The porter scooped Blooma into his arms and raced down the hallway with her; Murray trailed behind.

"Everything will be all right," shouted Jayne.

Just as the giant helped Blooma to her seat, the bell rang for the start of the final round of the day. The back of her head hurt and she felt a bump the size of an egg. It reminded Blooma of something she saw. Something about Jayne. Something important. If only she could remember.

Chapter Sixteen

SCHTICK: A GIMMICK TO DRAW ATTENTION TO ONE'S SELF

Mavis wiggled the parrot tattooed on her shoulder but she stayed quiet and didn't squawk. She'd been warned by Madame Director that one more screech would put her in jeopardy of forfeiting the tournament.

"We've received complaints about you all day," the director told Mavis. "This is a formal warning, Miss Gruber."

Mavis shrugged. Sammy the Parrot's face scrunched up in protest. "Yes, Ma'am," she demurred, but inside she roared with laughter. She had won seven out the eight games in the first two rounds, using calculated distractions besides the squawk. The best was mumbling the old line "Tickle your ass with a feather?" When the other players gasped and asked what she had said, she coyly murmured, "Mighty nasty weather. Yes, indeed."

As the last session of the day began, Mavis saw a huge man accompany Blooma to her seat. Mavis' lips contorted. Who was that man and was Blooma all right? She kept rubbing the back of her head and grimacing, which was unlike Blooma. Mavis wanted to shout "Pause!" or click a remote, or somehow stop time. She wanted to run over to

Blooma and find out what was going on. All Mavis could do was focus on her game, win quickly, and then see to Blooma.

But the first match was not going as planned. Her opponents had each won the earlier rounds, so they all had high points and skill. Now was not the time for Mavis to get distracted. Concentrate, damn it, she commanded herself. When it was her turn, she sat back in her chair, pretending to study her rack. Instead, she turned her eyes to Sammy and swore she saw him wink at her.

The other ladies at the table tapped their fingernails, clicked their teeth, and cleared their throats, but she'd resume when she was damned ready. There was no clock timing individual plays, although each round had to be completed within an hour, so she had every right to gather herself before making her next move, no matter how many old ladies she pissed off.

Mavis pulled out her stogie from her fanny pack and stuck it on her rack. The smell comforted her. "Don't have a hemorrhoid, Ladies, I'm not going to light it," she said, and discarded a tile, resuming play.

Madame Director rushed over when each lady raised her hand to complain, but as long as Mavis didn't smoke the cigar, there was nothing anyone could do.

Mavis called mahjong five turns later, and continued to win the remaining three games for a total of eleven wins on day one. She wanted to moon the ladies; instead, she settled for shaking her *tuches*, her buttocks hanging low from her thong underwear. Then she strode off to stand near Blooma's table so she would be there when her game was over.

Gertrude didn't notice Blooma's arrival or when Mavis finished her games to boos and "You're a *meshugenneh*." She was too busy railing against herself. She had lost the first four games of the day. The entire first round! She blamed Jayne. That woman was supposed to perform at lunch. Didn't she know she was Gertrude's muse, her inspiration? Gertrude bit the insides of her cheeks, so that her lips puckered. Snorting like a buffalo, she charged out of the game room after the loss and paced the deck during the short break between rounds one and two. Then came her serendipity moment. She rushed to her cabin and flipped through her cache of photos. She selected celebrities who swore by their good luck charms. Who needed Jayne when she had inspiration from Cameron Diaz, Michael Jordan, and Heidi Klum?

She returned to the game room hell-bent on winning. So what if the air was stifling, and those women with their manicured fingernails and helmet-heads were as determined as she was to win. She convinced herself that her opponents were *schmutzik* pieces of dirt whose photos would never don any walls. They were wannabes, pretenders. She was the real deal: Gertrude Friedman, a mahjong *maven*.

With renewed confidence, Gertrude bulldozed her way back through the second round, and played like hell was burning in her belly. She took the first game handily, and the next three games too, dismissing Jayne's unexpected absence. Her opponents exited the room, but Gertrude sat alone at her table applying a fresh coat of lipstick. From her purse, she took out the small cache of photos. Flipping through them, she placed a full-lipped kiss on the back of each, thanking them for her win.

The last round of the day, Gertrude was seated with three women who sat stiff and serious, their eyes focused and their minds alert. They were fast and skilled, click-clacking their way to victory, leaving Gertrude with only one win and the resolution to do better on day two.

Winnie hadn't had much luck. She won one game in the first round and lost the next three. She was playing as badly as Blooma, she thought, which was not at all acceptable. At first, concern for

Jayne distracted her; then she failed to find a viable hand. She was a good player, damn it. At the first break, Winnie returned to her room, looked in the mirror and gave herself a pep talk.

This is your time, Winnie said to herself as she put on her false eyelashes. If she looked good, she'd feel good. If she surrounded herself with strong people, she'd be strong. Her future was not dependent on Mavis or Gertrude or Blooma or Jayne. Make new connections. Find women like her on this cruise, women who appreciated Chateau Lafitte and lobster marinated in cognac, Gucci shoes and Shalini perfumes.

Before the bell sounded for the next round, Winnie strode into the tournament wearing a white chiffon dress with sheer beaded sleeves, a floral crown, diamond studded earrings and a matching necklace. "Look at me. Look at me. Look at me," each step said. She carried herself like a celebrity arriving at the Oscars, unlike the common *schleppers* in the room. One other woman caught Winnie's eye, a raven-haired stand-out wearing a sleeveless black leather body suit with silver rivets as seams, double chain necklaces, and an up-yours attitude. They nodded to each other as if in a secret sisterhood. Classy women stuck together, Winnie thought, and decided to approach this woman after the day's competition.

During the round, Winnie remained distracted and still couldn't find a hand. She picked and threw and shifted her tiles around, looking efficient and confident, but she was just listening for tiles that had already been thrown so she wouldn't give anyone else mahjong. In fact, the table ended up with three wall games where no one won. When the final round of the day ended and Winnie only had two wins to her name, she was disappointed, but not upset. So what? She was on her own. Sal was far far away, and Winnie was eager to find the black beauty who intrigued her. Winnie marched from the room fixated on befriending her, not even noticing Mavis leaning in the corner with her eyes focused on Blooma.

Chapter Seventeen

FARKAKTE: ALL MESSED UP

After Mavis' buttocks exposure, the women at her table raced to the director with complaints, stopping along the way to warn their friends what a crazy woman she was. Mavis didn't care. The tournament was about the game; she never was much good at playing in the sandbox. When Mavis was little, her mother had to go to the park when no one else was there, which was often because when the other mothers saw them coming, they bundled their kids up and ran. Mavis never had a close girlfriend until college and only then because Mavis had the drug connection for pot and pills. She and FiFi were so high all the time, they thought they were inseparable, but that dissolved as soon as Mavis' connections were arrested and both women dropped out of school.

It took seven decades for Mavis to realize that to have a friend, she had to be a friend. Even her husband Wally hadn't been a friend, a lover yes, a drug enabler, yes, but she cared more about herself than she did about him. Somehow Blooma had broken down a barrier inside Mavis and she felt nicer in her company. She wanted to please her, to protect her from gossips who called her *aiver buttel*, senile, lacking a brain. She watched Blooma play the end of the third round of mahjong, a beat behind everyone else. When the game ended, Mavis went to her side and knelt beside her. "Are you all right, Bloomie?"

Blooma squinted, trying to see Mavis in front of her. She felt woozy. "I need to lie down. Can you help me to our cabin?"

Murray was outside the tournament room when Mavis and Blooma emerged. He took her by the arm. Mavis reached out to chop him in two, but Blooma clasped his hand. "Oh Murray. I'm so happy to see you."

Mavis let out a shrill squawk, loud enough for Murray to jump. "What's going on?" she asked. "First Godzilla brings you into the tournament room. Now Tweedledum waits for you outside. Who's next? The goddamned Golem?"

"I'm Murray, a friend of Blooma and Jayne's. You must be Mavis. I've heard a lot about you." His cheeks puffed like butterballs.

Mavis' mouth twitched. "That I'm a bitch on wheels?" she spat even as she knew she should be putting Blooma's needs first or asking about the whereabouts of Jayne.

"You're one of a kind, I hear," said Murray, grinning ear to ear. "Now let's get our favorite lady to bed. Then you and I can chat."

Chat? Mavis thought. Chat? *Schmendriks* chat. She was beyond chatter. She wanted answers. Who was this pork chop chub? How did Blooma know him? Why was Blooma more *farmishted* than usual? What was going on with Jayne?

With Murray on one side and Mavis on the other, Blooma made it to the room. "I just need a short snooze," she said as her eyes closed.

Murray and Mavis went onto the balcony and stretched out on lounge chairs. Mavis withdrew her flask from her fanny pack. She took a swig and offered Murray a pull.

"Don't mind if I do," he said. His eyes popped as he drank. "Whiskey? I'm not surprised!"

"Keeps me on my toes," said Mavis, wiggling her sandaled feet. She shouldn't call attention to them, she thought, her bunions sharp and crusted, her nails yellow and craggy. She'd put down money that

Murray's feet were equally *farkakte*. "Ok, Murray, spill what you know. I'm waiting." She sipped more whiskey and stifled a Sammy-squawk, waiting for Murray to reply.

Mavis listened as Murray told her that he and Blooma had met playing bingo on the Thanksgiving Day Cruise and then they saw Jayne perform in the lounge in the evening. Murray praised Blooma's loyalty to Jayne, saying how she had told Jayne just that very morning in her cabin how talented she was and that she shouldn't be afraid to perform without her wigs and costumes.

Mavis listened quietly but volcano blasts of anger spewed through her. Her bottom lip pulled up and her cheeks sank in. This would mean Blooma had lied to her. Blooma! Her Blooma said she spent a quiet Thanksgiving reading and watching the Macy's Thanksgiving Day Parade, and that she never heard anyone knocking at the door. She must have been asleep, she said. And how Blooma was so excited to see Jayne perform because the only time she had seen her on stage was at the Watering Hole when they sang *Man Eater*.

Mavis chewed her tongue, her mouth jabbering soundlessly. She felt like she was in middle school and there was a party that even snot-nose Clarence went to and she hadn't been invited. She had begun to trust Blooma, to think of her with compassion. Look where that got her, thought Mavis. And what about Jayne? Befriending Blooma over the rest of us? What sort of *farshtunkene* shit was that? Did Blooma confide in Gertrude and Winnie? Those *yentas* were probably laughing at her right now, knowing that they put something over on her.

Mavis stood up too fast and felt her brain fall into her misshapen toes. "Well, Murray," she said, her voice thick, "*gai kucken afenyam.*" She pointed to the open sea. "The whole boatload of you can shit in the ocean."

When Mavis went into the cabin, she looked at Blooma sleeping peacefully, her mouth open and snoring in an easy cadence. "Two-faced liar," she mouthed, and flipped her the bird. She could have squawked like a parrot, but something inside her held her back from waking Blooma.

Mavis stopped at the bar, ordered three straight-up whiskeys, put them on a tray, and went to the twelfth floor deck. She found a lounge chair and downed one drink after another. As her anger festered, she lay back. Whiskey-dreams captured her mind: garlic clouds and choking dust, mottled hands and toothless mouths. Steam hissed from her ears as she imagined Blooma young again, infused with Murray's cherry glow. She pictured Gertrude and Winnie enjoying mandel bread and babke, while Mavis was home alone microwaving mac and cheese. She had an image of Jayne sitting at Blooma's table, sharing secrets that Mavis wanted to know.

Mavis released her knuckled grasp that punctured her palms and grabbed hold of the empty whiskey glasses. She stood by the railing and whipped them into the ocean. One for Blooma, one for Gertrude, and one for Winnie. "Friendship isn't worth the pain." She raised her trusty flask. "To me! Mavis the *Shlemiel* to believe that Blooma cared about me as much as I cared about her," and swallowed the dregs that remained at the bottom.

Gertrude wondered why she was alone on a ship of two thousand. Where were her so-called friends? She cruised by a few bars where she thought Mavis might be drinking. She was sure she could hear her squawking, but it was another yellow-haired wrinkled old lady laughing up an old geezer, getting him to buy her drinks. In exchange for what? Gertrude wondered. Who would want to sleep with a prune?

Gertrude thought Blooma might be lounging on a deck chair near the cafeteria, enjoying the late afternoon sun. She couldn't have gone too far, not the way she walked. No matter where Gertrude looked for the gray head of curls, Blooma was not to be found.

Winnie should be easy to spot. The tallest, boniest woman on the ship. But she too was missing.

Gertrude didn't want to sit around an empty room staring at blank walls. She could tape a few photos around to make it familiar and cozy, but the cabin boy would see them and think she was daft. So she went to the buffet and loaded her plate with brisket, stuffing, gravy, three types of bread, and pasta. Then she checked the *Cruise Daily* for evening entertainment. Jayne was scheduled to sing in the Blue Lounge at 11:00 PM. It was only 7:00.

Four hours to kill. In the mahjong room, she found three ladies seated around a table waiting for a fourth: one was a doughy *alter kaker* whose thick lips were outlined in red, but the fill had long since faded; the second was an ancient relic whose hands were mottled with brown spots and battled green with veins; and the third was a woman whose glasses were so thick she put every tile up to her eyeballs to identify it.

Gertrude tried asking them how they were doing. "*Vus machs da?*" But they only answered with grunts. She should turn the table over and get a rise out of them. Mavis would do that. Just play the game, she decided. Pass the time. Pretend she was a no-listening *farbissineh* who had nothing better to do with her life other than play mahjong all day and all night. When the tiles melted into each other and she couldn't tell a bam from a crac or a red dragon from a white, she closed her card and said good night. The women didn't make a move to leave. It was as if they were mahjong machines, waiting until a fourth showed up to rev into action.

Gertrude checked the time. 10:30 PM. She was eager to see Jayne's show—Jayne, whose goddess face beamed and whose body radiated good health. She took out a new folder of photos and studied the youthful faces of Raquel Welsh, Ann Margaret, and Jane Fonda, her bosom buddies for the evening. She glided into the Blue Lounge with them by her side. But no one noticed, like she was wearing an invisibility cloak, so she slunk to a dark corner and slouched in an overstuffed chair. Why go to the trouble of pretending to have friends? Just do what she always did, suck it up and push on.

What bolstered her spirits was the billboard on stage that shouted Jayne's World. Her Jayne. A headliner. She snapped Jayne's picture with her cell phone. She'd enlarge it on her printer at home. Maybe she'd make her own billboard and display it in her trophy room. She could put her arm around it. Talk to it. Make it larger than life.

Gertrude sat up straighter to catch the attention of Blooma, who sauntered into the room on the arm of a W.C. Fields clone. Where did she meet him? They looked like they'd known each other for decades. Then a decked out Winnie paraded in, dressed all in white, with a hat decorated with cockatoo feathers that sat on her head like a fan. Beside her was an equally tall woman dressed entirely in black. She wore a felt tam, tipped to the right. Curly black sideburns hung around her ears like the *payos* on Hasidic Jews. Her lips were orange-red; her oversized glasses were studded with jewels. To Gertrude, the pair looked like Bette Davis and Joan Crawford. Winnie's attention was entirely on the new woman. Who was this stranger? They sashayed to a front table. The people behind them had to move their chairs to see around them.

What was going on? Was this cruise an alternate universe? Was Gertrude the only person who couldn't find a friend?

Chapter Eighteen

SCHMALTZ: EXCESSIVELY SENTIMENTAL

Winnie discovered that the woman in black was an art connoisseur from Miami. She owned her own gallery but wasn't familiar with Jev and Sal's corporation, Authentic Restoration Art.

"I'd remember a name like that," said Hilda Lee. "It's an oxymoron."

Authentic Restoration, thought Winnie. Did those words cancel each other out? Hilda Lee seemed to think so.

"I'm always interested in the acquisition of fine pieces," she told Winnie.

A solution circled around Winnie's head as she sat beside the dazzling woman waiting for Jayne to perform. What if Hilda Lee bought some of the paintings in her home before Sal returned from his business trip? Surely she would pay handsomely for the masterpieces and Winnie would insist on cash. This woman could change her life and get her out from under that *mamzer* Sal.

Winnie spun a dream where she and her son BJ reconciled. They'd cruise around the world together, her treat. She'd hire the best therapist and together they'd go for counseling. Then BJ would understand that Winnie had been abused too. He'd know why his mother let

Brian Senior whack his son in the head for talking back or lock him in his room for lying. What could Winnie have done to help him? She would have been knocked unconscious and then what?

Winnie had seen BJ two years ago when he came for his inheritance money. Jev had the remarkable foresight to put a stipulation in his will that money from BJ's trust was available every three years on the anniversary of Jev's death. Winnie would also have to sign a release for the bank. That was just like Jev, insuring that BJ would have to see his mother at least every three years and perhaps even comfort her that Jev had passed.

BJ had shown up pen in hand. "Sign there," he demanded, brushing his dyed black hair off his forehead, revealing dilated eyes surrounded by black shadow and eyeliner.

"Stay for a while. There's so much I need to say to you," she pressed.

"Timeless horrors, Mother Dearest. I'm out," he said and was gone.

"Are you all right, Winnifred? You haven't heard a word I said," needled Hilda Lee. "Tell me about the artwork of your late husband."

Winnie closed her eyes and stretched her bony neck. "Jev liked impressionism, the kind you stand back to appreciate." She imagined the still life that blended vase and fruit and flower, and the painting of a sunset over an Italian villa, the grapes in the foreground plump for picking.

"Nothing modern? Nothing realistic?" asked Hilda Lee, who dug into her handbag for a stick of chewing gum. She took her time unwrapping it, folding it, and putting it into her mouth.

Winnie's mind wandered over the walls of her penthouse as the woman snapped her gum.

"There's a kaleidoscope of colors that looks like two birds in flight. And then there's the desperate woman clutching her three kids, one more ragged than the next."

Hilda Lee pointed her manicured finger at Winnie. "Fax me some photos."

Winnie's breath hitched. "Uh . . . uh," she stammered. She barely knew how to use her phone, never mind a fax machine; she'd have to figure it out fast. Sal was due home on Wednesday.

The lounge lights dimmed. "We'll talk after the show," said Winnie, glad to have more time to think this through.

A spotlight focused on the curtain. A black-stockinged leg appeared, long and muscular, tapping out a beat in her red stilettos. The light inched up her curves until her full lips threw kisses and she launched into her Carol Channing imitation.

Winnie's heart skipped, knowing that her Jayne was on stage. She put all other thoughts out of her mind.

In the back of the room, Gertrude tuned into the sexy voice. She felt pin drops of sweat trickling down her ample bosom, the same feeling she got when she looked at George Clooney, Marlon Brando, or Sting.

Murray popped out of his seat to whistle.

Blooma knew Jayne didn't need a catcall to get the audience's attention; she anticipated the talent about to unfold and she wanted to watch it all. This time she ordered a Shirley Temple, no falling asleep allowed. `

As Jayne performed, Mavis stumbled through the lounge, bumping into tables and stepping on feet. She tried to stay quiet, even though her heart thumped not only from her whiskey dreams and a nagging anger at Blooma, but also from hearing Jayne's dark-velvet voice.

Once seated on a stool at the bar, Mavis' eyes stalked the room. She saw Gertrude huddled in a corner; Blooma cuddled near Murray; and Winnie decked out beside a she-devil. Jayne strutted onto the stage in a shaggy blonde wig and a tight-waisted gown that ballooned her Dolly-Parton boobs. She sang *Islands in the Stream*, whispering the words "We rely on one another" as if she were singing only for Mavis.

Bull-shit, thought Mavis, focusing on her straight-up whiskey. The only person she could rely on was herself. That was the way she lived and goddamn it, she'd be a *schmuck* to change now. She didn't need that liar Blooma, or the *farbissineh* Gertrude, or the stuck-up Winnie. And Jayne was a phony too. No one had a natural body like that at sixty-three years old. Mavis raised her glass. "*L'chaim*, to me. Everyone else can *ikh hob dir in drerd*, go to fucking hell."

None of the other women seemed to notice Mavis stewing at the bar; they were wrapped up in the performance: Jayne belting out tunes, changing costumes, impersonating Elvis and Madonna, Michael Jackson, and Judy Garland.

Gertrude was amazed at how much Jayne resembled each celebrity, how the hair, the grin, the stretched legs, the way she stood made her a chameleon. Jayne was the composite of all the actors and actresses whom Gertrude admired. To have them all lumped into Jayne was mind-blowing and she imagined how Jayne would come to Gertrude's dinner table dressed like a different star each night. Gertrude was so excited, the corners of her lips turned up. Her private dreams had been answered in the embodiment of one woman, a woman accessible to her. Imagine that! All her life, Gertrude had wanted to be in the company of greatness, and now it was happening. She soared above the air watching this woman perform. She didn't need Mavis or Winnie or Blooma. Hell, she didn't need mahjong. She could devote the rest of her days to taking photos of Jayne as different personalities. She'd frame them and hang them throughout her home.

Winnie too was captivated by both Jayne and Hilda Lee, but she couldn't figure either woman out. Jayne impersonated singers, and was damn good at it. Like authentic restoration, thought Winnie. How was that for irony! And Hilda Lee had an art gallery and knew the business, but was she powerful enough to help Winnie become independent from Sal? From a distance, Hilda Lee was a vision of competence, but up close, she snapped her gum and drank bottom-shelf rum with diet coke, and had powder cracks in her pores. Jayne was strong and beautiful, but up close her skin was stretched thin, her makeup was garish, and her body resembled a Barbie doll. Winnie didn't know what to believe. Would Jayne remain a friend once her talent went viral? Did Hilda Lee have velvet paintings of Elvis and big-eyed children with pouty lips like those gas-station paintings.

At the end of Jayne's set, the audience rose to their feet. "More! More!" they shouted.

Jayne went behind her curtain and emerged wig-less, her own shoulder-length blond hair brushed back from her face. She wore a red terry robe sashed at the waist like she was in a living room ready to watch TV and eat popcorn. She sat on a bar stool, the mic a kiss away from her lips.

"My final tune is from the TV program *The Golden Girls*. I dedicate it to my golden ladies: Blooma, Gertrude, Mavis, and Winnie. I love them for their kindness, their generosity, their grit, and their dignity. This is for you."

Thank you for being a friend
Traveling down the road and back again
Your heart is true. You're a pal and a confidant.
My hat is off to you. Won't you stand and take a bow.

Jayne swept out her arms, inviting the women to stand. Gertrude was in the rear of the room, but Jayne saw her and waved. Gertrude hunched her shoulders, stood fast, and sat down faster. Mavis saluted with her middle finger and Sammy the Parrot squawked to the surprise and astonishment of the audience. Winnie raised her chin as if a puppet master's string were on her nose. Murray helped Blooma to her feet and she gave a sweet bow from the waist.

Jayne sang more verses, rotating through the audience, kissing each of her golden ladies on the cheek. Mavis accepted the kiss, then scraped it off like it was tar.

The audience chimed in with the chorus and formed a conga line that snaked through the room.

Thank you for being a friend
Thank you for being a friend
Thank you for being a friend

Winnie, Blooma, and Gertrude hummed along but did not fling their legs and belt "Thank you for being a friend." They nodded to the music, wrapped in the glow of Jayne's attention.

But Mavis jumped into the conga line, grinding and twerking her way through the crowd, out the door, and into the long corridor of the cruise ship. Now what? She had no choice but to return to hers and Blooma's room. She was still angry that Blooma had lied to her, but every bone in her body ached. As she turned into the hallway to her cabin, she saw Murray and Blooma at her door. Murray kissed Blooma's cheek and they said good night. Mavis slipped back to the elevator and as Murray turned the corner, Mavis bumped into him.

"Murray? Did you deliver our sleeping beauty?"

"Ah, Mavis. We were worried about you. She was so upset that you sat at the bar by yourself."

"She could have come over to me, you know," said Mavis, leaning against the wall, her chin tilted up. "Tell me, Murray, does she know what we talked about, how you told me that you two met on the Thanksgiving Day Cruise?"

"Gee, I don't know. When she woke from her nap, it was close to show time."

"So you waited on the balcony the whole time while she was sleeping?"

Murray blushed. "That lounge chair was comfortable."

Mavis thought about lying on the deck chair on the eleventh floor, how at the same time Murray slept under the blue sky and Blooma snoozed, both of them oblivious to Mavis' anger. She gave her shoulders a shake, causing her breasts to dance. "Let's put our little balcony conversation behind us, shall we? How about a nightcap?"

Murray's cheeks puffed and his shoulders shimmied. "What a fine idea. Maybe you can tell me what makes you so feisty."

"Feisty? I'm just a sweet little old lady."

"Sweet, my arse," said Murray.

"So you want to get to know me better?" Mavis teased.

"I'm always curious about the ladies," Murray said, "especially the bad girls."

Chapter Nineteen

FERDRAYT: DIZZY, CONFUSED

Gertrude waited in the lounge as the crowd thinned. She hoped Jayne would come to her table and give her another cheek-kiss. Gertrude clicked on photos on her phone and Jayne's headshot appeared. Where had she been hiding all those years? A talent like that just didn't materialize on a cruise ship. She wanted to know more about her.

Gertrude googled Jayne's World, but nothing was listed. She checked the images and lots of familiar Jaynes appeared: Jayne Mansfield. Jayne Meadows. Jayne Kennedy. Gertrude googled JANE. Jane Fonda. Jane Lynch. Jane Wyman. Jane Seymour. She realized with dismay that she didn't know Jayne's last name. How could that be? In truth, she only knew that this beautiful siren appeared a few months ago at her senior center and wanted to learn to play mahjong. Gertrude catalogued what she knew about Jayne: she could sing; she had a secret medical problem; she had sixteen thousand dollars from Gertrude, and three thousand dollars from Winnie, with a promise to pay them back. Beyond that, what the hell did she know? *Gornisht. Bupkis.* Nothing at all.

That would not do, thought Gertrude. She needed to investigate before making a fool out of herself.

Winnie and Hilda Lee left the lounge whispering to each other, like *haymisha* buddies.

"I feel like I've known you all my life," said Winnie.

"Do you want to see the artwork that's on display?" asked Hilda Lee. "I'll give you a private showing."

Winnie walked taller, pursing her thin lips, taking the woman's arm and pulling her closer. "Are you allowed to do that?"

"I always get my way," said Hilda Lee, smiling at Winnie.

They entered the glass elevator and descended to the fourth floor art gallery, passing first through the casino. Hilda Lee stopped to feed a dollar into a slot machine. Lights flashed and bells whistled. "One hit wonder," she said, and squeezed Winnie's hand.

Winnie saw her collect her ticket for $500 and put it cooly into her purse. If that were Winnie, beads of sweat would drip between her small breasts, her hands would be clammy, even her hair would shine. But this woman, this Hilda Lee, didn't register surprise or pleasure, thought Winnie, as if winning were her due. Oh how she wanted to be Hilda Lee.

Blooma lay on her bed but had trouble sleeping after the day's excitement. She was so proud of Jayne, getting up on stage, delighting the audience. Blooma couldn't understand why Mavis was so stand-offish. Murray said that Mavis had a hair up her *tuches* or something like that. Maybe Mavis was nervous that she might lose the tournament. Maybe Mavis was upset that Murray was Blooma's new friend. Maybe Mavis just needed alone time. She was a loner, after all. But Blooma saw a big heart under all that brashness. In Gertrude too. Both of them covered up their pain.

Blooma knew about pain, how it seeped from the corners of her body, causing her fingers to hurt and her brain to ache and her heart to break. When she looked at her friends, she saw years of struggle and anger. No one baked cookies for these women. No one added sugar to their tea. But Blooma thought they were coming around. Even Winnie. Now there was a woman with a hard heart. If only Blooma could bake something to cheer them all up, to change their attitudes, to make them happy. She had looked at each of them tonight when Jayne kissed their cheeks. If she hadn't been with Murray, she might have hobbled over to them and added her kiss too. But their cheeks looked cold to her and she couldn't understand why.

Gertrude seemed so icy, like she put up a wall around her and sat inside a refrigerator and wanted to stay that way. If Blooma had gotten close, she would have turned to frost. And Winnie was so taken with that woman in black, they had formed a circle around themselves that Blooma couldn't penetrate.

Blooma understood this feeling. Her Sarah had shut her out. The few times she had seen Sarah since Isaac declared her dead, Sarah pretended her mother was invisible, even though Blooma had appeared on the street corner near her house, even though Blooma had shown up at her office. Sarah had put up a shield and Blooma could not get past it. Her own daughter walked through her. So she knew the moment she looked at Mavis and Winnie and Gertrude that someone as weak as Blooma could never affect their mood, no matter how many sweets she baked.

Blooma went onto her balcony and looked out at the ocean and up to the sky. She needed to remember this night, how Jayne shone on the stage, how a star had been born. Blooma reached into her pocket and withdrew a napkin. She went back into the room and found a pen and wrote on the napkin: *Let me remember the moments. Let them be pleasant and sweet. There are so few remaining. May I enjoy the ones I have left.* She thought about throwing the napkin to the stars, to the sea, into the air, but she didn't. She chewed it and swallowed it; it tasted like challah, the bread of life. Now those words were part of her very soul.

As Blooma lay in bed waiting for Mavis to barge into the room, she reviewed the day: playing mahjong, taking her last pill, feeling faint, being helped by Mavis and that sweet man, the one with the round belly and suspenders and chubby fingers whose daughter booked Jayne on the cruise. For the life of her, though, she couldn't retrieve his name. Morris? Mickey? Moishe? It was on the tip of her tongue. What was the matter with her? She knew his name a few hours ago. She needed to take another magic pill but the little bottle was empty.

Winnie was too excited to sleep. She'd gone with Hilda Lee to her gallery and gushed over the artwork. The paintings were all about women. On horseback. At a masquerade ball. Playing a lute. In a garden. Defiant. Jubilant. Confident. Accomplished. One in particular spoke to her. It was of a woman in a white brocade dress and a gold cape. She wore a garland headband. Her eyebrows arched quizzically, as if she knew all the answers and no more questions existed.

Winnie fell in love with it, knowing that it depicted her. The best of her. The future of her. Hilda Lee told Winnie that it was an original and she had bought it directly from the artist. There were no prints, no Giclees. She would never see another like it anywhere.

"How much are you asking?"

"For a friend, four thousand."

Winnie was flummoxed that Hilda Lee called her a friend. She hadn't had a friend since forever. The mahjong women were acquaintances and they shared the game, but she didn't think of them as friends, more like, what was that word, frenemies? But she and Hilda Lee had an artistic bond and a personal flair. They were on the same wavelength. Winnie remembered how she had seen Jev the first time. He was tall and slender, like her. He was dressed in an expensive tailored suit with a matching tie, black socks and solid shoes—the obvious combination of class and character. She could tell. And there was something so familiar about his face that made her feel like they were meant for each other. That's how Winnie felt about Hilda Lee: class and character! A perfect match for Winnie.

But how would she explain a four thousand dollar check to Sal? That's when it struck her: no more Sal. The painting was her symbol of independence. She'd sell her share of the company and the penthouse and move. Why did she have to stay there and take his shit? She was divorcing him.

She wrote Hilda Lee a check on the spot. Fireworks and trumpets went off in Winnie's head. She was master of her universe from now on. Oh, how powerful she felt.

The alarm blared at 8:00 AM and Blooma stretched. She looked to see if Mavis was asleep, but the bed had not been slept in. Where was she? Blooma dressed quickly, put in her dentures and left the cabin in search of Mavis. She wanted to rent a scooter and race around the ship looking for her, but it was already 8:45, and the first round of the day began at 10:00.

Blooma scanned the cafeteria and saw Gertrude sitting alone. On the table was a finger-licked plate and a dozen crumpled napkins. "Have you seen Mavis?" Blooma asked.

Gertrude stared at Blooma. "Your shirt is inside out. And you have two different shoes on. Did you dress in the dark?"

Blooma looked at her feet. Sure enough, one sandal and one slipper.

"What's going on with you, Blooma? Who was that man you were sitting with last night at Jayne's performance? Why don't I know him?"

Blooma struggled to remember, knowing she had no memory pills left and her brain was likely to disintegrate into tiny molecules at any moment. They'd implode inside her and she'd burp them out, expelling all connection to the known world. *Ek Velt.* The end.

She closed her eyes tight, holding in the shaking nerves, and the letter M appeared, large and bold. "M. . . Murray. That's my friend Murray." Blooma sucked in air, relieved she remembered his name. Too bad she forgot to look in the mirror. Blooma started unbuttoning her shirt.

"Not here, Blooma. Let's go to your cabin and set you straight, but we have to hurry. We don't want to lose points for being late."

"You go along, Gertie, dear. I'll be fine."

"Let me at least get you to your cabin. Then I can meet you in the tournament room."

"You're a *mensch*, Gertrude. Do you know that? A real thoughtful lady."

If Blooma had slapped her in the face, Gertrude would have been less surprised. A *mensch*! A thoughtful woman! A good person! That's what Blooma thought of her? Gertrude was glad Blooma hadn't met up with her last night.

Gertrude had lain in bed for hours railing at her supposed friends, how they had forgotten her and had left her out. Her old nickname Intrude surfaced and stung her deeply. Like the time her suite mate in college made a sign and hung it on her bedroom door for all to see: Intruders stay away. Gertrude opened the door anyway because the sign could not have been for her. She and her suite mate talked every day after every class. Gertrude shared everything with her. She'd finally made a friend, so when the door opened and Patsy screamed go away, Gertrude was shocked. "Enough is enough," Patsy said. "Go bother someone else. I can't breathe with you constantly hovering around me."

That crushed Gertrude. She not only stayed away from Patsy, but she also failed to get close to anyone else at college. She felt the letters I - N - T - R - U - D - E branded on her forehead. It wasn't until she worked at Connelly Accounting and met Anthony that she made a connection with another human, even if he was married, even if each time with him was fleeting. She could talk and talk and tell him her deepest desires. He just nodded and said ah ha and never told anyone else her secrets. She suspected he was hard of hearing, but that made no difference to Gertrude. She let him in and he was always ready for her, when he wasn't home with his wife and kids, that was.

Now here was Blooma saying Gertrude was a decent person, worthy and good. She should only know, thought Gertrude. Last night, she had called her a *plyotkenitzeh* and a *yenta* and every other pejorative she could conjure for an old gossip. But Blooma hadn't meant to ignore her, Gertrude decided. She had just forgotten about her for a little bit. That wasn't unusual for Blooma.

Gertrude found a wheelchair outside the cafeteria. "Hop on, Blooma. Eighth floor. Room 822. That's your cabin, right?"

"I live at 92 Cortland Road in Boca Raton," said Blooma.

"I know that, but what about on the ship?" Gertrude didn't wait for an answer. She rummaged through Blooma's handbag and found her key. "So tell me, Blooma, this Murray. You and he looked cozy together last night."

"He's a honey," said Blooma.

"When did you meet him?"

"Meet who?" asked Blooma.

"Murray?"

"He's a honey."

"You just said that." Gertrude pushed the wheelchair faster. "You're *ferdrayt* in your head, Blooma. The man you sat beside. Murray. How do you know him?"

"Oh, him," said Blooma. "I think we're here."

"Here? What are you talking about?"

"*Oy gevult*, Gertrude, you just passed my cabin."

Blooma got out of the wheelchair as Gertrude opened the door. What they saw when they entered made them feel like they watching a B-rated movie. Mavis was on the bed and Murray was leaning over her, whispering in her ear and rubbing her shoulder.

The door shut with a thud and Mavis bolted up. "I lost track of time. Is the tournament starting?" She put on her shoes, raked fingers through her straw hair, and headed for the door.

"Just a minute, you *farshtunkene* hussy. What's going on here?" asked Gertrude. "I thought that man was Blooma's honey. You're a man eater for real."

Murray's face flushed. "We didn't do anything. She passed out and I was reviving her."

Blooma didn't know what to say. "Where were you all night?" she asked Mavis.

Mavis snapped, "What's it to you?"

"I was worried about you."

"No one gives a good goddamn about me. Least of all you," Mavis shouted.

"What are you yelling at her for? You're the one fooling around with her boyfriend," said Gertrude.

"Did you know, Gertrude, that these two met over Thanksgiving? Do you remember how worried we were about Blooma, how she didn't answer our knocks on her door, how we thought she might be dead? Well, she and her *putzy* friend were carousing on the ship with Jayne."

"Blooma, is that true?" asked Gertrude.

Murray answered for her. "This lovely lady and I had the good fortune to meet at a bingo game and then we went together to see Jayne's World in the lounge."

"Two weeks ago! On this cruise ship!" squawked Mavis.

Gertrude felt gobsmacked. "So she lied to us, and went behind our backs to see Jayne perform?"

"Exactly," said Mavis, her hair wild, her eyes pinpricks.

Gertrude grumped her head side to side, like she was weighing her thoughts. "So that makes it all right to fool around with her boyfriend? Our Blooma lying to us versus you canoodling with a man she likes?"

As all this filtered about the air, Blooma sat on a chair and listened. She heard her name and the word liar and lovely and *farshtunkene*. She heard the words boyfriend and lousy and two-faced. All the air deflated out of her and she became an empty balloon, trying to stay afloat but not succeeding. "Can we just go to the tournament and play?" she asked in a tiny voice.

The room grew still and the clock took on a glow. It was 9:50.

"We'll deal with this later," Mavis said, glaring at Gertrude and Blooma. "And you," she poked at Murray, "don't be such a pushover. There's no winning when you're a good guy. You could have had a little action, if you know what I mean." Mavis squawked and fled from the room.

Winnie looked around the tournament room. She didn't hear Mavis. She wondered if Madame Director had put a gag on her. Then she noticed that a few tables were missing their fourth players. Where was Gertrude? And Blooma?

As the bell sounded to begin play, Gertrude bustled in, her face an unusual high-color of red like her cheeks were on fire. She approached the director. "We had an emergency," she said.

"Who's We?" asked the Director.

Trailing Gertrude, Mavis strutted, and Blooma hobbled, still wearing mismatched shoes.

"Take your seats, Ladies. You'll each have twenty points deducted from your final score. Your excuse can go to the tribunal later if you'd like to challenge my decision."

Gertrude felt the Director's deep-set eyes staring at her. She turned her lips down and strode to her seat.

Mavis' head hurt. She had drunk too much last night and blacked out on Murray's bed. In the morning, he helped her back to her room to get ready for the tournament, but the minute she saw her bed, she passed out again. Damn, she was getting careless. At her age, she should know her limit. Now Gertrude and Blooma thought she was a hussy for real. But it was Blooma's fault, being deceitful in the first place. Tit for tat, thought Mavis. She looked down at her bare arms and felt Murray's warm hands trying to ease her back to consciousness. The poor *schlepper*, getting in the middle of her dysfunctional family. Time to concentrate on mahjong and win this game, she decided. Mavis sized up her opponents. With twenty points deducted right off the top, she would have to distract these *schmendriks*.

"So sorry to be late. I got caught *schtupping* my good friend's honey. You gotta take it when you can get it, don't you think?" Mavis didn't care if was true or not; she rattled her opponents for sure. On the third round of the Charleston, Mavis halted the passing, a legal move if she had no tiles to pass. She had plenty of unmatched tiles, but she knew the play would doubly throw their confidence. And it worked. Mavis beat them three out of the four games in the first round. Take that, Madame Director. Mavis ruled. Right Sammy? The parrot squawked loud and long and the women at Mavis' table high-tailed it out of the tournament room, grumbling and *kvetching* the whole way.

Mavis leaned back in her chair and closed her eyes. Her legs fell open and she felt a welcome breeze.

"You're out of control," hissed Gertrude as she whacked Mavis' legs together.

"Piss off," Mavis said. "I did nothing wrong."

"Haven't you learned anything in your old age? It's all about perception. If you look guilty, you are guilty," said Gertrude.

"And if you look *farmishted*, you are *farmishted*," said Mavis as she caught sight of Blooma teetering in her seat, trying to finish the third game in the round. It was already 10:45 and the full round would be over in fifteen minutes, barely enough time to complete the fourth match. The other women at Blooma's table seemed to look at her with steel eyes as they waited and waited for her to make a decision each time her turn came up.

The broadest of the three stood and began pacing behind her chair. Both Mavis and Gertrude stared at the woman's t-shirt: CUPIE PIE. She was one of THOSE *farbissinehs* bearing down on their Blooma!

Gertrude reached the table first. "Give Blooma time. She's just overwhelmed."

When Mavis drew near, she whispered into Blooma's ear, "Come on, Bloomala. Just throw a tile."

The Director saw the commotion and started toward the table as everyone else in the room turned in their direction.

"Yeah, dammit, just throw a fucking tile," demanded the Cupie Pie.

"Don't you dare talk to my friend that way!" shouted Mavis.

"Yeah!" said Gertrude, her body close enough to the Cupie Pie to knock her over.

Blooma began to rise, but Mavis gently pressed down on her shoulders to keep her seated. "We'll take care of this."

Together, as if on cue to some inner music, Mavis and Gertrude twerked into the Cupie Pie's backside, causing her to tumble onto the game board, scattering all the tiles, racks, and mahjong cards onto the floor.

"Now you've done it!" bellowed the Director, pointing to Mavis and then Gertrude. "Out, out, you two, OUT! On second thought, everyone at the table leave, except for you two!"

Winnie came to Blooma's aid. "Come on, Love. Let's get you back to your cabin."

"What happened?" Blooma asked, as she cradled Winnie's arm. "I feel like I'm in a movie and the film is rolling and I'm outside my body and my brain is floating away. I think I did something wrong. I just can't remember what."

Chapter Twenty

MESHUGENNEHS: CRAZIES

The Director alerted security and banished both Mavis and Gertrude from the rest of the tournament. Taking no chances, an officer escorted them to their rooms to pack their bags, then led them through the ship to a service elevator.

"You're one of the bad girls now, Gertrude," said Mavis, as she waved to the crowd of mahjong women who had gathered along the way to watch Mavis and Gertrude's walk of shame.

The guard took them to the rear deck of the ship, and set them up with lunch, snacks and beverages with strict orders for them not to leave the area. They were neither allowed to play any more rounds, nor attend the awards ceremony and banquet.

Mavis thought she'd be disappointed or angry that she didn't have the chance to gloat when she received top prize. After all, she had already won fifteen games, so her chances were damn good. Strangely, though, she felt heroic, like she saved her friend from public embarrassment and made the *farbissineh* Cupie Pie look foolish.

On the other hand, Gertrude hadn't been in the running. She'd won eight games and wasn't having fun. The photos she depended on for support just weren't giving her the energy she needed, so missing the afternoon rounds didn't deflate her; in fact, she felt relieved that she didn't have to try so hard to succeed. But more than that, she felt Jayne's absence and had hoped they would continue some sort of intimacy on this trip, which just hadn't happened.

After lunch, Mavis and Gertrude spent their internment pacing the stern of the boat and sharing one of Mavis' stogies in the open ocean air.

"We caused quite a commotion, don't you think?" said Gertrude.

"Those *alter kakers* will be talking about us until their dying day," chuckled Mavis.

Gertrude's mind wandered to Jayne's lounge act. She'd been to theaters and plays and improvisations, but she'd never known any of the performers personally. "Do you know Jayne's last name?" she asked Mavis.

Mavis twisted her lips. "Can't say I do. Then again, I don't know your last name either."

"Really? It's Friedman. Yours is Gruber. Blooma's is Gottlieb and Winnie's is Reichman. Why don't you know that?"

Mavis wondered if Gertrude was making the point that Mavis didn't care about anyone but herself. Or maybe Gertrude cared too much about everyone else. There were two sides to every story. "Maybe we should play Truth or Dare instead of mahjong," said Mavis, "and get to know each other a bit better."

"I've never played."

"Let's have a try. I'll go first. Choose to tell the truth or take a dare," said Mavis.

"Why do you get to go first?"

"Because I came up with the idea. Now choose: truth or dare."

Gertrude could imagine the dare: jump the guard, run through the ship naked, moon the Director. "Truth."

"Ok. What's the angriest you've ever been?"

Gertrude puffed on the cigar, giving herself time to think. She'd been angry as far back as she could remember. Her core was red-hot coals; if anyone got too close they'd burn.

"Come on, Woman. Fess up," said Mavis, yanking the cigar out of Gertrude's hand.

"When I was twelve, my mother told me she was taking me to a restaurant, just me. Not my sisters or my brothers. It was my special treat. I put on my best sweater and combed my hair the way the magazines said was stylish. I felt so grown up. She even let me sit in the front seat of the station wagon.

"We parked at a big brick building. On the second floor, was a long empty corridor and buzzing sounds. My mother led me to a room on the right. 'We're stopping here first,' she said. 'It'll only take a few minutes and then we'll go for lunch.' A man in a white lab coat took me into a big room and sat me in a white chair. 'Open your mouth, little lady.' Thirty minutes later I was minus two teeth. No novocaine. No laughing gas. And the teeth were stubborn and the *farshtunkene* dentist smiled as he pulled each one. And the blood got all over my best sweater. I thought we were going to a fancy schmancy place to celebrate my honor roll grades, or my first place trophy from the math team, or my science fair win. When the whole mess was over, my mother drove through the take-out lane at the fast food restaurant at the corner of my street."

"That's rough. Did you at least get a prize with your meal?"

"I got a barf bag and threw up for the next two days."

"Did you yell and scream at your mother?"

"I couldn't frigging talk, my gums were so swollen. And I was pissed. Not even an apology for tricking me. She never made it up to me either by taking just me somewhere nice. No white tablecloth. No bone china or polished silver. No mom and kid talk about me and what I was doing in school. Just paper-plate-and-plastic fork restaurants. To this day, I won't eat off a paper plate."

"I'll remember that when I invite you to dinner," said Mavis.

"You'd do that?"

"Probably not."

Gertrude stared at the ocean, the ripples rolling like tears. "Ok,

Mavis. That's the angriest I've ever been. After that, I lost trust in my mother. Do you know what that's like?"

Mavis lowered her chin to her chest and sighed. "It was the other way around for me. My mother lost trust in me."

Gertrude wanted to know the story of how Mavis' mother had lost faith in her, but Gertrude knew enough about Mavis that she'd have to be tricked into telling. "This is a *farshtunkene* game, but let's keep going. Truth or dare."

"Dare," said Mavis.

"Why am I not surprised? Okay, do an impression of your favorite celebrity."

Mavis wet the tips of her fingers and puffed out her hair so it was wild straw. She held the cigar like a fancy cigarette and raised her voice to a screeching pitch. "You know you're old if they discontinue your blood type." She opened her mouth wide and her eyes wider. "I have so many liver spots, I ought to come with a side of onions" Mavis winked hard and tapped out an ash. "Would you believe that I once entered a beauty contest? I must have been out of my mind. I not only came in last, I got 361 get-well cards. Va-Va-Va-Voom!" Mavis planted herself in front of Gertrude, paused for effect and bowed.

Gertrude's laugh echoed off the walls. "You're Phyllis Diller, right? You're a hoot! You should be on stage with Jayne."

"Yeah. I'm a natural." Mavis slapped Gertrude on the back. "Ok. Your turn again. Truth or dare."

"Dare," said Gertrude, holding her breath.

Mavis wanted Gertrude to be more messy and raw, to be all the colors in the crayon box, not just black and white and in rare moments, gray. "Give me your best snort."

"Snort, huh? I was sure you'd ask me to streak through the tournament and jiggle my *tuches* for the Director."

"Maybe next time. For now, an honest rip-roaring snort will do."

Gertrude pumped up her body, rotated her shoulders, and sucked air through the back of her throat. Then she spewed a torrent of blobby mucus out of her nose. An officer walking the deck jumped and Mavis swore a pod of dolphins dove for safety. The women bent over double, snorting with laughter.

When they caught their breaths, Gertrude piped up. "Ok. Your turn for truth, Mavis, if you're up to it."

"Shoot."

"What's the worst fear you have in life?"

Mavis flattened her hair and put Phyllis Diller away. "I can tell you what I'm not afraid of. Dying. Dying alone. Dying penniless. Dying friendless."

"That's not what I asked," Gertrude said.

Mavis' face crumpled. "I'm afraid that when I see my parents again in the after-life, they will spit on me."

Gertrude inched closer to Mavis. "Why?"

"I've told you enough. You asked my fear. Well there it is. Full-fledged phlegm in my face. I've shamed them. I've done nothing redeeming ever. I've lied and cheated and sold myself cheap. I've never given a damn about anyone other than myself."

"Is that true?"

"To them it was. And then I had the audacity to set their house on fire."

"Well, yeah, I'd be afraid of being spit on too. Yup, you win."

Mavis clenched her fist and jabbed it toward Gertrude. "You're not so bad, you know. We could go a few rounds in the boxing ring and put on a show. Phyllis Diller versus. . . who would you be?"

Gertrude returned the fist-bump. "Groucho Marx." She took the cigar from Mavis, raised a pinky and wiggled her eyebrows.

As the day stretched on, they lay on the deck chairs and snoozed. No one came close to them and they enjoyed the chance just to be.

When the ship docked, an officer escorted them off. Behind them on the access ramp, the mahjong women followed, including the four Cupie Pies who shouted, "*Meshugennehs!*"

Mavis turned and squawked, "You're *alta kaker farbissinehs*, all of you!"

"Yeah, you sourpuss *meiskeits*," shouted Gertrude. "Your faces are going to freeze like that!"

Mavis and Gertrude snorted and whacked each other on the back as they wove through the parking lot searching for the Lincoln Town Car. But their mood deflated when Winnie and Blooma approached, their faces solemn and drawn. Mavis and Gertrude believed that they had been protecting Blooma, but the truth was by doing that, they changed the experience for everyone, and not in a good way.

Chapter Twenty-One

RACHMONES: COMPASSION

The ride home from the tournament seemed endless for Blooma. She forced herself to think about sweet ingredients: sugar, cinnamon, honey, molasses. The list scrolled through her mind, erasing Gertrude and Winnie and Mavis and Murray and mahjong tiles that wouldn't behave. All she wanted to do was sit at her kitchen table and look at the picture on her refrigerator. She belonged in her own house, breathing yeasty air, sipping a *glazel tai*, and watching repeats of *The Golden Girls*.

Jayne parked in front of Blooma's condo and got out to help her with her luggage.

"Come and visit me soon. I'll make you fried challah, you'll like it." Blooma leaned in to whisper in her ear so the others couldn't hear. "I need more pills."

Blooma saw Jayne's eyes widen and hoped that was because she had a purse full of them and could provide them on the spot.

"Blooma, Sweetie, I just sold you an extra fourteen pills two weeks ago. You shouldn't take more than two a day. Please don't tell me they're gone."

"I needed them to make me smart for the tournament. I even won one game, but somehow my brain got lost and I didn't feel so well. I think it's what do you call it, withdrawal?"

"How many do you have left?"

"*Gonisht.* None," said Blooma.

"Honey, taking too many is dangerous." After she brought Blooma's bags to her front door, Jayne reached into her purse and withdrew three pills. "We'll talk about this on Wednesday at mahjong. Ok?"

Blooma's face lit up. "*Zie gezunt,* see you then." There'd be a second chance to get smarter and get to New York. Jayne would help her, she believed in her and in the magic pills.

Blooma hobbled into her house, relieved. Even so, she was weighted down by the weekend. It had gone so wrong. All that preparation, anticipation, and excitement and here she was, the tournament was over and she was tired and had an angry stomach, not to mention a heavy heart. She lay down fully dressed on the couch within sight of the refrigerator and the cherished picture of Sarah and her family. Sleep came fast.

She didn't stir until noon on Monday and then took a long nap in the afternoon. She could hardly wait to lay her head down again after *Wheel of Fortune.* She let thoughts wash over her, ignoring full-blown images of Sarah and her children at her doorstep and dismissing the memory of Murray's hugs as heartburn. He was still a robust mover and shaker and at some point he'd try for more than a kiss, which Blooma had no interest in pursuing. She never enjoyed sex with Isaac. She knew there was more to it than he had allowed her, but she wasn't about to begin discovering its afternoon delights at eighty-two. With Murray, she had the feeling he'd want her to cha cha and salsa and move her hips and shake her tush. She could never be his match. Mavis was more his style.

Blooma woke on Tuesday with Sarah's phone number in her hand. She couldn't remember how it had gotten there, but it gave her courage. She dialed the number and a child answered.

"Is this Mark?" Blooma asked.

"No, this is Andrew. Would you like to speak with Mark? He's in the bathroom right now, so he's busy."

"That's all right, Andrew. I'll talk to you. I'm Bubbe Blooma, your mommy's mommy, calling from Florida. How are you?"

"I think you'd better call back and speak to my mother. She's not home now, but my dad is. Do you want to talk to him?"

"Sure."

A man got on the phone, deep-voiced and curious. "Andrew says Bobby Bloom is on the phone. Do I know you?"

"I'm Sarah's mother, Blooma."

There was silence on his end and Blooma didn't want to fill it.

"Can I take a message for Sarah? She'll be home late tonight. She's been at a conference in California."

"So you and the boys are holding down the fort?"

"More like they're holding me hostage! I'm not a fort kind of guy," he laughed.

Blooma felt his energy sizzle through the phone. How she'd love to meet him, to tell him how welcome he was in her heart.

"I was wondering," stammered Blooma, "would you come to Florida to say good-bye to me?"

"Good bye? Where are you going?"

"It's not me who's going, it's my mind slipping away every day. I tried to capture it back by taking these magic pills, but they're not working so well any more. I want to see my family before I don't know that a family really existed, except on my refrigerator." Blooma thought about how the Japanese fabricated whole families to create a personal history. Was the refrigerator picture even real? Maybe this man on the other end of the phone had no knowledge of her. Maybe Sarah never said her mother was alive.

"Mother Blooma," he said, and the words caught her in the chest. "I'll tell Sarah you called and that you'd like for us to come to Florida to see you. I make no promises, but I'm a family man and I want the boys to meet you before the magic pills disappear completely."

"Charles, that's your name, right?"

"Sarah calls me Charlie."

"Charlie, may I call you son?"

"If that gives you peace, you may certainly call me son. What if you flew North to see us?"

Blooma didn't know what to tell him. Flying on a plane? Maneuvering through an airport? *Oy gevult.* Would she ever be strong enough? Brave enough? Smart enough? Somehow, she knew those days had passed.

"Maybe Sarah can call me when she's home from her trip?"

"No promises, but I'll ask," said Charlie.

Gertrude wanted to hug Jayne when she dropped her off after the cruise. "I wish we could have had more time together," Gertrude whispered to Jayne. "You're the only genuine woman I know. I so want to be you."

"You're better than I am," Jayne said. "You're the real deal."

Gertrude didn't know how to reply. The real deal? A *schlubby* nobody that nobody loves. A common *schlepper* who will live the rest of her years staring at photographs—not like Jayne: a doer, a personality, a player.

"Come for dinner after mahjong on Wednesday. I have something important to show you," said Gertrude.

Jayne pecked a kiss on Gertrude's cheek. "As long as you're serving *tzimmes*, I'll be there."

She needed to keep that woman in her life. How? How indeed? Numbers had made her self-sufficient, knowledgable about what worked and didn't. A business venture swirled through her mind, the profits accumulating and multiplying, making Jayne rich and maybe her too. Gertrude would supply the seed money at first, but once the plan became reality, she knew it would be a winner.

Gertrude had a lot to accomplish in the three days before Jayne would come to her house and be bowled over by her sensational idea. Go big or *gey schloffen*, her father had said. She was tired of sleepwalking through a dull life.

Gertrude retreated to her trophy room and identified all the celebrities whom Jayne could impersonate. She added the ones from the cruise ship and organized them into a portfolio. Gertrude's skin tingled with the possibilities. Never mind mere impersonation, never mind flattering imitation, her Jayne would revitalize the old stars and make them new again: Sammy Davis, Frank Sinatra, Connie Francis, Pat Boone. Jayne was a chameleon and Gertrude knew she could win over audiences. She'd be the next top star on *America's Got Talent*; she just needed the proper agent, and that would be Gertrude.

As Gertrude pored through the Internet for photos of singers she knew Jayne could sync with, she gravitated toward the backup groups, blowing up their photos. A blond bombshell who looked like Jayne was nowhere to be seen. Over and over she searched the names Jayne said she had sung with, but no luck, not even on YouTube. She decided that in her earlier life, Jayne must have had dark hair, so she focused on hair color. Still no resemblance. If Gertrude were to be her agent, she needed to make sure Jayne had bonafide credentials. Sinking her life savings into a charlatan was not in Gertrude's nature. When Jayne came for dinner after mahjong on Wednesday, she'd get her answers.

Chapter Twenty-Two

SCHMUTZ: DIRT

"Thanks for the memories," Mavis said to Jayne and Winnie when they dropped her off after the cruise. "Hey, that's a good tune. Can you impersonate Bob Hope?"

"I could try," said Jayne.

"What about Barbra Streisand?" Mavis crooned, "People who need people are the luckiest people in the world. Such a crock of shit." Mavis rotated her shoulder and squawked. "I don't need no stinking friends."

"What's that?" Winnie called from inside the car.

"*Gey gezunterheyt.* Go, have a good life."

Mavis stopped in the breezeway to stroke her motorcycle. "You and me, Pinkie. How about we go for a ride? I'm *fertummult*, upside down and inside out. I could use some fresh air."

Mavis put her suitcase in the carport and took the key to the motorcycle out of her fanny pack. She hopped on the roadster like she was fifty years old and sped along the perimeter of the village with the wind through her hair and the sun on her face.

Usually, if she passed any mahjong women, she'd flip them the bird and weave her bike toward them—veering out of the way before any of them fell down dead. Today, she needed to listen to her own thoughts; today, she avoided people.

She thought back to the Wednesday afternoon mahjong game the week before the cruise. Mavis had harped at Winnie for being slow and Blooma for being forgetful.

Gertrude had pointed a finger at Mavis when they were alone in the clubhouse. "You've never learned to shut the hell up, have you?"

"You should talk, motor *moyel*, with your jabbering lips yapping all the time," Mavis snapped.

Gertrude's bottom lip made puppet movements and Mavis imitated her. Gertrude stood with her hands clutching the corners of the table. Mavis stood too, although her frame was slight compared to Gertrude's girth. She imagined they were two gunslingers in an old western.

"I'm a cock rooster," Mavis shouted. "Don't mess with me."

Gertrude didn't back down. She too had gotten louder with age. "Your brain is fried, *tsedrait in kop!*" shouted Gertrude. "I should pull out your chin hairs until you howl."

"Try it. I like pain," Mavis said.

Those words caused them both to lower their gaze. The words stung too true. Mavis realized they each needed pain to feel alive. She needed it to rail at others, to tell them she was a force at seventy-eight, and Gertrude seemed to need pain to justify her meanness.

The women pounded on the table.

"I'm mad as hell," Mavis crowed.

Gertrude sort of remembered that line from the movie *Network* and blurted "and I don't give a goddam fuck anymore."

"That's the spirit," Mavis said, and tossed her the silver flask that she kept ready in her pocket. "Have a swig."

They both passed the flask a few times, and belched, loud enough for those North Tower *yentas* to hear them.

What Mavis wouldn't give for a pull on her flask as she drove Pinkie back to her carport. How could she have forgotten her flask?

It was as much a part of her as Sammy the Parrot. Was she losing her mind like Blooma. What was she doing, living from day to day, bottle to bottle?

She had behaved like a shrew on the ship. She knew she had hurt Blooma by flirting with Murray. It was so easy though, cornering him in the hallway to tease him, using her old charm, and it had worked. They went to the bar for a nightcap; then she followed him to his cabin. If only she could remember the details. Blackouts were a bitch. She passed out and he took her to her room in the morning, so tenderly, as if her head would split open and pour whiskey all over him.

She wondered why she was so defensive when Gertrude and Blooma barged into the room. Was she embarrassed? She was usually so loaded that nothing phased her. So what if Blooma lied about being on the cruise ship and seeing Jayne perform? Why was that such a crime? So what that it slipped her mind to tell her and Gertrude? Everything slipped Blooma's mind. Maybe it wasn't intentional. And if it had been, then maybe Blooma was growing a set. Standing on her own. Was that so bad?

Mavis let her thoughts wander to younger years. Greenwich Village. Reefers. Booze. The easy rider lifestyle. By the time she was thirty, she was high on free love and weed, Haight-Ashbury and cocaine, tramping through India and Thailand, hooking up with kingpins, gobbling quaaludes like candy. The people she hung with—drinking, drugging, *schtupping*—had balls of steel. Iron intentions. They slept on the sand, lit bonfires on the beach and danced naked till dawn. Debauchery burned through her skin, making her so tough she never got soft again.

Taking a break to try normal in her forties, she married Wally. Then she ignored him and went off to deal marijuana up the coast. Wally tried to rescue her but it was too late. Cancer was eating away at him and he had no strength left to save her. When she was arrested in Maryland for trafficking, she fled to Mexico with an alias, and Wally died while she surfed the waves in Oaxaca.

After the statute of limitations ran out and the charges were dropped, Mavis returned to her parents' house in western Massachusetts, where she fell asleep with a lit cigarette and set their house on fire. They didn't die, not right off. It took years of nursing homes and hospitals and hospice and waiting, which she did badly. She slept in the room over the garage, which had been spared in the fire. She used a space heater because the goddamn place wasn't heated, cooking everything on a portable burner. No wonder she drank.

And then her parents died within weeks of each other. She sold the property and went south to their condo in Florida, thinking she'd sell that too. But she was tired and the humidity made her lazy. She lounged at the pool and walked the beach. She took a job tending bar, but she entertained one time too many on the countertop and was fired. She drove a cab, but the *farshtunkene* drivers in Florida made her blood boil with road rage and the company received complaint after complaint. By sixty-five, she said fuck it and collected social security.

She'd been living in the condo for seventeen years, longer than she'd lived anywhere, but it never felt like home. She slept in her parents' bed, used their bureaus and couches and kitchen table, like the imposter she knew herself to be. It was her fault they were dead. She never smoked in the condo, she knew better. She gave up cigarettes, too fearful that an ash could slip into the mattress and burn down the place. Stogies required concentration.

It was time to stop rueing how she had destroyed her parents' lives and her husband's existence. Years ago, she had pieced together a shrine for Wally out of driftwood and plastic flowers. She lit a candle and had prayed to it every day. "Please forgive me. Let me find peace. I'm only me. A *farkakte* shithead. Doing wrong after wrong." Then she'd fill her flask and dull her pain.

In her heart, Mavis knew she was a coward. A bitch-faced coward. A wrinkled old woman who loved wiping her dirty hands on some else's clean linen. A woman who wasn't afraid of smelling bad, all the more reason for others to keep their distance. She draped herself in steel and rammed herself into every situation. But she was close to eighty and needed to rethink how to live her remaining years. Sammy the Parrot's colors were fading and his body shriveling. Before she knew it, they'd be six feet under squawking at worms.

She had to get sober and lift the fog off her brain.

Mavis entered the condo with new eyes, and went to work like a miner in a landslide. She gathered up the dead soldiers that lined the windows, that held plastic flowers, that were turned into lamps, and that lived under cushions and pillows. She cleaned out the bottles under the sink and in the garage and dumped them into the recycle bin where the garbage was collected. Then she tackled the cigar boxes she used to hold bills and receipts, keys and memorabilia; and the stacks of tissue boxes with the deed to the condo, bank notices, and receipts. Without stopping to think about booze—although the sweats and shivers overtook her at times—she organized her documents and trashed the rest.

She didn't own much clothing: a leather jacket, a few long sleeved shirts, t-shirts, halter tops, jeans, shorts, a bathing suit, underwear, socks, and two lace bras. She wore either flip-flops, sneakers or army boots. All her possessions could fit in the side pack of her motorcycle and on her body. If she were in trouble, she could make a fast escape. Trouble liked her. She loved having the bad girl reputation—she'd always been the rebel.

If Mavis sold the condo and left the complex, she might miss Gertrude's piss and vinegar that mirrored her own, and she had grown to enjoy Blooma's motherly *balabuste* nature. It reminded her of her own mother. But she could live just fine, thank you very much, without both of them. And snobbo-Winnie wasn't worth two shits, never mind one. If she never saw Jayne again, that would be all right too. The woman was foreign to her, a walking enigma. Mavis didn't need or want to solve puzzles.

But abandoning her parents' home, their quilts and comforters, their mismatched plates and ragged love seat caused an ache in Mavis' chest so strong that she thought she was having a heart attack. She lay on the mattress where her parents had slept, where they had hidden their money. Mavis reached into the folds to count her balance. Fifteen thousand dollars remained. Too bad so much cash had burned in the fire up north, but who the hell kept money in a mattress other than people like her parents who lived through the Depression.

Her only constant, other than booze, was mahjong. So many decades ago, it had been her mother's favorite game, every week the click-clack of the tiles, the fifty-cent victories, the excitement each year over a new card—how her mother *kvelled* over her ability to play a strategic game. The least Mavis could do was honor her mother and make the game a priority. But what had the game done for her? Brought her shame in the complex and on the cruise? Or was it her big mouth and loud hair and failing body and vile tongue? Where did the blame lie?

She needed a transition drink, at the very least a Xanax, or ten. Instead, she pulled the blanket over her and concentrated on stillness, willing a positive thought to filter through the bullshit.

Chapter Twenty-Three

SHPILKES: SITTING ON PINS AND NEEDLES

Winnie felt herself grow lighter as each woman exited the Lincoln Town Car after the cruise.

"Be a dear and help me get my bags and the painting up to my suite," Winnie asked Jayne, more like an order than a request.

"Sure thing," said Jayne, but when the trunk was opened, all of Jayne's possessions were piled high on top of Winnie's. "Tell ya what. Let me drop you at the club for a cocktail. I'll bring my bags to my place, then come back to give you a hand."

"Text me when you're downstairs and I'll come right out."

As Jayne sped off, Winnie exhaled. She relished the time alone before returning to her apartment. She didn't want to know which new paintings were missing and she absolutely didn't want to smell Sal's pervasive aftershave poisoning the air. Except for meeting Hilda Lee, the tournament had been a disaster. She had to endure the stares of the Cupie Pies all Sunday afternoon as if she were part of the Mavis and Gertrude gang. Winnie was so unnerved, she could barely concentrate on mahjong, losing the majority of matches. Poor Blooma hadn't come out of her room and forfeited the remaining rounds. Winnie had to bring her a plate of food from the banquet and explain to a crestfallen Murray that she just wasn't up to talking. It had nothing to do with him, she insisted. She just didn't want to see anyone.

But hope sparked anew for Winnie with the possibility that Hilda Lee might buy some of her paintings. She wanted to rise above the commoners in the village and from her forced friendships and from that despicable man Sal.

A full hour had passed. Winnie's glass of cabernet was polished off, and she hadn't heard from Jayne. Maybe Winnie shouldn't have trusted her. Maybe Sal was right that she wasn't who she pretended to be. Just as these thoughts barreled into her, Winnie's phone vibrated.

Waiting outside, said the text, *Jayne.*

Together, they rode the private elevator to the penthouse, Jayne handling the heavy trunk. Winnie chattered about the painting she had gifted Jayne. When she turned on the lights, the room sparkled like diamonds. The remaining pictures on the walls flooded the room with color.

"It's like touring the Guggenheim," said Jayne, twirling around, her eyes round as saucers.

Winnie saw how many empty spaces existed where fabulous paintings had once hung. "Come into my suite if you want to see true art." She unlocked her bedroom door with a key that was hidden in a planter. "My husband used to tell me the paintings in our room were just for his eyes and mine. You're my first and only guest." Out of respect for Jev, Winnie kept the door locked and off limits whether or not she was in her room. She never wanted Sal even near her private space, especially when she wasn't home. Not that she had anything to hide, but these paintings were exclusively hers, and not for sale.

The bedroom was spacious, with high ceilings and three walls filled with paintings. The largest and most striking was of an arch-browed woman with a smug expression. Jev liked to weave stories about her, calling her The Early Winnifred, before he met her when she was guarded and aloof.

Another painting was of a couple dancing, looking longingly into each other's eyes. "That's us, my Dear," Jev told her, although he had two left feet. No matter, thought Winnie, he had been her dance partner for thirty-four years.

But now that Winnie was on her own, this room was hers to embrace. "Where should I hang my new painting, Jayne? Give me some advice."

Jayne examined each canvas on the wall. She stopped short at a watercolor of a couple with crooked faces standing in a forest of white birch and ferns. The woman's eyelashes were false, her breasts contoured, and her Mona Lisa smile secretive. She draped a misshapen arm over the shoulder of a square-jawed man. His unibrow was thick, his cheeks rouged and his lips blood-red. The pair were the same height and neither of them had ears.

"This painting speaks to me," said Jayne, examining it from different angles.

Winnie wrinkled her nose. "I always thought the woman was too masculine and the man too feminine. The painting confuses me."

Jayne's eyes zeroed in on the two figures. "I think that's the point. Men and women are not so different." She looked directly at Winnie. "Each of us carries the traits of both sexes. Our natures are complementary."

"Men shouldn't wear makeup. It's just not natural," said Winnie.

"Maybe there's a bigger world out there where the edges blend and appearance is not the issue." Jayne sniffled and pursed her lips. "Men and women should support each other. Even if they're mismatched, they should find good in each other."

"Then you don't know Sal," groaned Winnie.

"Isn't there something redeeming about him? Maybe he has a softer side?"

Winnie recalled tender moments between Sal and Jev, but never between her and Sal, and they weren't going to start now. "Nope, he's a mean-hearted bastard through and through. He's all about proving that I'm weak and needy." If only there were a way to retaliate, to make him aware of her strength and her ability to stand on her own. Then Winnie realized her window of opportunity. "Help me unhook this painting that you like. I want you to have it as a gift."

"For me! I can't accept that. It must be worth a fortune."

"I have no idea of its value. Jev bought it at a yard sale. He said he liked its synergy."

"I agree with him."

"Then that's the best reason for you to have it."

Jayne gave Winnie a body-crushing hug. Winnie didn't have enough time to jump back and stiffened at the unexpected advance. "Fiddle faddle," Winnie said, freeing herself, "the painting is a celebration of your success and a thank you for driving. Now help me hang my new painting in its place."

Winnie admired how the new artwork she had bought from Hilda Lee made the room more hers. It was finally something she selected.

Jayne wandered around the room studying the women depicted in the portraits. "Almost every picture tells the same story about a woman dying to get free. All these ladies look so far away, like their souls are hiding."

"Jev chose these particular pieces for our bedroom. He said they made him happy, like he was looking at me through all the stages of my life. All they ever did was make me sad."

"Why don't you sell them?"

That's exactly what Winnie had hoped to do, sell them to Hilda Lee and be free from Sal.

"I have an idea," said Jayne. "I'll snap photos of a few and put them on eBay. Someone will buy them!" Jayne brought out her phone and clicked away.

"No, stop! Jev wouldn't want you doing that!" Winnie felt violated, like Jayne had undressed her.

"Sorry, Sweetie, I was just trying to help." Jayne put her phone away and turned her attention to a framed photograph of a rock band that was displayed on a bureau. "Those are some funky musicians."

Winnie gulped. The picture was of her son BJ and his band when he was in his thirties. A cigarette dangled from his mouth and sweat beamed from his body. His hair was a tangle of black knots and his eyes looked like a cougar had surprised him mid-bite. The tattoo on his neck blazed L.M.A. Winnie remembered when he came home with it and thrust his chin defiantly at her, revealing the tattoo.

"This is my message to you, Mother Dear. Leave Me Alone. I don't need anything from you or your sugar daddy." But BJ was never late cashing his trust fund check; when Jev died, BJ was first in line to collect his inheritance.

BJ was due for another visit in a year. Winnie wondered if he'd shorn his punk pose for vampire fangs or blackened teeth. She never expected the same person to walk through the door, and now that BJ was close to fifty, she wondered if one day he'd be in a suit and tie with his hair in a comb-over and his face pudgy-soft.

Jayne waved BJ's photo at Winnie. "Son of a gun. I know this group. I sang with them in New York in the nineties."

With a shaking finger, Winnie pointed to the man on the drums. "That's my son Brian. Do you remember him?"

"You're full of surprises, Winnie. Your son Brian, you say. I knew him with a different name. Llama, like the letters on his neck. L.M.A. Never spoke much to me, but a damn good drummer. You know, the band he played with, ah, The Hateful Dodgers, are in Miami this week. Is your son in the city?"

Winnie wanted to jump up and down and say, 'Yes, BJ called me last week and told me he'd be around, but that was impossible. "I don't know," she pouted.

"Well, let's fix that. I'll find out right now." She pressed a few buttons on her phone, typed in some words and within a minute she said, "Yup. The Hateful Dodgers are on stage Tuesday night. Shall we go? I'll drive."

BJ in Florida? Miami was forty miles from Boca Raton, not so far and yet it could be another galaxy. He'd never get in touch with her.

Her BJ. So removed. Maybe he'd let her in, just a little bit, now that she was old. Maybe he'd understand how scared and vulnerable she had been when he was a boy, how she had to put her interests before his or they never would have survived.

Winnie and Jayne made plans to drive into Miami on Tuesday.

After Jayne left, Winnie sat on the edge of her bed staring at her new painting of a woman in white: regal, above the fray, not at all sad or lonely, so different from all the others in the room. She thought about the painting she gave Jayne, the two figures dependent on each other, but from different worlds. Like her and Jev? Like her and BJ? Like her and Jayne? What story had Jev made up about that painting? He called it *"The Schmuck and the Mensch."* Winnie wondered now who was who? Was he the *schmuck* before Winnie came along and turned him into a *mensch*. Or was it the other way around?

Tuesday came too quickly for Winnie. She wasn't ready to see BJ. She didn't know what to wear. Casual? Hip and modern? She could put on black tights and boots and be punk too. She looked at her new painting for courage and chose white slacks and a silk blouse, belted with a gold looped chain. No hat. No gloves. No false eyelashes. She brushed her blond hair into a soft bun, leaving tendrils curling down her neck. She wore white-rimmed Gucci glasses, the ones that accented her eyes and cheekbones and matched her outfit.

Winnie met Jayne in the parking garage. To Winnie, Jayne looked crisp and confident wearing skinny jeans, a blue tank top, a white cardigan, and white sandals.

"Ready to see your son?" asked Jayne.

"I'm scared," said Winnie.

"When's the last time you saw him?"

"Two years ago. He came for money, not for me."

"Tell me about him so I can understand. We have a long ride and I'm a good listener," said Jayne.

Winnie sat in front, unlike when Sal drove and she would prop herself in the rear with her wide-brimmed hat and her mysterious smile. She felt different in the front seat with Jayne, more attentive and alert. What could she tell Jayne that wouldn't compromise the truth?

"Brian is my son from a previous marriage."

"Where's the father?"

"Dead, I hope. I haven't heard from Brian Senior in over forty years. May he burn in hell."

"Well, that's decisive."

"I hated that man. He took pride in beating me."

"I've known men like that."

Winnie looked at Jayne, so calm and polished. Could she have been a victim too? "What do you mean?"

Jayne kept her eyes on the road. "When you're a scrawny kid who likes to sing and dance, you're going to get pummeled."

"My good-for-nothing husband didn't pummel me because I was weak. He pummeled me because I was strong and he wanted to beat it out of me."

"Men like control," said Jayne.

"That's an understatement. I didn't know what to do. He said I deserved it and then he'd go after Brian Junior. I stopped fighting back. So did Brian. We just cowered in a corner and tried to hide."

"I hid as a kid too. My father was a lot like your husband. He beat me to make me stronger, or so he said. But it turned me inward."

"It turned my son against me. What about your mother? Did she stick up for you?"

"My mother was a saint, but she worked two jobs and wasn't home most of the time."

Winnie hadn't worked when she was married to Brian. He wanted her home, with a hot meal ready for him. She hated to cook and heated up mac and cheese or those TV dinners, which the man threw at her. "This is food? You expect me to eat this crap?" Then he'd drink himself into a stupor. But Winnie tried, she really did. She bought a Fanny Farmer cookbook and watched Julia Child on television. She learned to make American chop suey and sesame chicken, Tuscan pork chops and beef stew. It calmed him down for a while until she burned the meal or made the sauce too sticky or didn't add enough seasoning. She never knew when he'd explode.

When she married Jev, she never had to prepare a meal. They went out to eat or Sal cooked. It was never a priority like it was for Brian Senior. It was BJ who ate the burned chops or the runny oatmeal, and he never complained, until Jev showed him what life was supposed to look like: fine china, sterling silverware, clean fingernails and polite chatter. Winnie thought about her own father, a domineering presence who wouldn't take her back when she ran from Brian Senior and begged refuge in her childhood home. "You made your bed, Winnifred, now lie in it," he growled and closed the door on her.

"Did you forgive your father?" Jayne asked.

"I thank him every day for making me the person I am. If it weren't for him, I never would have struck out on my own, become my own person, embraced my true nature. I did what he didn't want me to do. I have him to thank for that."

If Winnie's father had helped her, BJ might have become soft, dependent, accepting. But she went back to Brian Senior, cooked and scoured and kowtowed to his needs, until he abandoned her and their son. Did their fate make BJ stronger? Was he his own person because he rebelled against her and made the best of a bad situation? Maybe she wasn't such a terrible mother after all.

When they arrived at the nightclub, Jayne parked the Lincoln Town Car and the women went inside. The band was not in sight. The bartender said they were on break and would resume in a half hour.

"Can we go back stage?" asked Jayne. "This woman's son is the drummer."

"I can ask," said the bartender. "Give me a minute."

If Winnie bit her nails they'd be ragged by now, but she didn't. In a few minutes, she'd be face to face with BJ, cheering for him, for his talent, for what she created.

She and Jayne sat at the bar, waiting.

A good looking man came in and stood behind them. "Ladies, you bring class to my nightclub. Let me buy you a drink."

Winnie's lips flattened, but Jayne smiled. "Two vodka martinis."

He took a seat beside Jayne. "Do you come here often?"

Winnie couldn't believe he asked that question. But Jayne didn't lose a beat. "My friend's son is in the band."

"Yeah? Which punk?"

"Llama, the drummer."

The man shook his head. "Llama isn't playing tonight. Seems like the band missed their flight. Got stuck in a snowstorm in New York. The gig's rescheduled for tomorrow."

Winnie stopped listening.

On their way home, Winnie lay on the back seat, too exhausted to sit in front, her eyes tearing at her missed opportunity.

"We'll come again," said Jayne.

"Sal will never drive me to see BJ."

"So I'll drive."

"You don't understand. It's not that simple."

"It's your car, right?" Jayne asked.

"Yes, but when Sal is home, he drives it."

"And you have no recourse?"

Re-course—options, choices, new directions—why must everything be so complicated? If only Samuel had lived, how happy they would have been. "I'm at a dead end," said Winnie.

Jayne pulled the car to the side of the road. "I'm at a dead end too and I need a favor."

Winnie crumpled into a whimpering mess. This was all too much for her. No BJ. Sal returning home soon. Winnie buying an expensive painting from Hilda Lee and giving Jayne one of Jev's favorites. And now this woman wanted a favor from her?

Jayne craned her neck. "Honey, you're overwhelmed. I get that way all the time."

"Like on the ship, not showing up to sing at the luncheon?" Winnie wanted to retract the words. It was wrong of her to expose Jayne's weakness like that.

"Exactly. But I'm going to fix that problem. I have a consultation tomorrow in Miami at 9:00 AM. If I can borrow your car for a few hours, I'd be sincerely grateful. Going by train is tricky and I can't miss this appointment."

Winnie weighed the request. Sal was due home Wednesday afternoon. What if he arrived on an earlier flight and the car wasn't in the garage? He knew Winnie would never drive it. He'd call the police and they'd find the car and Jayne would be arrested. But the Lincoln Town Car was, in actuality, hers. Why shouldn't she lend it to Jayne? Maybe she should go with her? She considered asking whom she was going to see? A therapist? An oncologist? A lawyer? A recording agent? It was none of Winnie's business.

Jayne's voice hesitated. "What if I take the painting you gave me and have it appraised by Hilda Lee after my appointment. If it's over-the-top valuable, I'll return it to you."

How valuable could it be, thought Winnie. Jev found it at a yard sale, but she watched *Antique Roadshow*. Maybe it was worth a few bucks and no one realized it. Winnie made up her mind. "I'll call Hilda Lee and tell her you're coming. Drop me off at my condo, then take the car. I trust you."

"Thank you Winnie. I owe you big time. Tell you what. I'll return the car to the garage as soon as possible and leave your key under the front mat."

"The earlier the better," said Winnie.

Chapter Twenty-Four

BRACHA: A PRAYER OFFERING PRAISE

Wednesday dawned sunny. It was the first mahjong day since the cruise. Winnie woke to the gaze of the woman in white staring at her from the wall. So regal. So assured. So Winnie. She had called Hilda Lee that morning to tell her Jayne was bringing a painting for appraisal. She described it briefly, but couldn't answer the barrage of questions about the medium and who painted it and how it was framed. It was Jev's art; what did Winnie know? She'd find out soon enough. Jayne would be back in time to go to mahjong, way before Sal got home to see that the car had extra mileage on it. Would he check? Why would he care? Winnie wondered which painting he'd take next and if he'd realize that *The Couple in the Countryside* was missing.

By noon, Winnie was pacing the penthouse deciding whether or not to call Jayne's cell. She still had one hour before mahjong, but Winnie's antennae were up, telling her that something was *nisht gut*. At 12:15, Winnie called Hilda Lee.

"Ah, Winnifred, I'm researching the picture that Miss Day left with me. I have some concerns about its authenticity."

Miss Day? That must be Jayne's last name, thought Winnie. She was relieved to know that Jayne had followed through with Hilda Lee and was probably on her way back to Boca. She looked out the window, searching down the road for the black Lincoln Town Car. Winnie could hear Hilda snapping her gum.

"Miss Day also downloaded a few pictures from your collection onto my computer. I hope that's all right."

Winnie's heart seized. What right did Jayne have to do that, she fumed. But if the paintings had value, they'd be Winnie's ticket out. Winnie's stomach rumbled at Jayne's *chutzpah*, but it was too late now to do anything about it.

"Miss Day was reluctant to leave your painting with me, but I said I could return it you by the end of the week. By then I should have a definitive answer," said Hilda Lee.

That would mean Hilda Lee would come to her apartment and see the paintings for herself. What about Sal? She'd send him on a fool's errand. That would be funny if she weren't so scared about his discovering that she was plotting to sell the paintings to Hilda and get out from under him.

"Winnifred, are you there?"

"Yes, Hilda. Any guesses as to their value?"

"There's a common theme among them that reminds me of an impressionistic German style called Sinnende Frau, which literally means reflective woman."

Winnie liked the sound of that. Had that been what Jev thought of her, reflective—how she was deep and always thinking?

"I have a few hunches to follow. Miss Day said your husband found the artwork at yard sales. He had quite an eye."

"My Jev was a connoisseur of good art. Indeed, he had a sharp eye. He married me, didn't he!" Winnie laughed.

"Give me a few days and I'll give you a call. In the meantime, your treasure is safe with me."

Winnie had no choice but to go along with Hilda Lee. But where on earth was Jayne? Winnie took the elevator to the garage to see if the car was there, but the space was still empty. Jayne had promised to return the car as early as possible. Did her appointment run late? Was there traffic? She called Jayne's cell, but it went straight to voice mail.

Winnie made an enormous decision. She went upstairs to her room and found her tennis shoes. She got her new wide-brimmed yellow hat and a bottle of water and set out by foot to the senior center, which was a half-hour walk. For once, she would not be late due to someone else's negligence.

Mavis considered walking to the senior center. She didn't trust herself on the motorcycle. Wasn't that the balls? Drunk most of her life, she drove just dandy. Sober for three days and she couldn't see straight. What kind of divine justice was that? She needed to get to the senior center fast, before she dove under the covers chugging a gallon of wine.

For once, she didn't care if she won the game. She just wanted to lose herself playing. She wanted to sit across from Gertrude and watch her face contort as she played a tile that Mavis knew she knew might need. Mavis wanted to eat Blooma's pastry and laugh at Winnie's hat, which was probably a shade of yellow ever since Jayne told her that was her color. The tournament didn't pan out like Mavis had expected, but she came home with a determination to clean up her act. Whatever that meant.

That morning when she knelt before Wally's shrine, she was sober when she apologized to him. "I'm sorry, Baby. I didn't do enough right by you. That's my story, always. I do just the minimum to stay on the right side of right but my foot slips. Have I been all wrong? If that's so, then I'm a fucking failure and a fraud. Pretending to be a squawking renegade when all along I'm a mouse. I'm going straight until I can figure out my next ten years. Any advice you can give me, I'll listen."

Mavis patted the motorcycle on her way through the carport. "You're a good girl and I'm glad I have you, but you're wrong too. Why haven't I realized that? And what can I do about it now, way after the fact?"

She remembered the day the motorcycle made itself available to her. It's not like the woman on the side of the road who was surrounded by EMTs and had a pool of blood under her head was going to need it. It had flung the poor woman far in the distance, in a whole other lane of traffic. The motorcycle veered way to the right and landed in a ditch.

Mavis had been on her way back from the chiropractor and traffic had stopped right near the complex entrance, close enough for Mavis to walk. "Drop me here," she said to the taxi driver. She made her way to the side of the road where she saw the motorcycle, just lying there. She glanced around. Traffic began to crawl, opening to two lanes on the right. No one seemed to notice the shriveled old lady tottering along the green strip of grass, getting closer and closer to the motor-cycle. It was a lady's Kawasaki Eliminator, with a pink saddle, and low to the ground, like Mavis. It had no damage whatsoever from the accident. "I should take it back to that poor girl," said Mavis, but the wild Mavis took over, the woman whose impulses got her into trouble, and before she could think twice about the wrong she was doing, she had hopped on and drove into the complex.

She patted the pink saddle and wondered if was too late to make amends. She straddled the seat, revved the engine, and motored for-ward. The vibration comforted her like an old friend, even if her eyes wobbled and her legs shook.

Blooma waited by the house phone throughout the Wednesday morning. She should have given her son-in-law her cell number, but she barely remembered it on a good day. And she hardly ever turned on the phone. It was for emergencies only. Well, wasn't a call from her daughter an emergency? Maybe she should call again and leave the number?

She had no pills left but had high hopes that Jayne would supply her with more at mahjong. She didn't feel like her brain was totally empty. It was loaded with images of Sarah as a baby and a toddler and a teen. She imagined her on her wedding day and her graduation from medical school. Isaac refused to go and he wouldn't allow Blooma out of the house. He called her weak and said if she went, she'd be dead to him too. What choice did she have but to watch the clock and imagine her beautiful Sarah receiving her diploma, saying her vows, and later giving birth to her sons?

While she waited for the phone to ring, Blooma made her signature pastry: strudel with raisins and nuts. She wondered if her grandsons would like her to add chocolate chips. Everything tasted better with a *bissel* chocolate. Sarah loved sweets. Charlie sounded like he was a sweets man too. His voice was buttery and smooth. Isaac's was like gravel, especially at the end.

Even though she wanted more than anything to hear her daughter's voice, she wanted to play mahjong. After all, it was Wednesday and she had her routine. Even though Mavis tried to steal Murray, Blooma didn't fault her. At their age, every man was fair game. She'd be willing to share him. When she and Winnie got off the ship, she loved seeing Gertrude and Mavis carousing together, bent over in laughter. That Gertrude so rarely laughed; Blooma was afraid her face would crack. She'd look a lot younger if she smiled. After all, Gertrude was the baby of the group, only sixty-eight. A *pisher* compared to her, thought Blooma.

It was 12:30 when the strudel was packed and ready and still no phone call. Blooma picked up the receiver.

The phone rang in Brooklyn and a voice answered. "The LaSister family is not home. Please leave a message and we'll call you back."

Blooma cleared her throat. "Sarah, this is your mother, Blooma Gold Gottlieb. I'm going out to play mahjong now and I'll turn on my cell phone. My number is 810-262-1267, I think. Please call. *Ich hob dir lieb, mein kind.*" She probably wouldn't understand the Yiddish, but Blooma had to tell her daughter that she loved her.

Blooma hobbled to the senior center with her warm strudel and heavy heart, but her brain felt lighter. Jayne would refill her magic pills and her mind would continue to improve. Maybe she could get on that plane to New York.

Gertrude woke on mahjong morning surrounded by more celebrities' pictures than she could count. She was so happy she had invested in a great colored printer. She had a stack of Jayne's photos which she placed beside all the singers Jayne could impersonate. She made a list of songs that Jayne could sing. This was a win-win—Jayne on stage with Gertrude as her manager.

Maybe Gertrude would travel around the world on a cruise liner with Jayne, sharing her room, helping her with her costumes, listening to her practice, encouraging her, supporting her. Loving her. Why not! Gertrude was a shrewd business woman. She had contributed plenty of ideas at the accounting firm and they all showed a profit. Together she and Jayne would score big time. Gertrude was confident Jayne would like her business plan. In just a few hours, Jayne would tell Gertrude the full story of her early life so that Gertrude's second life could begin, a life of style and glory and satisfaction and Jayne.

Since it was Wednesday, Gertrude set her mind on mahjong mode. Everything was ready for Jayne, down to a PowerPoint presentation. Gertrude got her purse and went out the door, mounted her three-wheel bicycle and pedaled to the senior center.

Chapter Twenty-Five

CHUTZPAH: BRAVADO

The four women sat around the mahjong table as if the cruise had never happened. Each pushed private thoughts out of her mind and concentrated on the tiles. When a door squeaked, they all looked up, hoping it was Jayne, but four other women walked in, their t-shirts suspiciously the same: the Cupie Pies.

The broadest one, the *farbissiner* who had been twerked by Mavis and Gertrude, poked the air with an accusing finger. "We have a bone to pick with you, you *valtshers.*"

"Call us vultures and I'll pick the meat off your bones before you can whistle Dixie," said Mavis, puffing out her chest and meeting them mid-room. Gertrude rushed to stand beside her.

Winnie and Blooma rose as one and flanked their friends.

"You ruined the tournament for everyone. Squawking, drinking, and snorting like pigs. You should be ashamed of yourselves," said the tall one, whose eyes bugged out like double doorknobs.

"We took a vote on the ship and have banished you from all future tournaments," said the frizzy gray mop-head.

Mavis leaned in and brought up a wad of phlegm.

"No, Mavis, don't give them the satisfaction," said Gertrude, putting an arm around Mavis' shoulder. "They're no-talent floozies, the four of them. And they smell like stale onions."

"Yeah, stale onions," repeated Blooma.

"And they play a lousy game of mahjong," said Winnie.

"You should talk," said the hatchet-faced one. "You play like a duck with a stick up its butt."

"I'll have you know she came in fourth at the tournament!" said Gertrude, putting her other arm around Winnie, knowing this was a lie, but what the hell.

"Yeah, fourth!" repeated Blooma, who held up four fingers and planted herself in front of Mavis, Gertrude, and Winnie, like a tiny elf.

The four Cupie Pies surged forward.

"None of you can play in a cruise ship tournament ever again! In fact, we blackball you from all mahjong competition from this day forward," said the tall one.

"*Feh*! Is that all? We don't need the likes of you to play mahjong," said Gertrude. "And we'll still beat you at Karaoke!" She took a happy breath. "We have Jayne on our side!"

The apple-barrel woman laughed. "You mean that cross-dressing imposter with the fake titties?"

Gertrude's face reddened and her lips trembled. She charged toward the Cupie Pies, her fists pumping. "No one insults our friend and gets away with it."

Mavis followed, squawking like Sammy was being tortured. Winnie screamed banshee-like, and Blooma rattled off Yiddish swears with a ferocity that she never knew she possessed: *Farkakte mamzers. Farshtunkene shtick drecks. Gai kaken!*

The Cupie Pies tried to stand their ground, but the apple-barrel one started to cry and ran out of the common room. The others followed.

Mavis, Gertrude, Winnie, and Blooma hugged each other and giggled.

"*Oy gevult!* We told them!" said Blooma.

"We're a gang to be reckoned with," said Winnie.

"No messing with us!" said Gertrude.

"You got that right," said Mavis.

They continued playing mahjong, pausing to meet each other's eyes and burst out laughing. There was a niggle at the back of each woman's mind, about what the apple-barrel said about Jayne, that she was a cross-dressing imposter.

Mavis had experience with cross-dressing. One of her boyfriends liked wearing her panties and she thought he was sexier than she was in them. They both got a hoot out of that.

Blooma understood cross-dressing to be a religious thing. Like wearing necklaces and bracelets that had to do with Jesus. She had no problem with that, although she never saw Jayne wear a cross.

Gertrude knew down-deep that Jayne might very well be an imposter. What if she did have fake boobs? What if she wasn't a female at all? Gertrude thought about John Travolta playing the mother in *Hairspray* and Dustin Hoffman in the role of a female actress in *Tootsie* and Robin Williams as the nanny in *Mrs. Doubtfire*. How about that hottie RuPaul? Men in drag could be gorgeous. Gertrude made a mental note to print out their photos and put them in her day folder. Jayne made a more beautiful woman than any of them. That might explain Gertrude's physical attraction and her erotic dreams about sleeping with Jayne. Gertrude knew she wasn't a lesbian, although there was nothing wrong with that. If Jayne were a man, maybe she'd have a chance to really lie by his side. She'd be all right if Jayne were a she by day and a he by night. Gertrude decided she'd accept Jayne as she was. That's what friends were for. Who was she to judge?

Winnie too thought about men who dressed in women's clothing. She had caught a glimpse of Sal by accident through an opening in the door central to both apartments. He was in a lady's slip and had on a wig. She knew it was Sal because he had a mustache during those years. Jev had come in from the other side of the house and didn't know Winnie was close by. He shut the door quickly, but not quick enough. Winnie lingered a long time imprinted with the image of a mustached man in pink lingerie. She finally decided he was imitating one of the paintings for an ad campaign. That was the only reasonable explanation Winnie could tolerate.

None of them mentioned aloud what the apple-barrel woman had said. Instead the click-clack of tiles dominated the room, until a door slammed and they all looked up.

Winnie saw the Lincoln Town Car parked outside the senior center. First she felt relieved that the car was safe; then anger bubbled in her chest that Jayne hadn't parked it in the garage like she said she would. At least Winnie wouldn't have to walk home. Besides, she was eager to talk about what Hilda Lee had to say about the painting and she needed to scold Jayne about sharing the other works, although Winnie was curious about them too.

Gertrude wriggled in her seat when the door opened; she was so excited to see Jayne. Her business plan promised to make them both millionaires. And her suspicion about Jayne being a man fueled her desire.

Blooma sighed, knowing her magic pills would be refilled.

But instead of Jayne entering the commons room, a square-jawed man with close-cropped hair barged in as if he were going to rip the chairs out of the floor and whip them around.

"Winnifred, where's the painting?" he roared.

Winnie gulped. "What painting would that be?"

"You know damn well. *The Couple in the Countryside.*"

"Do you mean the one in my private room where you have no right to trespass?"

"Nothing is private in that penthouse. It all belongs to me. So I'll say it one more time, Winnifred." Sal stomped toward Winnie, his voice booming off the walls. "Where is that painting?"

Mavis stood up and stopped the man from ramming into Winnie. "What's it to you?"

Sal shoved Mavis. She recovered quickly and jumped Sal from

behind, wrapping her legs around his waist and pounding on his shoulders. "No one pushes me out of the way, you *bulvahn.*"

Sal whipped around, tossing Mavis like a doll onto the floor. Blooma ran to help her.

"No one does that to our friend, and gets away with it," said Gertrude. She put her entire weight into her wide hips and knocked into Sal's side.

"Bitches, all of you." Sal recovered his balance and grabbed Winnie by the chin. "Where is the painting?"

"That painting is mine," Winnie insisted. "Jev bought it at a yard sale and gave it to me."

Sal laughed like the roof would explode. "Yard sale? That's what he told you? I knew you were a fool, but Jev? I can't believe he let you think that the paintings in your room were yours. They're mine. They're all part of my business."

"Our business," Winnie said.

"My fucking business. You've never had a say in it."

"I own forty-five percent."

"That's bullshit. Show me in a document where it says that? Nowhere. Your percentage of the business decreased yearly. Jev wanted to ease you out slowly. You're just about at zero now. All you own is that car out there."

Winnie stood up. She was eye level with Sal. "You're lying. I have papers to prove it."

"No you don't. You never bothered to read the fine print, Winnifred. The condo and the artwork were in a trust that reverted to me after a stated period of time. And that time is gone. So I'll repeat the question. Where is my painting? What have you done with it?"

"I gave it to a friend as a gift."

Sal looked around at the other three women in the room. Mavis stood crooked against the wall, rubbing her lower back. Blooma held out a piece of babke to Sal, but he tossed it to the floor. Gertrude gulped because she guessed who the recipient of the painting was.

"You'd better get that painting before I rip your cold heart out."

"She has a warm heart," said Blooma. "You must not know her very well."

"Old lady, Winnifred has greedy green bile beating in her chest. She wants one thing, money."

"And you don't?" asked Winnie, her voice gaining strength.

Sal grabbed Winnie behind the shoulders and pushed her out the door. "Now, Winnifred, now. I want that painting now."

The women ran after Sal, but his stride was no match for them. He shoved Winnie into the Lincoln Town Car and shut the door. Winnie didn't even try to escape. Sal got into the front and sped away.

"Call the police!" said Gertrude.

"And tell them what? That Sal kidnapped his dead boss's wife and wants to find a painting that she gave to Jayne," squawked Mavis.

"How do you know she gave it to Jayne?" asked Blooma.

Gertrude and Mavis gaped at her.

"Why am I the last to understand everything?" asked Blooma, cleaning up the mahjong table. "I guess we're done for the day."

"Not by a long shot," came a voice from the rear of the room.

"Jayne!" said Gertrude, who ran to her and flung her arms around her, then jumped back, all red in the face. "You heard the whole thing? Why didn't you save Winnie from that monster?"

"Revealing myself would have made the situation worse. What we need to do now is beat that slimy salamander to Hilda Lee's studio in Miami."

"Why?" asked Blooma.

"This morning, I brought the painting to Hilda Lee for appraisal. We need to get it to Winnie as soon as possible. She can decide what to do with it after that."

Mavis closed her eyes and pinched the bridge of her nose. "There's only one way to get there." She paused, taking a deep breath. "On Pinkie."

Her motorcycle was parked in the handicap spot like usual. Mavis knew she was in no condition to drive, so she threw Jayne the key as they raced out the door. Mavis climbed onto the passenger seat, her tailbone hurting.

"Text Winnie," she called to Gertrude, who was fast approaching Pinkie. "Tell her we're driving to Miami to get the painting."

"What about me? I want to go too," cried Gertrude.

"You and Blooma head to Winnie's. Be on guard. We'll call your cell to keep you posted on how we're doing."

"How will we get to Winnie's?" asked Blooma.

"On my bicycle. You fit snugly in the basket," said Gertrude.

Chapter Twenty-Six

GEFERLECH: DANGEROUS

Winnie hadn't let on that she saw Jayne hiding in the back of the mahjong room. Exposing her would be the end of Jayne. Done. Gone. Pummeled into the ground. Jayne needed to get to the gallery to retrieve the painting and get it to Winnie. After that, Winnie wasn't sure what to do. Give it to Sal? Stand up to him and keep it for herself? Hide it? Sell it to Hilda Lee?

Sal's voice boomed off the interior of the Lincoln Town Car. "You don't have any friends unless you mean Queen Jayne. Does she have the painting?"

Winnie stayed silent.

"Answer me or I'll smash your face in."

"You wouldn't dare."

"Try me."

In the rear view mirror, Winnie saw his nostrils flare and his eyes blaze. He made a fist and whacked it on the ceiling causing a rip in the fabric.

Winnie thought about her first husband Brian, how she never stood up to him, how she cowered whenever he came close. Had she learned nothing in forty years? "If you hurt me, you'll never get the painting." She wasn't going to be a victim. Not again. "Let's consider a deal. I'll pay you for the painting and then we'll be even. You can have all the others. I don't want them."

By then, Sal had pulled alongside the curb at the high rise. He steadied his voice and turned to face Winnie. "You're not understanding, Winnifred. That painting is valuable and could get us into trouble if the wrong people find it."

"Now it's us you're concerned about?"

Sal's shoulders slumped. "I'm appealing to your devotion to Jev. He would want you to tell me where it is."

"Then you have to be nice to me."

Steam rose off Sal's head. "There's no nice in my vocabulary. This is as good as it gets."

"What can I have in exchange?"

"I won't kill you."

"You wouldn't get away with it. My friends would hunt you down."

"Those stupid old women," he roared.

"They have more strength than you've ever had. You're a fat ass bully with no guts. Jev kept you around because you made him money. Now I want you out of my life forever. So let's make a deal."

"The only deal we're making is right now. Don't you fucking move and I won't kill you." Sal got out of the car and slammed the door shut, ending all conversation, turning Winnie into jello.

Winnie curled into a ball in the back seat and cried. What was she going to do? Sal's words boomeranged off every fragile bone: the business belonged to him and the penthouse belonged to him. According to Sal, the painting was priceless and if it wasn't returned, they'd be in serious trouble.

How had Winnie been so blind? Whoever brought home that many paintings from yard sales? On some level, she knew that the paintings had value, but it was Jev's business, not hers. She was happy to reap the benefits, no questions asked.

And what about her marriage to Jev? Was it all a farce? Jev's love for her had been mostly platonic, even when he courted her. He loved her for her beauty, he said. He worshipped her. Sex wasn't necessary when two people respected each other. Why hadn't Winnie realized that he was plenty virile when he was with Sal? A woman of convenience? It dawned on her what that meant. An invisible person who suited a need—to appear married, to appease his parents, to pretend that he wasn't in love with a man.

If Sal was telling the truth, Winnie had nothing of her own except the damned Lincoln Town Car. It was impossible that Jev had shut her out of the business. Wasn't it? She thought back to the signing with the lawyer. She and Jev were there and so was Sal. The lawyer summarized the details, Jev nodded and handed her a pen. "Sign here, Winnifred."

She recalled looking him in the eye. "And what if you die? What happens then?" And he said, "Don't you worry your pretty head about it. A rich man will come along and scoop you up before I'm six feet under." Was that Jev's way of telling her he expected her to move on after his death? But she hadn't moved on. She liked the penthouse. She liked the beautiful artwork. It was Sal she hated. Where were those damn papers anyway? Probably in Sal's safe! She'd need a jackhammer to excavate them.

So now what? Her son hated her. Her friends tolerated her; otherwise, they'd have no mahjong game, although they did stick up for her against Sal. Winnie recalled the image of Mavis flying across the room and Gertrude shoving Sal out of the way. She saw Blooma spit in the babke that she offered Sal and she saw Jayne signaling a thumbs up from the rear of the senior center, giving Winnie support. Maybe she had misjudged them all. Maybe she had misjudged herself too. She had to get it together before her chance for independence disappeared.

Winnie wondered how much time had passed. She took out her phone: 3:00. There was a text from Jayne: *On our way to get the painting. We've got your back.*

Think. She commanded herself. She sat up and looked around.

She caught a flash of Sal's jacket in the lobby. He held a large canvas, which he leaned against the wall. Winnie crouched down in the seat so he wouldn't see her watching. He covered the painting with a blanket and then re-entered the elevator. He was raiding the house! Stripping it of paintings. He was going to put them in the car, dump her in the ocean and be on his way.

The minute the elevator doors closed, Winnie climbed into the front seat. She searched under the mat for the key she hoped Jayne had left there. And she had. *Danken Got!* Thank God. OK. She could do this. Shaking, she turned on the ignition, keeping an eye on the elevator door, which still hadn't opened. She pulled away from the curb and onto the street, gunning the car, making a fast escape. But she had no idea what to do next other than avoid crashing. She could drive to Hilda Lee's gallery. It was somewhere in downtown Miami. But she wasn't about to stop and ask directions, and every time she asked Siri for help, the damn phone never understood what she was talking about. Think, Winnifred. Think. She knew how to find the nightclub where BJ would perform. She had watched how Jayne got there, feeling throughout the ride like a magnet was pulling her closer to see her son. She could get there again. At the next traffic signal, she whipped out her phone and texted Jayne: *Meet me at the nightclub at 4.*

Chapter Twenty-Seven

OY VEY, NISHT GUT: OH DAMN, NOT GOOD

Mavis' coccyx bone ached where she had landed and she squirmed on the seat of the motorcycle as she and Jayne sped down the highway toward the art gallery.

"I think something in me is broken," she whispered to Jayne. The wind caught her words.

Weaving in and out of traffic, Jayne pulled the motorcycle up to Hilda Lee's studio in record time. When Hilda Lee saw the two bedraggled women enter the gallery, her face drained of color. Mavis compared her to the Pillsbury dough boy before he went into the oven.

"I didn't expect you until Friday," Hilda Lee said, rushing to them. "I haven't finished my research."

"No matter," said Jayne. "I need the painting now."

"It would be irresponsible of me not to inform you and Winnie about what I've learned so far."

Mavis' bones twitched, and not just the coccyx. She felt a chill run from her toes through her *tuches*. "Something bad?"

Hilda Lee pointed to a room at the rear of the store. "There's coffee and snacks in the conference area. Have a seat. I'll be right with you."

"I'd prefer to stand," said Mavis, rubbing her backside. She watched from the doorway as Hilda Lee made a phone call. A big *macha*, thought Mavis, making us wait. Who did she think she was?

Hilda Lee's heels clicked as she entered the room, took a seat at the mahogany table, and folded her manicured fingers together.

Mavis stood behind Jayne, balancing herself on the frame of her chair for support.

Hilda Lee started slowly. "The painting resembles the art of Conrad Felixmüller, a twentieth century German artist."

Mavis shrugged. She had painted in the twentieth century and her drawings were worth *bupkis*.

"According to my Internet investigation, barely any of Felixmüller's works have survived. Most were destroyed when the Nazis confiscated all impressionistic art they deemed degenerate."

Mavis shrugged again. She'd been known to create degenerate art. Lots of body parts in compromising positions. "So what's the problem?" asked Mavis.

"If this is truly the work of Felixmüller, then its existence is an enigma," said Hilda Lee. "Why would it be in this country? Who would have brought it here? And if it is authentic, then someone must have stolen it, which means that the person who possesses it would be under suspicion."

Jayne swiveled in her seat to eyeball Mavis. "Winnie said her husband found it in a yard sale. But he was an art dealer. Surely he knew the value of the painting."

"But we don't know that. So what do we do now?" said Mavis.

"We call Winnie," said Jayne, who took out her phone, read the missed message about meeting Winnie at 4:00, and showed it to Mavis.

"Do you know how to get to the nightclub?" asked Mavis.

Jayne nodded and turned to Hilda Lee. "What about the artwork in the snapshots I provided from my phone?"

"I believe they're also early twentieth century impressionistic art. They could be forgeries, maybe not."

"Let me get this straight," said Mavis. "Winnie has a shitload of paintings in her place that are either worthless forgeries or stolen originals worth millions?"

Hilda Lee raised a sculptured eyebrow. "It's a possibility."

Mavis' shoulder twitched. "Give us the painting. We're taking it with us."

"I don't advise that," she said.

"*Feh*," said Mavis. "We didn't ask you."

"I am the legal owner. Winnie gave it to me as a gift," said Jayne, "so it's my responsibility. Wrap it up."

The painting was too big to fit in the pannier on the bike, so Mavis tucked it under her arm and held tight to the motorcycle's frame with her other hand. She still felt wobbly and her tailbone hurt. "When will we be there?" asked Mavis like a child wanting time to disappear.

"Ten minutes, at most," said Jayne.

Knowing that the more pissed off she felt, the better she'd endure the pain, Mavis channeled her anger toward Sal. How had Winnie tolerated that *mamzer* all these years? Mavis would have kicked him in the balls, assaulted him while he slept, put a pillow over his face, added garlic to his coffee. She thought it had been many years since Winnie's husband died. Why hadn't she moved on? Why was she stuck?

Then she realized what was really pissing her off. She was no better than Winnie, staying in a place that held no hope. A two-bedroom condo that belonged to her parents. A scratched-up kitchen table with three bridge chairs. A sagging sofa and an old TV. A corner shrine for her Wally and a framed picture of the old house in Massachusetts that burned down. Outside, she owned a patch of green with a dying lemon tree, a driveway littered with metal junk, and a platform for Pinkie so the rains wouldn't eat away at her.

Where had Mavis' spirit gone? To swearing at old people? Trying to mow them down and laughing about it? Chugging whiskey, taking pills to sleep and guzzling coffee to stay awake?

Mavis sizzled with anger, letting it steam through her body and pour out her ears. That piss and vinegar turmoil set her blood boiling. If only she could drink it instead of booze. How was she ever going to get unstuck? Certainly not playing mahjong each Wednesday. That was too sad if that was all she had to anticipate. She was seventy-eight. She'd be eighty in two years and then what? Die? Her whole body ached from being shoved to the ground by that bastard Sal.

Jayne accessed the highway. The nightclub was only two exits north from Hilda Lee's gallery. "Hold on, Mavis. We're going to fly."

Weaving in and out of traffic, they sped along, Pinkie spewing out thick fumes of exhaust, but they were getting close to the off ramp—which is when Mavis saw the red flash of light and heard a police car's siren. For them?

Pull over, signaled the officer and Jayne had no choice but to obey.

"License and registration, Ma'am," said the officer.

"Did I do something wrong, Sir?" she drawled.

"Going 85 in a 65 mile per hour zone on an old motorcycle, that looks problematic to me. License and registration, please."

Jayne handed the policeman her license, but Mavis didn't budge.

"This is a James Day's license, clearly not yours. Step away from the vehicle. You too, Ma'am," said the officer.

Mavis caught a look at the photo on the license. The hair was blonde, but short. The face had pale lips, plain eyes, and stubble on the chin.

"That's me, Officer. I swear. I'm a female impersonator by profession. Isn't that right, Mavis?"

Mavis nodded rapidly, the wrinkles around her mouth stretching into a dozen frowns.

"Registration, please," said the officer.

"The motorcycle belongs to my passenger, Sir."

"Maybe it's in the saddlebag," said Mavis, who rummaged through the side pockets. "Nope. I don't see it. Must have fallen out."

The policeman examined the motorcycle, then took Mavis' name and address and told them both to stand by the guard rail. He went to his cruiser and spoke into a phone. Mavis watched his expression as he listened to the dispatcher. She saw him grimace, and then he was by her side with handcuffs at the ready.

"Come with me, Ma'am," he said to Mavis, turning her around and securing her wrists.

Mavis didn't squawk or put up a fight.

Jayne, however, spat out words like bullets. "We're not criminals. I drove over the speed limit and she doesn't have her registration. That merits a ticket, if I know anything about the law."

"Funny thing about updating a data base," said the officer. "That vehicle's vin number popped up faster than toast. Looks like the motorcycle was stolen so I have no choice but to bring the lady in for questioning."

The policeman recited the Miranda Rights and opened the back door for Mavis.

"I'm coming too. Where she goes, I go," said Jayne.

"Yup, you're part of the problem, Ma'am, or Sir, or whatever. Come along. We'll deal with this at the precinct."

"What about our handbags and the package we were transporting?" asked Jayne.

The officer grumbled, retrieved their property and filled out an inventory form for Mavis and Jayne to sign.

In the back of the cruiser, Jayne elbowed Mavis. "What's going on?"

"With me? What about with you, Mr. James Day? What's that *farkakte* bullshit?"

Jayne slouched. "I was going to tell you all so many times, but I chickened out. I'm undergoing gender reassignment."

Mavis' eyebrows knotted together. She waggled them up and down until her lips could form the words she had been thinking for a long time. "So you're a guy?"

"Not anymore."

"So you've been chopped?"

"Mavis, you're being crude."

"Call me whatever you'd like, but I want to know what's what with a man who looks like a woman, acts like a woman, but pees like a man."

"I've undergone hormone treatments for two years. This morning, I met with a surgeon in Miami and scheduled my operation."

"*Veyismer!* I know a lot of *fegeles*, but this is different, right?"

"I'm not gay, although there's nothing wrong with that. I've always believed that I was a woman in a man's body. I don't remember feeling any different. As an adult, when I entertained, I became the person I wanted to be. But I want it all. Like you say, *emmis*. That's the truth. Now what's the deal with the motorcycle and the registration? Is the bike stolen?"

Mavis clammed up. She wasn't ready to tell Jayne, even if Jayne had been honest with her. Jayne's confession had been brave, but Mavis was a coward. How could she tell Jayne that she stole the motorcycle from a ditch when the poor driver was lying in the road. Sure, there were people helping her. Police. Medics. A whole gang of motorcyclists. The woman was put on a stretcher and taken to the hospital where she recovered. But Mavis had taken advantage of an unexpected opportunity, to be a big shot on wheels, to have freedom in the village, to be alive again in a way she hadn't experienced in oh so many years. How could she tell that to Jayne? At the time, she thought she'd hold on to the motorcycle until the girl was out of the hospital. She even called to check on her, but Mavis couldn't remember what they talked about and whether or not she mentioned returning Pinkie at some point or another. Either way, it never happened.

Seemed like the police hadn't forgotten because as soon as Mavis stepped into the station, she was booked for possession of a stolen vehicle. And when Mavis' fingerprints were taken, her criminal record from thirty-five years ago showed how she fled her court sentencing on a misdemeanor drug charge in Maryland. The statute of limitations was way over, but the theft of the motorcycle was a felony. Seventy-eight or twenty-eight, it didn't matter to the law.

Chapter Twenty-Eight

SHANDA: A SCANDAL

Winnie put on blinders as she drove to the nightclub. No green cars flashed. No lanes wobbled. Nothing distracted her. Forty miles and she would make it. Come hell or high water.

On the freeway, she glanced in the rear view mirror, thinking Sal would be pressing in on her. But nothing was out of the ordinary. Just Florida traffic crawling along. She slowed her pace, letting her heart cool. She moved into a center lane and allowed her fingers to relax on the steering wheel. The white knuckles turned pink and she breathed. She'd get to the nightclub, meet up with Jayne, retrieve the painting and use it as a bargaining chip against Sal. Maybe BJ would be there to protect her. Maybe they'd reconcile? Maybe L.M.A. would find a new translation: *Love Masters All. Lovely Mother Arrives.*

As Winnie neared the nightclub, she saw a crowd of young people gathering in the lot, so she parked on the street. A van pulled up to the front entrance, and a large man got out—no one she recognized. He pushed back the crowd and slipped open the van's side door. As soon as the figure stepped out, the crowd erupted. They raised their phones and snapped pictures.

"Llama! Llama!" they chanted.

BJ strode through the admirers shaking hands, giving fist bumps, grinning. He wore a silver vest, a black shirt and flared-bottom pants. His hair was styled with feathers and braids, his body lean, his shoulders wide. The rest of the band followed, but Llama received the adulation.

Winnie was floored as she watched the spectacle. Her son. Famous. Larger than life. An icon of punk rock. Llama. L.M.A. *Lavish monetary allowance. Look! Ma! Attention!* Winnie laughed out loud. BJ was followed inside by the crowd; she could hear the deep bass of instruments thrumming through the door. It banged into her heart and magnetized her to the spot. When Winnie's phone rang, she thought it was BJ calling. He had seen the Lincoln Town Car and he was acknowledging her presence. But the phone said Jayne.

"Where are you?" asked Winnie.

"At the Miami Police Station on 2nd Avenue. Come quick and bring your checkbook. You need to put up bail for Mavis and pay a fine for me."

"What's going on?" asked Winnie.

"Just get here. Mavis is in big trouble."

Winnie had barely known how to find the nightclub, never mind 2nd Avenue. BJ will help, but she knew even as she considered running in and pleading with him that it wouldn't work. She'd get trampled by the crowd and BJ would leave her on the floor.

Winnie called Hilda Lee. "You've got to help me. When Jayne and Mavis left your gallery, they were stopped by the police."

"So the police confiscated the painting?"

"What are you talking about?"

"*The Couple in the Countryside.* If it's the real deal, and not a forgery, it's worth millions. Chances are, though, it would be here illegally." Hilda Lee paused for effect. "Didn't you get my message? Your cell said the mailbox was full, so I called your home phone and left a message."

"What exactly did you say on the phone?"

"Just what I told your friends. That I think the painting is an original Conrad Felixmüller and it's priceless."

"When did you call?"

"Around 3:15. Before your buddies grabbed the painting and fled."

"Damn it, Hilda. Sal must have heard that message. I'm betting on it."

"Who's Sal? I thought you lived alone."

Winnie sank into the seat. Her mind whirred. Sal would trace the call and hire a car to take him to Hilda's gallery. "Hilda, I'm at The Vagabond, a nightclub in Miami. Do you know where it is?"

"Sure I know it. But what the hell are you doing there, in the day time no less!"

"Can you come and get me? I'm in a black Lincoln Town Car on a side street. Come now, please. We need to find out what's going on with Jayne and Mavis."

"And the painting!"

"Hurry," Winnie said, but Hilda Lee had already hung up.

Needing air, Winnie locked the door and paced back and forth along the sidewalk thinking wildly. Who was Conrad Felixmüller? How did Jev get his painting? Were the other paintings valuable too? What did all of this mean? The only thing she was dead sure about was that Sal was going to kill her when he found her.

After what seemed like forever, Winnie heard beeping as a red car pulled in front of the Lincoln Town Car.

"Get in," said Hilda Lee, shouting out the window. "You have a lot of explaining to do."

"How far is the police station?" Winnie asked.

"Ten minutes without traffic."

Winnie sank into the seat, took out her phone and called Gertrude.

"Are you at my building?" asked Winnie.

"We sure are," said Gertrude, feeling like John Wayne or Gary Cooper. "We're your back up!"

"Have you seen Sal?"

"We saw him get into a gray car about an hour ago. I think it was one of those Ubers. There's been no sign of him since then."

"Can you look in the lobby to see if there's something stacked against the wall?"

Gertrude walked to the building and put her nose against the glass door. "I see something large and square covered in blankets."

"You and Blooma have to get inside. I took the car so he had no place to stash the paintings. You have to move them to someplace secure. Can you do that? Don't let Sal see you. If he comes, run."

"Run? Have you met me?" asked Gertrude.

"You know what I mean. Get the hell out of his way. He's dead set on getting those paintings for himself. He'd stop at nothing. Even hurting you."

Gertrude repeated the conversation to Blooma.

"*Oy gevult*. How are we going to get in the lobby?"

"Pretend you forgot your key when the next person goes in or out. Look confused, *farmishted*. That's easy for you to do," laughed Gertrude.

Blooma didn't think it was funny, but she understood her role. Rummaging through her purse, she waited by the front door of the building. Her dimples crunched into her cheeks and her lips puckered as she tried to appear frustrated. She upped the act by talking to herself. "*Dumkop*. Where are those keys?"

Within minutes, a man who looked older than Blooma, shuffled up. He had a silver loop ring attached to his belt and fumbled through a half dozen keys before he unlocked the door.

"After you, my dear." The man looked Blooma over. "Have we met? I don't recognize you. I thought I knew everyone in this building, I've been here so long. Did you just move in?"

Blooma wondered if she had blown her cover, and looked like an imposter, but the man's eyes twinkled.

"Do you like strudel?" she asked.

"Are you offering?"

Oy vey, thought Blooma. Now what should she say?

Gertrude intervened. "Bloomie, we're going to be late! Now help me carry these packages to the car."

"We don't have a car, do we?" Blooma asked. She turned to the man, "Do you?"

"I do. But I don't drive it anymore. It's rusting in the parking lot."

Gertrude jumped at the opportunity. "I have a proposition for you. We'll trade you strudel for trunk space in your car."

"I'm listening," said the man, patting his round belly.

Gertrude drew the blanket away from the canvases. "These are a bunch of paintings that belong to my sister, Winnifred Reichman. Do you know her? She lives on the top floor."

"I've seen her from a distance. So she's your sister?"

Gertrude piped up. "She sure is. We need to hide them before her ex-brother-in-law claims them. Will you help us?"

"I'll make you chocolate bubke too," smiled Blooma, her dimples deeper.

The man winked at Blooma. "Call me Hymie," he turned to Gertrude. "Is the brother-in-law big?"

"Only in his own mind," said Gertrude.

Gertrude carried the largest canvas. Blooma balanced two smaller ones under each arm. And Hymie stacked three together and held them in front of his growling stomach. It was slow going, but they were doing it.

Hymie unlocked the trunk, which was clean as a whistle. Gertrude stacked the paintings inside, covering them with the blanket. She didn't examine or study them. She was too afraid Sal would show up any minute.

Blooma and Gertrude thanked Hymie, wrote down his phone and apartment numbers, and promised they'd return soon.

"Don't forget the strudel!" Hymie called. "And the bubke! This is

RUTH E. WEINER

the most excitement I've had in years." He shuffled to the elevator and hit the button.

Blooma blew him a kiss and the doors closed.

"You're a regular man-magnet," Gertrude teased.

"*Oy vey!*" Blooma blushed.

Gertrude laughed until her belly shook. "Now let's go to your house, get the goodies and bring them back."

Gertrude got on her bike, helped Blooma into the back basket, and pedaled to Blooma's. Gertrude sat in the kitchen and dialed Winnie's cell. "We did it! We hid the paintings in Hymie's trunk," she yelled when Winnie answered.

"Whose trunk?"

"A nice man who lives in your apartment building."

"Are you still at my place? Has Sal shown his face?"

"We got away clean!" said Gertrude.

"I hate to ask you to go back there, but I have to know when Sal shows up again. I'm afraid he's on my tail even as we speak. Call me if you see him," said Winnie.

"Blooma, pack up the pastry. We're on the job again. And bring a kitchen knife. A sharp one."

"A kitchen knife?"

"I have an idea. I'll explain later."

Blooma put the food and the knife into her pocketbook and skittled to the door. She noticed a red flash on the phone. Another message from her pharmacy, she thought. It could wait.

Chapter Twenty-Nine

ODER GOR, ODER GORNISHT: ALL OR NOTHING

Winnie hung up the phone with Gertrude just as Hilda Lee pulled into the police station parking lot. The ride had lasted forever, stopping at every red light, crawling the whole way. Winnie and Hilda Lee walked around the block to the front entrance, but something black and shiny on the street caught Winnie's attention, her Lincoln Town Car. Was that Sal in the driver's seat? How could that be?

Sal must have heard Hilda's message and hired an Uber to go to her gallery. Maybe he saw Hilda leave her store, so he followed her to the nightclub. When he saw Winnie get into the red car, he must have spotted the Lincoln Town Car. After all, he had a key. And that damn traffic gave him the advantage of catching up to them. That's the only plausible version that made any sense. But he wouldn't dare come inside the police station after hearing Hilda Lee's implication about the paintings on the answering machine. Would he?

Winnie flung the police station door open. "That goddamn monster is following me. He's going to kill me," she screamed.

Policemen ran toward her from all angles, their weapons drawn. "Explain the problem, Ma'am," said the sergeant.

"Salvatore Sarno threatened my life. I gifted a painting to Jayne Day, I believe she's in your custody, and she and my friend Mavis Gruber, who's also in your custody, retrieved it from Hilda Lee's Art Gallery on 5th Avenue. Salvatore is outside right now in a black Lincoln Town Car, circling the building, waiting for me to come out. He said he'd kill me if I don't give him the painting."

Hilda Lee's eyebrows arched to the ceiling. "You're safe now, Winnifred, but the painting must be located immediately. Officers, we think it's worth millions."

A lieutenant approached the women. "We checked the surroundings. There's no one out there in a Lincoln Town Car. Why don't you just sit down and tell us what's going on."

Winnie straightened her spine and pursed her lips. "We're here to get our friends out of jail."

"And find the painting," Hilda Lee snapped.

The lieutenant led them into a small room with large panes of glass on three sides. "And your friends would be James Day and Mavis Gruber."

Winnie thought the officer said James, but she must be mistaken. James, Jayne. The names sounded similar. "Exactly. May we see them."

The sergeant brought Jayne to them. "The arresting officer dropped all charges against you, Mr. Day. You're free to leave."

Mister, thought Winnie. Mr. James Day? Her hearing was definitely intact. She was sure of that. She looked at Jayne, her makeup precise, her curvy figure on display. What was going on? First though she needed to find out about Mavis.

"Thank God you're here," Jayne said, "Mavis is in a bad way."

Hilda Lee stepped forward. "Do you have the painting?"

"Is that all that's on your mind? Our friend is suffering in a prison cell and you're worried about a damn painting," said Jayne.

Winnie held up her hands. "Let's take care of one thing at a time. What do I have to do to get Mavis out of here?"

Hilda snapped her gum like her teeth would crack.

Before Winnie could consult an officer, a siren whirred outside.

Winnie imagined the police finding Sal, handcuffing him and shoving him up the stairs into the station. Instead, EMTs rolled in a bed.

"Where is she?" asked a young man wearing a badge with a red cross on it.

"Ms. Gruber is in the first cell on the left.

Jayne, Winnie, and Hilda Lee were too stunned to talk. Within a few minutes, the EMTs rolled Mavis toward the door.

"Now what's going on?" asked Jayne.

Mavis lifted her head from the gurney. "Spasms in my *tuches* from that *farshtunkene* asshole throwing me down." Mavis screamed in pain. Winnie heard an extra dose of Sammy the Parrot squawking.

"Where are you taking her?" asked Winnie.

"To Jackson Memorial Hospital."

"What about the felony charge?" asked Jayne.

The EMT shook his head. "She has a police escort, Ma'am. You'll have to check with them."

The lieutenant on duty approached the gaggle of women who all shouted at him at once. "Mavis Gruber's papers have been filed and she is officially a prisoner of Florida. But right now she needs medical attention. Her health is in danger."

"How can I help her?" asked Winnie.

"Posting bail would be the next step," said the officer.

"Then let's get that done," said Winnie. "But first can you tell me the charges leveled against her?"

Jayne pulled Winnie aside. "Mavis was arrested for stealing her motorcycle."

Winnie shook her head. "Do you mean that noisy piece of junk that she drives?"

"That's as much as I've been told. Maybe you can get to the bottom of this."

"Lieutenant," Hilda Lee snapped. "We have a bigger problem than an old lady having back pains. I have reason to believe the painting that was in Mavis Gruber's possession, which I assume you now have, was stolen from Germany during World War II and is worth millions. What are you going to do about that?"

"And who exactly are you?" the lieutenant asked.

"Hilda Lee. Owner of Lee Art Gallery on 5th Avenue. Perhaps you've heard of me?"

The officer ushered Hilda Lee, Winnie, and Jayne back into the conference room. He wrote notes as Hilda Lee explained. Winnie templed her fingers over her forehead and listened.

"I met Winnifred Reichman on a cruise ship recently. She bought a lovely painting from me and I offered to appraise the artwork in her apartment, which she said had been left to her by her deceased husband."

"Is that true, Mrs. Reichman?" asked the officer.

"Yes, so far," said Winnie, without looking up.

"Yesterday, Jayne Day came into my gallery with *The Couple in the Countryside*, a watercolor given to her by Mrs. Reichman. She asked that it be appraised. She also provided me with snapshots of other paintings from the Reichman apartment."

"Is the person sitting there known to you as Jayne Day?" the lieutenant asked Hilda Lee.

"Yes, Officer."

Jayne piped up, "I told Mrs. Reichman that if the painting were valuable, she should keep it for herself."

"That's very generous of you. Why would you do that?" asked the officer.

"She's my friend, and I didn't want to cheat her out of something special," said Jayne.

Winnie tilted her chin. Her friend, she repeated to herself. Someone who cared about her well-being, more than Jev, her husband of thirty-five years, or Sal, her so-called partner in business.

"Go on, Ms. Lee."

"My suspicions rose when I saw the signature on the painting.

C. Felixmüller. I researched the name on the Internet and in my art books and located other watercolor images he had created. Then I compared them to the photographs that Jayne Day took. They were one and the same."

"So the Reichmans have a collection of Felixmüller paintings. That isn't a crime," said the officer.

"It is if my suspicions are correct and the paintings, which were stolen during World War II by the Nazis, are just surfacing now," said Hilda Lee.

"Mrs. Reichman, what do you know about this?"

"The first I heard of this was what Hilda Lee told me today. My husband died five years ago and since then Salvatore Sarno has run Authentic Restoration Art. I've never been involved. In fact, I own nothing related to the business."

"You have other portraits in your home besides the ones Ms. Lee has spoken about? Right? Do you own your own home?"

"There are dozens more paintings where I live in the Boca Raton Senior Living Community. And no, the penthouse is in Salvatore Sarno's name, not mine. My deceased husband made arrangements for me to live there until I remarry." Winnie wanted all the blame to fall on Sal, not on her. She realized what the officer was thinking: that she knew all about the stolen art. But she hadn't. Had she just been too blind to notice? "And, Lieutenant, you can bet your bottom dollar that right now Salvatore Sarno is stuffing those paintings in a car and will disappear before you can say *fuckacktah mamzer*."

"I beg your pardon?" said the officer.

"He's a bastard and he'll stop at nothing to ensure those paintings belong only to him. He assaulted my friend Mavis Gruber and threatened to kill me if I didn't hand over *The Couple in the Countryside*."

The officer grimaced. "So the injuries to the woman who was just brought to the hospital were caused by this Salvatore Sarno?"

"She came to my defense at the senior center in Boca Raton when Sal was threatening me. He threw her across the room," said Winnie.

The officer stood and paced. "We'd better get the Boca Raton police department involved. We can detain Salvatore Sarno because he caused bodily harm to Ms. Gruber and threatened your life. After that we can address the problem of the paintings."

The lieutenant left the room and Winnie could hear him on the phone talking with the Boca Raton police.

"What about Mavis Gruber?" Winnie asked the other officer who had remained in the room.

"She'll need a lawyer," he said without explanation.

Jayne positioned her chair so she was eye-to-eye with Winnie. "Here's the story. Mavis obtained the motorcycle fifteen years ago from a girl who had been in an accident and could no longer ride. She had planned on returning it when the girl was better, but she never did."

The policeman raised his eyebrows. "That's not the version we have on file. The motorcycle was stolen after the woman riding it was involved in an accident. It is the same vehicle that Ms. Gruber claimed was hers. That's grand larceny, James."

Winnie threw her hands into the air. "Why are they calling you James? I'm so confused. Mavis is arrested for a felony, my paintings were stolen by Nazis, and Sal is selling them on the black market."

"That's about right," said Jayne. She took out her license and handed it to Winnie. "I was born James Day. About two years ago, I decided I could no longer live a lie, so I began hormone therapy."

Winnie looked at the photo on the license and then studied the woman in front of her, the curve of her breasts, the smoothness of her face, the luster of her blond hair. "So you're a man impersonating a woman, like in your nightclub act?"

Jayne shook her head. "I was never a man, except for my plumbing, if you know what I mean."

"So you're still plumbed like a man?"

"Not for long. I borrowed your car this morning to keep an appointment with the doctor who will perform my surgery."

"When will that happen?"

"After I've raised enough money."

"I knew it!" said Hilda Lee, popping out of her chair and pointing her long-nailed finger at Jayne. "You were going to sell Winnie's painting and use the money for yourself for your operation. You're a fraud and a thief."

"Now wait one minute," said Winnie. "Jayne offered to get the appraisal. The painting has nothing to do with her needing money. Does it?"

Jayne lowered her eyes. "I never had dental problems. The checks you and Gertrude wrote went to the doctor I met with today."

"So Jayne is not only a fraud and a thief, but an embezzler too?" said Hilda.

Winnie's palms began to sweat and her head throbbed. *Jayne sure fooled me. I trusted her, and she used me, shamelessly. What if she had told me why she needed the money? Would I have given her the time of day?* Winnie watched Jayne's face crumble into tears. "So you lied to me about everything and now you want me to forgive and forget?"

"I never meant to hurt anyone. Please don't hate me." Jayne dropped her chin to her chest. Her shoulders shook and her breathing came in quick bursts.

Winnie felt drawn to Jayne's pain and although she didn't like physical contact, she placed her hand on top of Jayne's. "There's so much I don't understand but there's one thing I'm learning. Each day I pretend to be classy and high born. The truth is I grew up poor. My first husband beat me. My son resents me. And my ex-husband owned a blood business. Who am I to judge anyone?"

Hilda Lee zoomed in on Winnie. "Stop this ridiculous tell-all garbage. You can be Eliza Doolittle for all I care. What needs to be done immediately is to secure that artwork before it goes underground. Do you hear me?"

Jayne squeezed Winnie's hand. "She's right. Let's nail that bastard Sal before he gets away."

The lieutenant returned. "I've been in contact with the Boca Raton police. They are acquiring a warrant to enter your apartment, Mrs. Reichman. My advice is to be at your condominium as soon as possible. The Boca Raton police will need to question you."

"Now you're talking," said Hilda Lee. "Get in my car, Ladies, and I use that term loosely. We have to get to the bottom of this."

Hilda Lee brought the car around as Winnie posted bail for Mavis. She felt a stab of guilt as she thought of Mavis lying alone in a hospital room, but Mavis had nurses surrounding her and emergency care. At the moment, what more could Winnie do to help her?

Jayne got into the front seat and Winnie commanded the back.

"How could I have deceived myself for so long?" Winnie asked.

"Revealing the truth is like lighting a match. It can bring light or it can set your world on fire," said Jayne.

"You should know," said Hilda Lee, snapping her gum.

Jayne's words roared in Winnie's mind. It was time to light the match, she decided. For Jayne too, if truth be told.

Winnie called Gertrude on her cell. "Any sign of Sal?"

"Not yet," said Gertrude.

"Be careful, Gertie. Sal is dangerous. The Boca Raton police have been notified and they're on their way. Don't do anything foolish."

"Someone's coming," said Gertrude. "I'll call you back."

Chapter Thirty

MEGILLAH: A LONG INVOLVED STORY

As Gertrude and Blooma approached the high rise, the Lincoln Town Car screeched around the corner and came to a halt. Sal got out and raced into the lobby; within a few minutes, he tore out of the building and ran its perimeter, once, twice, around and around, searching, mumbling, swearing. "Fuck. Fuck. Fuck. Where are those paintings?" He charged back into the lobby and the women saw him enter the elevator.

"Now," said Gertrude.

They took the knife that Blooma had brought and snuck up to the Lincoln Town Car. Together they held the shaft and plunged it into the rear tire. It barely made a dent. They tried again and again, expecting a huge gash, but they weren't strong enough.

Gertrude and Blooma hid behind the bushes in front of the condo and texted Winnie. "We tried to slash the tire of the Town Car," said Gertrude. "It's not flat yet, but it's thinking about it."

"*Oy gevult!*" said Blooma into the phone. "That man will go postal."

Gertrude hung up fast as Sal emerged again from the elevator. He carried a large frame, which he brought to the car and put in the trunk. He went back into the lobby and onto the elevator.

Blooma and Gertrude snuck to the car. They had watched him carefully and knew that he hadn't locked it, so they popped the trunk and retrieved the painting. They stashed it behind the dumpster.

When Sal reappeared, he stacked several paintings in the back seat and covered them with a blanket. Then, he returned again to the elevator. Once more Blooma and Gertrude retrieved the paintings and set them behind the dumpster. The next time, Sal emerged with a canvas the size of a bay window. He leaned this against the side of the building, then he entered the elevator again.

Once more, Blooma and Gertrude snuck close to the car and stabbed at the tire, but ran out of time to hide when they heard the door of the condo opening.

"You! Thieves! Stop right there. What do you think you're doing?" Sal screamed. "You stole the paintings from the lobby. Didn't you? They belong to me and I want them back."

As if on cue, Hymie shuffled toward them down the walkway. "I heard all the commotion. Are you the bad brother-in-law taking these charming ladies' paintings?" he looked at Gertrude. "He's really big! I thought you said he was small."

"I said only his mind was small."

Sal grabbed Blooma around the waist and lifted her like a feather. "Tell me what you did with them or I'll throw you to the ground."

"Like you did to Mavis, you big *fashtukenah* bully," shouted Gertrude. "Leave her alone. She has nothing to do with any of this."

"So you do?" Sal roared.

"Why do you have to be so loud?" said Hymie, covering his ears. "You'll wake the dead!"

"It's 7:00 PM, old man. Time for you to feed your goldfish. This is none of your business."

"It certainly is. I'm the one who has your precious paintings, I'll have you know," said Hymie.

"*Oy gevult!*" said Blooma.

"Step away from that lovely lady and I'll show you where they are."

Sal cast off Blooma like a rag doll. Luckily Gertrude was there to keep her upright. Blooma wasn't about to be played with like that. She gathered all her strength and whacked Sal with her massive pocketbook, the knife protruding just enough to graze his jaw.

"Damn you," said Sal, lunging for Blooma's purse and grabbing the knife.

In the distance, Gertrude tuned in to a siren coming their way which was hardly unusual in the complex. "Hear that?" boomed Gertrude, pumping up her voice, showing him that his efforts were of no use and that the calvary was coming to their rescue. "The police are on to you, Salvatore Sarno. You can't get away with this."

"Shut up, bitch-face," said Sal, wielding the knife. "Now, you, old man. Get me my paintings. NOW!"

"Put down the knife and I'll do what you ask," said Hymie.

"The hell I will," said Sal, throwing Blooma over his shoulder with the knife aimed at her back. "Paintings, now, or I'll hurt this doddering fool."

Gertrude knew he'd do it too, but as she looked toward the street, she realized the calvary was indeed coming, but Sal was too caught up in his rage for it to register. She lowered her voice and tried for calmness. "Put her down, Sal, and I'll take you to the paintings."

Sal lowered Blooma who sank to the ground as Gertrude walked toward the parking lot. Hymie shuffled behind as Blooma rose to follow. When the police cars were in plain sight, Gertrude dropped and rolled, exposing Sal and the knife he was wielding.

"What the fuck?" Sal said, swinging his arms like scissors, trying to hurt anything within range.

"You're done for now," said Hymie. "See what happens when you're mean to old people."

Blue lights flashed, squad cars surrounded them, and a sergeant called out, "Cease what you're doing and raise your hands. All of you."

Blooma's hands shot up. Gertrude and Hymie's too.

Sal dropped the knife and squared his shoulders. "These people must be brought to justice. They've been running a fraudulent art ring for years out of this building. I caught them absconding with paintings that they claim are authentic." He spit on the ground. "All in the name of greed. Shame on them."

"That's not true," said Gertrude, although she hadn't a clue as to the real story.

Sal waved her away. "I have proof. That car belongs to Winnifred Reichman, the mastermind of the whole scam. It has paintings in it that she's selling as if they were the real deal. They're worthless fakes and she's making millions."

The policemen checked the interior of the car and opened the trunk. "Empty. No evidence of wrong-doing here."

"But that's impossible," said Sal.

A red car screamed to a halt and Winnie, Jayne, and Hilda Lee jumped out. The gang was all there, thought Gertrude, except for Mavis? Where was that woman? Probably trailing behind on her motorcycle.

"There's your thief. Winnifred Reichman," Sal said, his voice commanding. "Question her, not me. I'm an upstanding businessman and I have rights."

Sergeant Monti, the officer in charge, continued to listen to Sal, and then approached Winnie. "What can you tell us about these paintings, Mrs. Reichman?"

"I can fill you in," said Hilda Lee who had examined the artwork near the dumpster. "I own Lee's Gallery in Miami and am an authority on art. As I told the Miami police, I believe the paintings in Winnifred's home were stolen by the Nazis in World War II and sold internationally on the black market. I'd stake my career on the authenticity of these paintings."

At that moment, Hymie beeped his horn like he was in a parade. He brought his car around to the front, driving five miles per hour the whole way and beaming like a hero. "I've got your paintings, my lovely ladies."

The police examined the artwork, but were far from experts. "Sir, I'm afraid we have to impound your car as evidence until we get this straightened out," said Sergeant Monti.

"At last, I found a way to get this junk box off my hands," said Hymie, who got out of the car to the applause of the onlookers.

The sergeant looked from Sal to the women surrounding him, their eyes needling porcupine quills into his body. "There's a lot to process here. Let's all take a step back and I'll hear from each of you separately. We'll get to the bottom of this."

A call came in from the dispatcher. "Yes, sir. Yes, sir," said the sergeant, turning to Sal. "Salvatore Sarno, we have credible evidence from the Miami police department that you assaulted Mavis Gruber and that you threatened the life of Winnifred Reichman. If convicted, you face up to fifteen years in prison and a $10,000 fine. We need statements from all involved, but for now, Mr. Sarno, you're under arrest."

"But the paintings, they're mine. These women have stolen them from me," he railed.

"One problem at a time," said the sergeant. "For now, you're coming with us. We have a lot to discuss."

"There's nothing to discuss. A bunch of worthless old biddies took something that belongs to me and I defended my rights," Sal tried to wrestle out of the police officer's grip.

"So you feel justified throwing a seventy-eight year old woman across a room and dumping an eighty-two year old woman onto the ground. Shame on you. *Zol dir vase tzibbeles fun pupik!*" shouted Gertrude.

Blooma translated, her dimples on full display, "Onions should grow from your navel!"

"What's more, you're a worthless *schtick drek*," said Jayne, proud that she knew the words for a piece of shit in Yiddish.

The women breathed with relief as an officer handcuffed Sal and forced him into the back of the cruiser. As the car sped away, the bystanders cheered. Even the Cupie Pies, who had shown up in their dress t-shirts, clapped as if this were a show put on for their entertainment.

"Now, Mrs. Reichman," said the sergeant, "let's address the problem of the paintings."

Winnie offered her key to a detective. "Let me show you around the penthouse. I think you'll find it stripped of a lot of artwork, but there's still enough to corroborate what's been going on."

Winnie trailed the officers through the apartment as they catalogued the art. Hilda Lee was on their heels.

"Mon Dieu, Winnifred, you can't tell me you thought this was yard sale art! This one is a Picasso. Its cubes of color are like raucous pigeons. I'm sure of it. And that one is definitely by Maria Casper-Filser. So refined and precise. Oh, the pink chrysanthemums and yellow bud vase. So perfect. To think that these paintings existed in your apartment. The painting I sold you pales in comparison."

"That's not true," said Winnie, as she took it off her bedroom wall and admired it. "This painting was my choice. The others might have been magnificent to someone, but not to me. All those sad faces made me feel tiny, unimportant. So much complexity surrounded me. I felt so simple. But your painting made me feel like a queen. It gave me hope."

Hilda Lee nodded but Winnie had the feeling she wasn't listening. Her eyes were too filled with newspaper clippings with her as the central authority, how she was the one to uncover this bounty of confiscated art from Nazi Germany in a Boca Raton apartment. Winnie hoped she was imagining how Hilda Lee would dominate the narrative in the coming weeks. Winnie needed a shoulder to lean on and a heart to hear her. Would Hilda Lee be capable of that?

The police cordoned off the apartment as a crime scene but first allowed Winnie to retrieve her clothing and toiletries, as well as the new painting that she had bought from Hilda Lee. She filled a second suitcase with jewelry, the photo of BJ, her shoes, gloves, and yellow hats. Everything else remained as official business.

"What will happen to the paintings?" Hilda Lee asked the detective in charge. "I'm a certified art dealer and I'm right here, right now. I could research them for you."

The police took her card. "We'll be in touch."

Winnie entered the elevator, her head pounding. She wondered what would come next for her. "Can you recommend a hotel nearby?"

"Nonsense, Winnifred. Stay with me for a few days," said Hilda Lee. "The police and I will keep in close contact, so you'll have direct knowledge of what's going on with the artwork in your apartment and with that thief Salvatore Sarno."

Winnie didn't care about the art or Sal. She didn't care about the penthouse. She stopped caring about Jev's reputation the minute she realized she had been duped, used as a front for Jev and Sal's amusement. A marriage of convenience! How had she been so blind?

Jev had kept her on a pedestal, away from reality. She was the perfect woman, to be admired, pampered, dressed, and shown off, rarely touched or hugged or kissed. Once Jev died, she became less than a person, spending hours up and down the aisles of department stores or sitting in a hair salon or sipping a dry martini with a patron of the arts waiting for Sal to collect her. Her only special day was Wednesday when she played mahjong. On that one day, she belonged to herself to make her own mistakes and earn her wins.

When Winnie exited the elevator with Hilda Lee, she saw the blue lights from the police cruisers still whirring. She felt weighted down by so many paintings of brooding ladies with peacock hats, ancient men with green faces, and haunted spirits swirling through space. The tears streamed down Winnie's face, blurring her understanding of what lay ahead.

A policeman was closing his notebook and rising from the bench where Gertrude, Blooma, and Hymie had been sitting. "We'll be in contact with you as more evidence comes to light," he said and tipped his hat to the trio.

Blooma tilted her chin toward Hymie, "I have your strudel and babke."

"I would hope so!" he said, patting his belly. He saw Winnie emerge from the building. "That woman sure is lucky to have such courageous sisters."

Gertrude heard the word sisters and frowned. She had three actual sisters, none of whom she'd heard from in years. Was sixty-eight too old to reconnect? Did sisters have to share blood to be sisters?

Blooma thought about the lie they had told Hymie, implying that she, Gertrude and Winnie were sisters. They were her family now. And Jayne, beautiful Jayne. And of course Mavis. It dawned on Blooma that she hadn't seen Mavis. Where was she?

Jayne had stayed in the background throughout most of the ordeal, but now that Winnie and Hilda had come out of the building, she rushed over to them, Gertrude and Blooma joining them.

"Winnifred's had enough excitement for one day," said Hilda Lee, waving them all off. "Come along, Winnie Dear. There's nothing left for you to do here."

"Thank you all for your help," Winnie managed to say. "I'm going to stay at Hilda Lee's for a few days. I'll be in touch." Winnie gave Jayne the key to the Lincoln Town Car. "Keep it safe," she said as Hilda Lee took Winnie by the arm and led her away.

What a *farbissineh* that Hilda was, thought Gertrude, like she was better than the hoi polloi in the complex. Gertrude wheeled her bike around and helped Blooma into the back. Her eyes drooped and she curled into the wire basket.

As everyone began to scatter, the Lincoln Town Car farted and its back tire collapsed. Gertrude and Blooma burst into laughter. Jayne stood on the curb surveying the scene. "I'll fix the flat tire in the morning," she told them.

Gertrude heard Jayne's words and stopped mid-pedal. "We'll meet you here at 9AM, if that's all right. We want to hear what happened in Miami."

Gertrude was eager to share with Jayne the dreams she had for them. After the tire was fixed would be a good time. Imagine that beautiful creature knowing how to fix a flat. Jayne was so full of surprises. With any luck, they'd swing by Gertrude's condo and watch the PowerPoint she had created. Maybe Blooma would come too. And Mavis. Where the hell was Mavis?

Chapter Thirty-Two

MITZVAH: GOOD DEED

The hospital room where the EMTs dumped Mavis had no windows, a tiny doorless bathroom, no phone and no TV. It was in the basement of the building because Mavis was a prisoner. A policeman was stationed outside her room and checked on her every hour. The best part were the drugs: a *bissell* of this, a *bissel* of that. Before she knew it, she was in LaLa land, cooing not squawking, on the edge of constant laughter. Nothing hurt, not even her insides.

Weird images flopped around in her mind. A monster throwing her to the ground. A man dressed up like a woman. Two people in a garden crumbling into chalk.

After dinnertime, the lieutenant pulled a chair beside Mavis' bedside. "You're being moved to a regular room in a few minutes. No more police guard, but you still have to answer to the felony charge, Miss Gruber."

"Call me Mavis," she groaned. Mavis had a married name once, but she reclaimed Gruber after her parents' died. It made transfer of property so much easier. No one ever called her Miss Gruber unless they wanted to eat mud.

"How's your back feeling?" asked the lieutenant.

"Like a horse kicked the tail out of me." Mavis remembered a drop-down drag-out fight long ago with a horse when she had won. Not this time.

"I just have a few questions before I release you on your own recognizance."

"So I'm not a flight risk?" squawked Mavis. "Did you hear that Sammy?"

"Your friend Winnifred Reichman posted your bail, so after you get the okay from a physician in the morning, you may leave the hospital. Remember that you have a court date which you must attend."

"I get it, Officer."

"Tell me, Mavis, how long have you possessed the motorcycle?"

"Ah, fifteen years, give or take."

"And in all that time, did you try to get in touch with its owner?"

"I did, yes, as a matter of fact."

"And what happened?"

"I got this pang of conscience a few weeks after the accident. I had learned the woman's name from the newspaper reports, so I found her phone number and called."

"How did you identify yourself?"

"I told her I knew what had happened to her motorcycle."

"Then what?"

"She said she didn't want it, that it was too painful. She hung up on me."

Mavis squirmed in the bed. She'd had enough interrogation. She wanted him to leave.

"I have a royal pain in my *tuches*," said Mavis. "I'm bringing charges against that madman Sal for assaulting an old woman. Do you hear me, Officer?"

The lieutenant nodded, "He's already in custody for assaulting you and your friends."

"*Danken Got.* Thank God. And what about Jayne? Is she still in the hoosegow?" Mavis wondered where they'd put her, with the men or with the women.

"She was released. No charges were brought against Mr. Day."

"Did she go home with Winnifred?"

"I couldn't say."

"Then what the hell are you still doing here? *Gai avek.* Give me some peace."

The officer backed out of the room. "Sleep well, Ma'am."

Mavis' new hospital room had a spectacular view of Miami, but she couldn't get comfortable in the bed. Her coccyx bone had been bruised and no amount of *kvetching* would make it better, so she stopped complaining, asked for more pain meds, and dozed.

The lieutenant on the case seemed to take a liking to Mavis because he showed up at the foot of her bed the next morning.

"Mavis, can you hear me?"

She lay with the covers over the bottom of her face, so no one would see that she slept with her mouth open. Catching flies, her father always said. She was feeble enough lying in that *fashtunekeneh* bed, she didn't want to make it worse.

"There's someone here who'd like to see you. Are you up for visitors?" he asked.

"Do I have a choice?" squawked Mavis.

A forty-something year old woman walked in, her brown hair in tight curls, her nose, eyebrows and upper lip pierced. Tattoos ran along her arms: rainbows, bouquets of roses, chipmunks, everything Mavis never wanted.

"Meet Allyson McFee," said the lieutenant.

Mavis had heard that name somewhere. Ally McFee maybe? On the television? On the radio?

The younger woman commandeered the room. "I'm here to thank you."

Mavis tried to sit up, but her bones ached. "Do I know you?"

"No, but you're the one who took my motorcycle, right? The police contacted me last night and told me the woman was in custody and the motorcycle would be returned to me after the paperwork was complete."

"Why on earth would you thank me?" This woman had a hole in her head, thought Mavis. It was probably a trick to see how sane she was. If she gave the wrong answers, she'd be thrown in the loony bin, never to escape.

The woman brought over a chair and the lieutenant left the room. "When I was in my twenties, I ran with a gang of bikers who harassed people about their race or their size or anything that would get a reaction. Then they'd beat them up for what was in their pockets. It didn't matter if it was a quarter or a hundred dollars, each conquest added a notch to their ego."

"So you were a *schmendrick* like them?"

"If *schmendrick* means loser, then that's what I was. On the day of the accident, a heist was planned. They did it even as I was being operated on for a shattered femur."

"What did they do?"

"They robbed ATMs along the coast of Florida near Miami, shooting up the parking lots, scaring people, and causing chaos."

"The *schmendriks* got caught, I figure."

"Of course they did. They were stupid fucks, pardon my expression."

"So you're thanking me because I took your motorcycle and you never resumed your life of crime."

"How did you know?"

"*Sachel,*" said Mavis, pointing to her head. "I got smarts." Clearly, this woman didn't, thought Mavis.

"Once I realized what could have happened to me, I changed course. I went back to school, got a degree in music therapy, and have worked with young people ever since, showing them the right path."

"So why are you here? It's been fifteen years since the accident."

"You called me while I was recuperating. I remember that. And you said something that made a difference."

"*Nu*, don't keep me in suspense. I could use a life lesson just about now."

"You said, 'If you can, do!' I think you meant you took the motorcycle on impulse, but I heard those words and woke myself up. I've lived clean ever since."

Mavis didn't remember any part of the conversation. If you can, do? What kind of expression was that? She recalled her mother saying Mavis, you're capable. Mavis, you're wasting your time. Get out and do what's right. Mavis, stop drinking. You can do it. "That still doesn't explain why you're here," she told the young woman.

"The police called me to press charges against you. How could I do that? You've given me a gift all these years, so now I give you my gift. I've signed the motorcycle over to you. She's all yours legitimately."

"Great, now that my tailbone is broken, I can't drive the damn thing."

"If you can—do!" said Allyson. "If not, pass it forward."

The woman bent over Mavis and pecked her on the cheek. She smelled like damp earth and cinnamon.

Chapter Thirty-One

MISHPOCHEH: FAMILY

The next morning, Jayne set to work changing the tire. She wore overalls and tucked her hair under a baseball cap. She wore sneakers and a sweatshirt and no make up.

Gertrude and Blooma knew she'd be there, so Gertrude helped Blooma into the wire basket again and off they went.

"I'm going to drop a few pounds doing this," said Gertrude.

"Not if you eat a whole bubke when you're finished," said Blooma, remembering how Gertrude devoured a blueberry cake and dug into the bubke last night at Blooma's table after catching their breath after the crazy day.

When they came upon the Lincoln Town Car, Gertrude wondered why Jayne had hired someone to change the tire. She had been so adamant about doing it herself. "Hey, you there, *Chaim Pipick*, who gave you permission to touch that car?" Gertrude called.

Jayne raised her head and Gertrude had a flash of déjà vu. On the ship she recalled how Jayne changed costumes and wigs between tunes. Gertrude remembered seeing her in profile getting into the Elvis jumpsuit, thinking how manly she looked. Gertrude knew Jayne was an impersonator, but she had never seen her up close devoid of female attributes. Without question, Gertrude now understood the true reality of Jayne's identity.

Blooma just said, "Hi, Fella, you're doing a great job."

Gertrude nudged her. "That's our Jayne."

Blooma tsked. "No way. That's a *schlepper* paid to do the work."

Jayne removed the baseball cap and her hair tumbled around her face.

Blooma's face crumpled and she whispered to Gertrude, "She's our Jayne all right, but something's different."

Gertrude elbowed her. "That's because she's a dude."

"Why am I always the last to know these things. I wasn't born under a rock, was I?"

"You take people at face value," said Gertrude. "I'm suspicious right away and play bad scenarios in my head. But Jayne as a man, that's one scenario I didn't expect to believe."

Jayne asked the women to sit on the curb as she changed the tire. "I was born James Day," she began, "a seven pound bouncing boy, but as I grew I realized I didn't enjoy what my father enjoyed. I preferred to cook with my mom or shop with my sister. By the time I was a teenager, I snuck out of the house wearing my sister's clothes. This was before I went through puberty, so my face was hairless and no one questioned that I was female. But then my voice changed and my body betrayed me."

Gertrude watched as Jayne hoisted the spare tire out of the boot and rolled it along the ground. She saw how Jayne loosened the lug nuts from the hub cap and cranked up the car. She was a natural at this, not even breaking a nail. Gertrude wished she had mechanical skills, but she hadn't been allowed to take metal shop or mechanics in school no matter how much she desired to learn. She wondered if she should have been born a boy.

Jayne changed the tire and secured the bolts as she finished her story. "When I got out from under my parents' roof, I went to New York and became a backup singer for rock groups. Sometimes I dressed as

James and sometimes as Jayne depending on what the singer needed. I thought I could go solo, the first transgender singer, playing both male and female roles. That was 1990 and it went over badly. I got horrendous reviews and stuck to small venues in Podunk towns after that, mostly doing female impersonations. But I wanted a true gender reassignment, so I went to a doctor two years ago, and began the process."

Blooma considered the magic pills Jayne had given her. "Are the pills you gave me part of your treatment?"

"They are, Blooma. They have hormones in them and I thought they might boost your assets."

"They did until I got befuddled."

"Because you put too much faith in them."

"People believe what they want to believe," said Blooma. "But I know when someone is sincere. You have a sweet soul, *a ziseh neshomah*. Take it from me. Embrace life each day in a way that's true for you before it's too late."

Gertrude gasped at Blooma's lucidity. Maybe her brain was on the mend. "Do Winnie and Mavis know your background?"

"I told them yesterday at the police station."

"I'm *farmishted* again," said Blooma. "The police station came to the complex last night and Mavis wasn't there at all."

Mavis was probably sleeping off a drunk, thought Gertrude, and missed all the excitement.

Jayne took each woman's hand. "Remember how Sal threw Mavis across the room yesterday? Well, her coccyx was bruised and she was rushed to the hospital."

"That's terrible," said Blooma. "Why didn't you or Winnie tell us?"

"I guess we were so caught up with Sal and the painting that we lost sight of what's really important," said Jayne.

"And that would be?" asked Gertrude.

"Taking care of each other," said Blooma. "Thinking about each other. Being there."

"So what happens next?" Gertrude asked Jayne.

"I can't tell you what will happen to Winnie or Mavis. But I know my fate. Yesterday morning I had an appointment with a surgeon. Thanks to the money I received from you and Winnie, I was able to pay for half the procedure in advance. But I can't schedule the operation until I assure the doctor of full payment."

Gertrude wanted Jayne in her life. She wanted to show her the PowerPoint and share her dream with her. They'd make a great team. "Jayne, I have a business venture for you to consider. Come to my house and let me share it with you."

Gertrude watched as Jayne put the tools away. As she was about to close the trunk, Gertrude saw a manilla envelope poking up from under the rug with Winnie's name on it. *For Winnifred Reichman, after my passing. Jev Reichman.*

"There's something else in here," said Jayne, who uncovered a box wrapped in duct tape under the spot where the spare tire had rested. She shook it gently. "It doesn't make a sound, so it's not jewelry."

Gertrude saw how thickly it was sealed, so it had to contain something valuable. "Winnie's at Hilda Lee's. We should get these to her as soon as possible, don't you think?"

"And we should visit Mavis at the hospital," said Blooma.

"Let's go," said Jayne. "The car's ready."

"Will you have time to come to my condo before we leave?" asked Gertrude.

"Maybe later, Honey Pie. Winnie and Mavis need us first."

After the lieutenant and Allyson McFee left Mavis' room, the doctor came in to examine her.

"Are you ready to go home?" he asked.

Mavis shrugged. Home? Alone with *farkakte* ghosts. What a life. How was she going to get there? By taxi? That was so not all right, thought Mavis. She called Winnie.

"Thank you for posting bail," said Mavis, choking up.

"When will you be released? We've been worried about you," said Winnie.

"*Gae in dred.* No one gives a good goddamn about me," said Mavis.

"Then why would I have bailed you out? And why are Gertrude, Blooma, and Jayne driving into Miami right now to visit you?"

Jayne had texted Winnie to say they'd be at the gallery in an hour.

"*Emmis?* Is that true? And what about you? Are you coming to get me out of this place?"

"As soon as they pick me up."

When the Lincoln Town Car edged close to Hilda Lee's gallery, Winnie emerged carrying her suitcases and the painting she had bought from Hilda Lee.

"We thought you were staying a while," said Gertrude.

"Hilda Lee is a difficult woman."

Gertrude coughed.

"She kept me up all night telling me how stupid I was to let that Sal character control me. Thank God I never told her about my first husband Brian. She'd think I was a real doormat."

Hmmm, thought Gertrude. We never knew about Brian either. Maybe Winnie is finally trusting us?

"Then she lit into me about not recognizing great art when it was right in front of my face. Finally, she let me go to sleep but woke me up at seven this morning to begin research on the damn paintings. That's the last thing I wanted to do: read about degenerate art confiscated by the Nazis during World War II, knowing that Jev and Sal made a profit over poor Jewish victims of the Holocaust. How shameful. I don't want to know."

"Breathe, Winnila, breathe," said Blooma, patting the seat beside her. "Come. Sit with me."

"I have something for you that might make you feel better," said Jayne. She handed her the manila envelope and the box. "We found it hidden under the spare tire in the trunk."

Winnie saw that each was sealed shut with duct tape. That was Jev's signal that something was to be dealt with in private. The envelope would have to wait.

"*Nu*, so aren't you going to open it?" asked Gertrude.

Winnie balanced it in her hands. "It would be just like Jev to remind me how I should be nice to Sal because he had a sad childhood. I don't need another lecture. It's been hidden this long. It can wait until I'm good and ready." She set it on her lap, closed her eyes, and concentrated on breathing.

As Jayne drove, Blooma remembered that the light on the phone still blinked and she never checked to see who it was from. At first she thought it might have been her pharmacy, but maybe it was from Sarah. Blooma had given up hope, but it could have been her, right? Her son-in-law Charlie said he would try. Maybe he convinced her. On the other hand, it could be Murray calling or even Hymie, her new admirer. Or one of those telemarketers wanting her to invest in Nigeria.

Gertrude kept thinking about Jayne's operation and how brave she was to undergo surgery. Gertrude made a decision, then and there. She'd fund Jayne's surgery, then she'd invite her to convalesce in her home. Gertrude knew she'd have a good bedside manner with Jayne, and she had the perfect distraction while Jayne recuperated. Going through photos. Listening to recordings. Selecting a playlist. Making marketing plans. They were going to have such fun.

Winnie caressed the envelope and the box, intuiting what was inside. Maybe there were papers that gave her sole ownership of the penthouse. Maybe there was an explanation of the paintings? Maybe there was a love letter somewhere tucked in there. Maybe there were divorce papers that Jev never filed? And maybe it was an entreaty to do what Sal told her to do and not ask any questions. She needed alone time to find out.

But first they entered the hospital. Mavis was lying in bed, her face covered, but the blanket was being sucked down by her breath and breathed out like a tent. She looked so tiny, her blond stick-straw hair fanned out on the pillow.

Winnie, Gertrude, Blooma and Jayne tiptoed in.

"*Kacka mun*! Cut it out! I'm not dying. You don't have to be quiet," said Mavis, trying to sit up.

The women flurried around her, fixing her pillow, offering her water, making sure the TV remote was within her grasp. Mavis remembered how she and Gertrude had sat by Blooma's side the night Blooma passed out at Karaoke. Maybe these women did care about her. Mavis let out a Sammy the Parrot squawk. "Get me out of here, pronto! That *farkakte* doctor wants to put me in a nursing home. He says I shouldn't live alone in my condition."

"They're just covering their asses," said Gertrude.

"*Meshugennehs*!" squawked Mavis. "I've lived on my own my whole long life. These people are crazy."

"You need help until you're on your feet again," said Winnie. She inhaled deeply. "If you let me, I'll stay with you for a few weeks while the police conduct their investigation."

Mavis rolled her eyes. Winnie in her house was like taking a step backward. Winnie brought high-heeled shoes, white gloves, hats and mirrors. Mavis didn't live like that. "I don't know. I think you'd be miserable at my place."

"Can I make that decision once we try it?"

"You can't even make soup!"

"I make pancakes, and an egg with a hole in it, and smoothies. The rest, I'll learn. Remember, I cooked for a little boy once."

"And how did he turn out?" asked Mavis.

Winnie wouldn't tell them he was a vegetarian. He swore off meat, not for moral purposes, but because Winnie burned every steak, chop, and meatball she ever cooked. "He's the picture of health. I saw him the other day. He's playing drums for the group Hateful Dodgers."

"The Hateful Dodgers?" crooned a nurse who had come in with a folder of papers for Mavis to sign. "I saw them on *The Morning Show* being interviewed by Robin Roberts. Great music!"

"What do you think of Llama?" asked Jayne.

"A hunk!" said the nurse.

"Good looking stock," said Jayne, nodding at Winnie with an I-told-you-so stare.

The nurse looked at Winnie. "Are you a relative of Llama's?"

"I'm his mother," she said.

"Wow. He talked about you in the interview. An audience tweet asked about his name."

Oh God, thought Winnie. L.M.A. *Leave me alone.* That's what he told his audience? That he wanted his mother to leave him alone... forever!

"He said he owed his name to his mother who taught him how to stand on his own two feet and never look back."

"He said that?"

"Something like that," she said. "You should be proud."

Winnie's eyes teared. "He needed me after all."

"Even to tell him what not to do," said Mavis.

"I could do that for you. Tell you what not to do and you could end up famous like my son," said Winnie.

"You can come on one condition. That you learn to drive Pinky."

"Who's Pinky?" asked Winnie.

"My motorcycle," Mavis squawked.

"Isn't that why you got canned," said Gertrude, "and why Winnie had to post bail?"

"You're back in the money, Winnie. I'm as free as Sammy. The owner didn't press charges. In fact, she gave me the motorcycle and thanked me for changing her life."

"*Oy gevult!*" said Blooma. "I don't understand a thing you're saying. Why am I always the last one to get it?"

"Blooma, when I'm better, I'll explain everything when I take you on a ride through the village. It's the freest feeling ever," said Mavis.

"Just what I need right now," said Winnie. "Freedom."

"Me too," said Mavis.

No one disagreed.

Chapter Thirty-Three

BESHERT: DESTINY

Winnie was glad to be sequestered at Mavis'. Journalists from all corners of the globe wanted to interview the unsuspecting woman whose apartment had been filled with priceless treasures. Newspapers, television, the Internet ran stories about the haul of Nazi plunder found in the Boca Raton penthouse. Winnie wore sunglasses and a baseball cap to avoid recognition.

The apartment had contained works by Pablo Picasso, Henri de Toulouse-Lautrec, Oskar Kokoschka, Canaletto, Pierre-August Renoir, Franz Marc, Maria Casper-Filser, Conrad Felixmüller and Gustav Courbet. "A total of 121 framed and 600 unframed works, among them works by famous artists, were seized," wrote the United Press International. "There were oil paintings, works in India ink, pencil, watercolors, lithographs and prints, concrete indications that [some of it] was so-called 'degenerate art' or stolen art."

"How could you not know?" Hilda Lee reproached. "What kind of asshole are you?"

Winnie ceased any connection with her. She didn't need admonishment; she needed support and a good lawyer.

Out of the blue and to Winnie's endless delight, BJ called to say he'd catch up after the commotion died down. He didn't need or want the notoriety. "I'm feeling your pain, Mother. I always liked Jev. He was a generous guy. But that prick Sal could never be trusted; he probably thought I had the hots for Jev. Salvatore deserves the trouble he's in, bullying the little guy, making us feel unwanted. All along he was a thief. Worse than a thief! Making money off the victims of the Holocaust."

So BJ didn't blame her! He saw her as a victim too. Maybe it wasn't too late for healing between them to begin. They'd reconnect, she knew it, once this ordeal was over.

After the women brought Mavis home and all was quiet in the condo, Winnie opened the manila envelope and the box that Jayne had retrieved from the trunk. Winnie sat at the kitchen table with a glass of white wine and read Jev's words:

Dearest Winnifred,

I figure I'm dead if you're reading this, or maybe Sal has found this and he's reading it. If it's Sal, then Go to Hell, old Sport, I'll meet you at the corner of shit and shinola.

My wife Winnie, I owe you an explanation about why I didn't want you involved in the business and why I cut you out of my will (except for the car—with the hopes that you'd find this letter, eventually). Sal built our business around priceless artwork which was believed lost for decades, stolen or destroyed by the Nazis. He had a connection in Argentina. At first I resisted, but money is compelling and Sal was so insistent that we weren't hurting anyone.

He persuaded me to stay quiet about what he'd found, what he bought and what he smuggled into the United States. I take full responsibility for my actions, but you, my sweet Winnifred, are innocent of any wrongdoing, except for loving the wrong man. I was never true to our vows. Sal was in my life long before you and held a control over me that I could not shake. I tried. When you and I were alone in our room, I tried. Truly I did.

My deepest regret is marrying you under false pretenses. My parents wanted a grandson. They didn't know I wasn't interested in women. When I met you, I found my match and their foil. You were gracious, loving, unquestioning, and accepting. My parents died believing we'd have an heir to carry on their name.

Please forgive me and use the money in the box to move forward. None of it was gotten through the sale of stolen art. It was honestly earned and honestly saved. Not every sale was illegal. I swear.

So here it is: my gratitude and undying love (that's a joke, Winnifred!). I hope this tidy little sum will keep you in the lifestyle you deserve.

Jev

Winnie didn't cry. She had shed enough tears. She unsealed the box and counted out the money: $250,000. No one knew about it, least of all Sal, who was taken away in handcuffs never to see sunlight again, she hoped.

She tucked the letter and the box under the twin bed where she slept in Mavis' house. She liked how small the room was, how it contained all she needed. One painting hung from the wall: the one she had bought from Hilda Lee. One framed photo graced the bureau: BJ and his band. In the closet were her favorite dresses, hats, and shoes. In the bureau were her underwear and basics. She shared a bathroom with Mavis and controlled the kitchen, heating soup in the microwave and serving it with Blooma's challah. Winnie and Mavis sat together on the couch and watched *Judge Judy* and *Wheel of Fortune*, betting nickels on the outcomes.

Maybe she'd use the money from Jev to travel. Maybe to help Jayne transition. Maybe to find the descendants of the artists whose paintings were stolen or the families whose art was confiscated. She didn't know and didn't have to decide. Living with Mavis wasn't forever, but it was all right for now.

Mavis didn't mind having Winnie around, especially for meals, which Winnie didn't exactly cook, but read directions well for the microwave, called for take-out, and welcomed the Meals on Wheels brigade. Mavis had rarely eaten a full dinner in the last twenty years in someone else's company. How strange. It hadn't bothered her until Winnie sat across from her. They didn't talk much, but their silence was compatible.

The motorcycle had arrived during the week with a large pink bow and a thank you note from Allyson McFee. *Get well soon*, it said. All those years she never ventured out of the complex with Pinkie, knowing it would get her in trouble—and it did, but it also brought a peace she hadn't expected.

Imagine beginning the ninth decade of her life with no regrets. If she and the girls went to the ocean to dump their sins, she'd have an empty purse and she would not call herself a coward ever again. What she did to her parents' house was a tragic accident. How she neglected Wally was immature ignorance. How she played up Sammy the Parrot and swore like a sailor was boastful acting. Perhaps by eighty, she'd learn the difference between willful acts of aggression and thoughtful withdrawal of reaction. She had two more years to get it right.

On a mahjong game day in April, the women planned a party at the senior center. There was so much to celebrate: Jayne's surgery, financed by Gertrude and Winnie with an IOU from Jayne to pay back every cent; Winnie's liberation from Sal, whose lawyer worked every angle but couldn't hide the facts; Mavis' return to good health even though she had to sit on a rubber doughnut; and Jayne's World Productions official launch with Gertrude Friedman as manager.

Mahjong began at 1:00 as usual. Blooma had arrived early. She brought her award-winning *schlissel challah*, a honey and wheat bread guaranteed to fill everyone's home with blessings. She hadn't baked it in forty years, ever since it won *Yankee Magazine's* award, but if ever there were a time for blessings, it was now.

Blooma had finally retrieved the message on her answering machine and to her everlasting delight she heard the voice she treasured: "Mother, this is Sarah. We are planning a visit during the boys' school vacation. Be ready! We might be more than you can handle. Call me back."

Blooma returned the call, and mother and daughter reconnected. Nothing was said about Isaac. He no longer existed, but Blooma talked briefly about her friends, trying to paint a positive picture: Crazy Mavis, the *meshugenneh* who broke every rule; Winnie, the *gansa macha* big-shot whose husband looted Nazi Germany art; Gertrude, a real *mensch* who pretended to be a jerk; and Jayne, a gorgeous woman who had been a man. Blooma didn't go into more detail; she wanted Sarah to judge for herself.

For the first hour of mahjong it was the same-old, same-old. Mavis won three; Gertrude won one; Winnie and Blooma won *bupkis*. Then the day took a turn. Jayne appeared. She was dressed in a t-shirt that said, *Thanks for the Memories*, which began her tribute.

She followed it up with Barbra Streisand's *People*, but she wasn't impersonating the singers. She was just belting out the words. For the third song, she sat on a stool and looked at the four women at the table. "Thank you for being my friend."

Mavis wondered how a woman like that had entered their lives. "I have a question, Jaynie. Why us?"

"What do you mean?"

Gertrude had always thought about that, as had Winnie. Blooma believed in *beshert*, what was to be was to be.

Jayne took a stool and sat on it like she was going to sing a ballad. "I am going to tell you the God's honest truth."

"Here comes the big story, the *gunsa megillah*," said Mavis, rolling Sammy the Parrot on her shoulder.

"And one you might not like," said Jayne.

"If it's about how you found us, we'll like it," said Blooma.

"Here goes. You know I was down on my luck, singing in bars and getting nowhere. I was frustrated as James and not comfortable yet as Jayne. That's when I noticed two letters to the editor in the *Sunrise Gazette* on the Internet. They were written with such passion about keeping the commons room open for mahjong games. They said the police accused you of gambling but the letters refuted that and said you played for companionship and friendly competition."

"So you read my letter?" asked Gertrude.

"Our letters were on the Internet? Does that mean they went viral?" asked Winnie.

"Not exactly," said Jayne. "I stumbled upon them by accident. Random googling."

"So that's why you came to our complex? To nickel and dime us in mahjong?" asked Mavis.

"I thought you might have some extra money for a down-and-out singer," said Jayne.

"And you succeeded," said Gertrude, her face suddenly crashing into frowns.

"Not the way I expected," said Jayne. "I've come to love you like sisters. I never knew women could be so generous and you've proven to me that friendship is worth more than money."

"So we'd still be your friends if Gertrude and I stopped payment on the checks?" said Winnie, who, like Gertrude, had advanced Jayne money for her surgery.

Blooma scolded Winnie. "You gave Jayne money because you believe in her and you trust her."

"All bonds are built on trust," said Jayne. "It's true that I came to the complex because I thought there was a group of women who had money to burn. What I hadn't counted on was the strength and courage I've gained because of all of you."

Jayne cleared her throat, reached into a bag and brought out a bouquet of red roses. "For my Blooma, a woman who loves unconditionally.

May everything come up roses for you, Sweet Lady." She dipped into the bag again. "And for my lovable *meshugenneh*, Mavis. Did I use the word right?"

"Damn straight," laughed Mavis. "What do you think, Sammy?" Mavis shimmied her shoulder and Sammy danced.

Jayne gifted her with a parrot motorcycle spinner, emblazoned with color, and emboldened with the words *Born to be Wild*. "Presenting your alter-ego!"

"For an *alter kaker!*" said Mavis.

"You're the youngest older person I know," said Jayne.

Jayne's attention turned to Winnie. "At first I thought we'd never have a meeting of minds. You're so different from me. Classy. Cultured. Sophisticated. What I've learned is you're down to earth and true." Jayne pinned a gold star on Winnie's yellow beret. "This is your badge of courage. Let it shine."

Gertrude sat on *schpilkes* waiting for her turn. Why did she have to be last? Did Jayne forget her? Was she an afterthought? Then Jayne bestowed a kiss on each of Gertrude's cheeks, just like celebrities do. "With you beside me, I can do anything," said Jayne, who gave Gertrude a framed photograph of the two of them standing in front of a banner marquis: "Jayne Day and Gertrude Friedman, BFFs."

Jayne returned to the front of the room and sang a quiet tune, "Oh how happy you have made me. Oh how happy you have made me."

When she finished, Winnie, Mavis, Gertrude and Blooma broke into a rendition of "For she's a jolly good fellow, she's a jolly good fellow, she's a jolly good fellow, that nobody can deny." That hadn't been rehearsed. It was *emmis*, the truth, as each woman felt it.

At the back of the room, balloons rose into the air and shouts of joy rang out as two young boys ran to their grandmother and wrapped their arms around her.

"Bubbe, mommy says you'll fly back to New York with us. Is that true?" asked Andrew.

"Bubbe, can we bake bubke together?" asked Mark.

"Yes, yes, and lots more yeses," said Blooma.

"We're going to miss you, Blooma!" said Jayne.

"I won't be gone for long. Then again, they might want me to stay."

Winnie broke into a bright smile. "I've booked a trip to New York City. BJ is playing there in a few weeks and he's invited me as his guest! Imagine that. Me and BJ! What if we come to your daughter's house? We can celebrate family together!"

"And Jayne's World will be on tour beginning in June. The cruise leaves from New York. We'll come early and spend time with you too," said Gertrude.

Mavis squawked, "Who's going to play mahjong with me when you all leave? And don't say the *farkakte* Cupie Pies!"

"Join me in New York," said Winnie. "We'll have an adventure."

That sounded like a righteous plan, thought Mavis. It was about time for her to travel the world again.

"Let's all meet up at my Sarah's house and we'll have a mini-mahjong tournament," said Blooma.

"*Kayn-ahora.* Knock on wood! From your lips to God's ears," said Mavis. "Now fill up your plates with *schissel challah*, boys, and sit your *tucheses* down next to your Bubbe. We're going to teach you mahjong."

As they played, Jayne perched on a stool and *kvelled* over each of her ladies and the two adoring boys who followed every pick and throw, calling out the discards for Blooma. Every so often, Jayne broke into song and the women swayed to the words: "For good times and bad times, I'll be on your side forever more. That's what friends are for! That's what friends are for..."

The End

Printed in the USA
CPSIA information can be obtained
at www.ICGtesting.com
LVHW022147051023
760329LV00034B/1002